NIGHTMARES *of* WEIRDWOOD

NIGHTMARES OF WEIRDWOOD

Thieves of Weirdwood Book 3

NEWBERY HONOR–WINNING AUTHOR

CHRISTIAN McKAY HEIDICKER

Illustrations by Anna Earley

A WILLIAM SHIVERING TALE

Henry Holt and Company
New York

Henry Holt and Company, *Publishers since 1866*
Henry Holt® is a registered trademark of Macmillan Publishing Group, LLC
120 Broadway, New York, NY 10271 · mackids.com

Our books may be purchased in bulk for promotional, educational,
or business use. Please contact your local bookseller or the Macmillan
Corporate and Premium Sales Department at (800) 221-7945 ext. 5442 or
by email at MacmillanSpecialMarkets@macmillan.com.

Library of Congress Control Number: 2021916953

First edition, 2022
Book design by Trisha Previte
Printed in the United States of America by Lakeside Book Company,
Harrisonburg, Virginia

ISBN 978-1-250-30292-2 (hardcover)
1   3   5   7   9   10   8   6   4   2

For Luke Minaker, Russ Uttley, and Paul Pattison,
Shaper of Cosmos, Mystical Strategist, and Orchestrator Supreme:
Thank you for letting me play in your world.

There are many who don't wish to sleep
for fear of nightmares.
Sadly, there are many who don't wish to wake
for the same fear.

—Richelle E. Goodrich

NIGHTMARES *of* WEIRDWOOD

THE FIERY PLAINS

The Blazing General was home at last.

After being taken by the strange, flameless humans and spending months imprisoned in that small wire box beside other flameless creatures, far from the sizzling warmth of his family . . . his roaring mane had begun to flicker out. His red coal skin dimmed black with cold. He had feared he would be extinguished and never see his herd again.

But now, he was back, reignited on the Fiery Plains, where the orange brush roared into the sky and the grasses crackled pleasantly underhoof. He had his herd of flaming bulls, and all was bright and burning.

As the Blazing General led his family toward the chewy flames of the Smoldering Gorge, he heard a whinnying behind him. And another. Grunts of fear. He turned and saw a blankness, brighter than the heart of a flame. It expanded across the Fiery Plains, enveloping the tail end of his herd. *Absorbing* them.

The general's molten eyes ignited with fury. The whiteness was *human*-shaped. He huffed sparks, lowered his horns, and charged at the figure. He had to protect his herd from those cold metal cages. He had to protect the ember in his wife's belly.

When the Blazing General's horns reached the human shape, he expected to pierce through. For blood to spill. For this nightmare to end. But the shape unraveled the general's horns like bark stripped from a tree. It reached his coal-bright skin and began not to extinguish it . . . but to *erase* it. And the general learned there is nothing colder than nothingness.

THE INFINITE HOSPITAL

The floating nurse was thirsty. She had not drunk her quota of tears that day.

She still needed to tell the little ones, tucked in their sheets,

that they would not see their parents again. That this, the hospital that stretched to the horizon and beyond, was their home now. The little ones would weep at the news, and their sadness would be hers to reap until the end of time.

When a figure appeared, impossibly, at the end of the infinite hallway, the nurse shrank back. She did not recognize this thing. She did not think she could make it cry. The figure was dissolving the infinite hospital, vanishing the little ones from their beds before their tears could be harvested . . .

And now it was coming for her.

The floating nurse began to shriek, her thirst unquenched forevermore.

THE TREASURE BOLT

Having defeated Luckless Chuck and imprisoned the pirate captain in the belly of the golden whale, the Merry Rogues stood on the deck of their stolen ship and watched the moonlight cascade across the waves. The seas were safe again.

"Now that's what I call a whale of a time," Tuck said.

"I would call *that* a punning crime," Mim said.

"You both owe me a dime," said Gus. He sighed. "I wish the boss was here."

"As do I," said Tuck, pulling him close.

"Nah," said Mim, wiping away a tear. "He'd just take all the credit."

Gus spotted something out to sea and wrinkled his nose. "What's that when it's at home, then?"

A white spot had formed on the horizon. It wasn't the moon. It was human-shaped.

"It's gobbling up all the fishes!" Tuck said.

"And our golden whale beside!" said Gus.

They watched in horrified awe.

"Looks a bit . . . *familiar*, don't it?" Mim said.

"Boss?" whispered Tuck, staring at the figure.

"That ain't the boss . . . ," Gus said, then swallowed. "I don't think."

"Whatever it is, it's about to meet the *Merry Rogues!*" Mim gallantly stepped to the ship's wheel, steering *The Treasure Bolt* toward the blank figure. "In honor of Garnett Lacroix!"

"The world's most cavalier outlaw!"

"Who never blushed when shouting *hurr—*!"

The ship, the Rogues, and the high seas were swallowed up as if by a drain.

1
HEROES

It was another picture-perfect day in the DappleWood. The sun smiled, the grasses hushed, and Arthur Benton entertained an audience of chickens, ducks, squirrels, rabbits, reptiles, toads, and (he tried not to meet their beady little eyes) *mice*.

"Yesterday," Arthur called from the stage of the DappleWood amphitheater, "I concluded the tale of my meteoric rise from humble street thief to unpaid consultant of the Wardens of Weirdwood, defenders of humans and Fae-born alike!"

The air shook with stomping paws and clapping wings as a barnyard excitement spread through the audience. Arthur's crowds had grown so large that Pyra had brewed him a special potion that made his voice carry to the critters all the way in the back.

"Having rid Kingsport of unspeakable horrors," Arthur continued, "brought a monster hospital screeching out of the sky, and gracefully retired the Gentleman Thief Garnett

Lacroix, I was ready for the next step in my magical education." Arthur arched an eyebrow. "But fate had other plans."

The crowd grew rapt and silent.

"As you'll remember," Arthur said, voice low and urgent, "Weirdwood Manor was on the fritz, leaping wildly from pocket-world to pocket-world, like an untethered balloon on too much caffeine."

In the front row, a squirrel scout raised her paw. "What's caffeine?"

"Please hold your questions till the end," Arthur said.

He proceeded to tell his captive critter audience about his descent into the Manor's Abyssment to try and stop the root-chewing Scarabs.

"Breeth, who was still a ghost at the time, bested those Scarabs by possessing Ludwig, the giant plant carpenter. You've probably seen them around town. It's good to keep friends nearby. They can get you out of any pickle."

The squirrel scout's paw shot into the air, then was quickly lowered again.

Arthur neglected to mention that the Scarabs had been his fault . . . or that he was mind-controlled after inhaling the spores of a psychotic mushroom . . . or that Lady Weirdwood ejected him from the Manor for abusing magic with a dragon-bone Quill. But it was difficult to weave an inspiring tale around those less-than-flattering moments. And after the trauma of seeing their town erased, the DappleWood citizens could use some inspiration.

"I decided to return to Kingsport to focus on more *charitable* efforts." He paced the stage, telling the DappleWood citizens how he had written obituaries to console Kingsport's grieving citizens. He expounded, breathlessly, on being chased by the Order of Eldar—"one with teeth of rust, one with a tongue of silver, and one with skin of stone"—through multiple pocket-worlds to the Whirling City, where the dragons dwell, and finally back to the Manor where Lady Weirdwood dueled the dragon duchess by magically spending her years and wisdom.

He didn't mention the horrible death of Huamei the dragon boy. There were bunnies in the audience, after all.

As the sun dipped into purple twilight, Arthur finished his tale with the Battle of the Great Elsewhere. "At the climax of the fight, I discovered that *I* had created the storm cloud city with the very obituaries I had written!" He brought his voice to a stage whisper, waggling his fingers as if each was a wand of indescribable power. "Little did I know I could spin a story so convincing that it magically appeared as an entire pocket-world unto itself—*ghosts included.*"

The audience gasped.

"*Whooooaaaaaaa,*" a lone hedgehog said.

Arthur didn't think his audience needed to know that these ghosts were not the beloved souls of the dearly departed. They were copies. Mirages. Magical creations. It turned out there was only one way to reach the afterlife. And it wasn't pleasant.

"And so," Arthur said, voice rising in triumph, "I convinced my newfound ghost army to knock that evil Order through the clouds, where they could rust, command, and smash no more!"

The audience burst into applause, feathers and dander wafting throughout the theater.

"Some might use the power to create pocket-worlds to give themselves untold riches," Arthur shouted over the cheers, "but I wanted to help those who had lost their homes." He spread his hands toward the sky. "So, I created the DappleWood!" He cleared his throat and mumbled, "With the citizens' input, of course."

The crowd didn't hear him. The birds chirped and squawked, the reptiles chomped their teeth and whirled their tails, and the rodents squeaked and shivered with excitement.

Arthur bowed deep. "And that, my dear chickens, lizards, and m-m-mice is how I became a Novitiate with the world-skipping, Rift-fixing, lifesaving Wardens of Weirdwood! Any questions?"

A portly frog raised his slimy hand. "What—*brr-brrt*—happened next?"

Arthur shook his finger at the frog with a grin. "You'll just have to wait until tomorrow's performance! Any other questions?"

A fox kit raised a trembling paw and spoke with a lisp. "I*th* the Nothing Man gonna come back and era*the* u*th*?"

There was a murmur among the audience.

The hairs on the back of Arthur's neck prickled. Of all the parts he'd left out of his story, the Eraser was the scariest. He didn't want these innocent critters to worry that the entity that had erased their town was still on the loose, spreading through the pocket-worlds and leaving massive Voids in its wake. That it could show up at any moment and erase the DappleWood and all its citizens forever. That their storybook lives were as fragile as a page.

Arthur looked out across the fuzzy, feathered, and scaled faces of his audience. He didn't have the stomach to reveal that the Eraser was actually Garnett Lacroix. That Arthur had created this terrifying Void when he retired the Gentleman Thief from existence. How could the DappleWood citizens believe they were safe if they knew that one of the people who was meant to protect them had caused all their problems in the first place?

"If the Eraser so much as *glances* at the DappleWood," Arthur said, "the Wardens and I will splash it with so much ink, they'll start calling it the *Pen*."

It wasn't Arthur's best joke, but the crowd still chuckled with relief. The truth was he had no idea how to defeat the Eraser. No one did. Still, he winked at the fox kit and watched the fear melt from her whiskers.

"Any more questions?" Arthur said. "Happier ones?"

A mouse maiden shyly raised her paw and squeaked, "D-do you have a girlfriend?"

Arthur couldn't keep his skin from crawling. The only rodentish creature he could stand to be around was Audrey. But the ferret seamstress was still missing.

"I did have a girlfriend once," he said whimsically, staring toward the darkening clouds. "But she's a rook now."

One of the spring chickens whispered to another, "*Told* ya he was into birds."

Arthur clapped his hands. "This concludes today's performance! I'll see you all back here tomorrow!"

As the DappleWood citizens waddled, skittered, and slithered toward the exits, Arthur left through the backstage, stepping into a lonely twist of alley. It was here, away from his adoring fans, that he finally let his shoulders sag and his smile fade. He tucked his hands in his pockets and headed toward Audrey's house.

The sky was a masterpiece that night. A swirl of purples with faint threads of gold, as if painted to suit Arthur's mood. He didn't like to lie. Not anymore. But every time he stepped onto that stage it reignited his confidence. It reminded him that it was important to tell stories. It was important to have heroes that inspired you to continue when everything seemed hopeless. Arthur had had Garnett Lacroix to guide him. And the DappleWood citizens had the Wardens of Weirdwood. And they had Arthur.

He stepped out of the alley into the open street, which wound through the charming little cottages in one direction and stretched in the other direction through golden fields to a happy little wood on the town's horizon.

"It's him!"

"Hee hee hee!"

"Shh-hh-hh! Stop laughing!"

A troop of squirrel scouts had spotted Arthur and was hopping up and down, chittering and waving their paws. Arthur quickly put on a smile and waved back.

"Can't wait for the next part of the story!" one of the scouts cried.

"It's gonna be a doozy!" Arthur called back.

"Oh my gosh, he answered!"

"I am *freaking* out!"

"Quiet! He's still looking at us!"

Arthur turned his back, and his smile vanished. What would he tell his audience the next day? After the Wardens lost the Manor, the stories had come to a screeching halt. Maybe he could feign sickness. Or hide for a few days and have Sekhmet tell his eager audience that he was on a secret mission to recover Wally.

Arthur sighed. He still couldn't get his head around it. How could his best friend betray the Wardens of Weirdwood by stealing their Manor? The Wardens saved people's lives from dangerous Fae-born. They were *heroes*. Had Graham brainwashed Wally? Was Arthur's best friend a bad guy now?

"*Yoo-hoo!*" a voice bellowed from above. "Arsur!"

Arthur looked up and found Ludwig hailing him from the thatched roof of the claw salon. The giant descended the rungs of a ladder. In a sling on his back was Baby Weirdwood—BW for short—red-faced and blinking in the fading sunlight.

"Hey, Ludwig," Arthur said. "What are you working on up there?"

"Oh, I am just fixing ze structures of your imaginings," Ludwig said, wiping some sugary sweat from his forehead. He chuckled. "You may know what a building looks like, but zat does not mean you know how to make zem to stand!"

Arthur swallowed some embarrassment. "Sorry about that."

"Do not be sorry!" the giant said. "Zis is vhat I am for!" He removed the sling from his back. "Here," he said, thrusting BW toward Arthur. "Zis little vun has had enough sawdust for vun day. And she is not paid in ze sunlight like I am!"

"Oh, no, no, no." Arthur quickly stuffed his hands in his

pockets. "I can't babysit. I, uh, have to do my Novitiate work. Amelia told me to practice my spells."

While Lady Weirdwood was indisposed in infant form, the staff's captain had tasked him with simple writing assignments—creating new items in the DappleWood that were preferably helpful and definitely harmless. A wheel maybe. Or a butter churn.

But Arthur had yet to complete a single assignment. The traumatizing events of the last adventure had frozen him up. He couldn't write a single word without flashing back to the moment when the Eraser had nearly wiped him from this earth. He couldn't even *think* about writing without dwelling on all the damage caused by the entity he had created. The merest slip of his pen could create horrible side effects on this innocent little town. No one wanted a bloodthirsty butter churn.

"I understand," Ludwig said, re-shouldering BW's sling. "To be honest, it is a struggle to fix zese houses vithout Veston here to make ze plants blossom vis his vhistle." The giant gazed up at the roof, tears streaming down his cheeks like tree sap. "Vorking is ze only sing zat helps me not to sink about him."

Arthur swallowed some guilt. Weston was Ludwig's gardener twin. *Had* been his twin. The Eraser had squeezed Weston's head until there was nothing left. Arthur had kept that horrifying part of the story from his audience as well.

"Here," Arthur said, reaching out for the baby. "I'll find someone to watch her."

"Oh, *sank* you, Arsur!" Ludwig said, handing him the sling, which was made from the old architect's wedding dress.

Arthur tried not to grimace. Holding a baby was weird—a wobbly mass of fat and bones.

Ludwig pinched BW's tiny cheek with his massive fingers. "Ze little vun misses her snake, no?"

Arthur wrinkled his eyebrows. "Are snakes good for babies?"

"Zey are for zis vun! Ha ha."

"Good thing it isn't the kind of snake with a rattle, then."

"Oh! I get it! You are always to make ze best comedy jokes!"

The giant scaled the ladder back to the roof while Arthur stared into BW's eyes. Deep in her tiny pupils, he thought he could see the shiny blue dust of a forming galaxy.

"You'd better not pee on me," he told her. Once the architect was back to her old self, he'd never be able to look the old woman in the eye again.

Arthur sighed, tossed the sling and baby around his back like a lump of dough, and set off to find a proper babysitter. He started with the Dozen-Acre Meadow where Sekhmet and her father, Linus, ran drills among the dandelions with two other Wardens, Willa and Cadence. They tossed a ball of leaves through the evening air.

"Linus!" Arthur called, waving his hands. Of all the Wardens, Sekhmet's dad was the kindest. "Hey! Linus! It's Arthur! Over here!"

Linus used his swords to create an explosion of green fireworks that carried the leaf ball straight up to Willa, who swooped in on her furry moth wings and caught it before dropping it to Cadence, who lightly juggled it with his drumsticks, then passed it to Sekhmet, who used her flaming swords to create a waft of wind that blew the ball back to her father.

"*Linus!*" Arthur called again. "Linus! Linus! Linus!"

Linus finally noticed him and he holstered his swords, running over. "How can I help you, Arthur?"

"Could you take her?" Arthur said, holding out BW. "Ludwig's sick of babysitting, and I don't like babies."

"As you can see, we're training right now," Linus said, smiling at BW.

Arthur peered over Linus's shoulder to where the other Wardens continued to keep the leaf ball aloft. "You realize the Eraser is nothing like a ball, right?"

"You never know when juggling a ball-sized object will come in handy!" Linus said, jogging back toward the Wardens.

"Um, I think you do?" Arthur called after him.

When Linus didn't turn around, Arthur fluttered his lips and continued his search.

Next, he found Ahura, Sekhmet's mom, near the town's border. The cartographer was working on a map of the newly created DappleWood. The drawings on her paper swayed with the same breeze that ruffled the nearby trees. Ahura had been sketching day and night, using her Mimic Maps to try and find a way out of this pocket-world so the Wardens could return to their Manor. But the town's wooded border was impenetrable, as if they were trapped inside a snow globe.

Arthur cleared his throat. "Um, Ahura?"

The cartographer didn't so much as glance up. Her lips

moved as she drew, clearly performing calculations in her head. Arthur left her to her work.

He considered dropping BW with one of the critter citizens, but he wasn't sure they were big enough to lift her. He was just about to give up looking for a babysitter altogether when he spotted a strawberry-blond girl near the back of one of the market's tents.

"Breeth!" Arthur said, running up to her. "Am I glad to see you! I've been bragging about your heroic acts at my shows . . . Um, Breeth?"

The girl had stuck her hand through the back flap of the tent and was fishing around for something.

Arthur stepped closer. "*Breeth!*"

She whirled, startled.

"Didn't you hear me?" Arthur said. "I said your name three times."

Breeth's jaw clenched. She scowled at the ground and kicked up dust. Arthur didn't understand what Wally saw in this kid. She was always so *surly*.

His nose caught the silvery scent of melting metal, and he peered through the tent's parted back flap, where he saw a collection of gleaming pitchforks and scythes.

"What are you doing at the blacksmith's?"

Breeth's eyes darted around the street, then landed on the distant fields. "Thought I'd help farm a bit," she said, swallowing her words. "Nothin' else to do 'round here."

"Well!" Arthur said, slipping the sling off his back and wiping a viscous strand of baby drool from his shoulder. "Do I ever have something to keep you occupied!"

He presented BW, and Breeth's comically angry face relaxed into something almost sweet. *Finally*, Arthur thought with relief.

But the moment Breeth reached out for the baby, BW's face went as bright as a tomato. The baby started to cry. And then scream. And then make an ungodly sound that Arthur couldn't believe came out of such a small human.

Breeth's hands jerked back. She scowled at the baby, almost like she didn't trust her, then turned and ran down the lane.

"Wait!" Arthur called after her. "She's probably just gassy! You can do whatever it is people do to . . . ungas her. *Please!*"

Breeth didn't look back, and the smell of melting metal faded.

Arthur frowned at BW, who had stopped crying the instant Breeth left. "You really blew that for us."

In response, BW made raspberries with her lips.

Arthur looked down the little lane. He had one option left. The thought made his shoulders hunch to his ears. But the only thing more terrifying than asking Amelia for a favor was the prospect of changing a diaper.

Teeth clenched, Arthur headed up the hill toward the DappleWood's observatory, passing the greenhouse on the way. Ludwig hadn't gotten around to fixing the glass building yet, and Arthur couldn't help but wince at his own imagination's shoddy construction. It was embarrassing having his first drafts on display like this. One of the window panels was so ill-fitted, it had an inch of space on two sides.

He reached the observatory entrance, raised his hand to knock, then paused when he heard a voice within.

"Try spreading yourself out like butter."

Arthur pressed his ear to the door.

"I'm *aware* you're not made of butter," Amelia continued sharply. "Just *imagine* you are, and then spread yourself out like that!"

Silence.

"Yes, yes, I miss toast too," Amelia said with a frustrated sigh. "If you would *please* pay attention, perhaps we can share a slice back in the Manor."

Arthur plugged his other ear to listen more closely. Who was creating Rifts? And *why*?

Before he could get any more information, BW, for no reason whatsoever, burst out with an extremely loud, *"Bah!"* Arthur quickly knocked on the door, lest Amelia think he was spying.

Something thumped heavily inside. There was shuffling and scraping, and then the door opened just a crack. "What is it, Arthur?" Amelia said. Her one blue eye was haunted, like she hadn't slept in days.

Arthur peered beyond her into the gloom of the observatory. No one was there.

"Who were you talking to?" he asked.

"Myself."

She started to shut the door in his face.

"Wait!" He unlooped the sling from his shoulder and brought the baby around to his chest. "Someone needs to watch BW while the Wardens waste time playing catch."

Amelia tried closing the door again.

Arthur caught it with his foot this time. "I can't babysit right now! I need to do my exercises."

Amelia's lip curled. "How are they coming?"

"Good! Great. Couldn't be better, honestly. I wonder why writers always say writing is hard. It's not hard. Not for me, anyway. Heh."

Amelia's eye narrowed, as if it could see straight through his lies. "You *must* practice, Arthur. Keep your skills as sharp as possible. The Wardens might not realize it, but you are our best chance at defeating the Eraser. With your knowledge of the Gentleman Thief, you're the only one who can draw Garnett Lacroix to its surface, possibly eradicating it."

Arthur scratched the back of his neck in discomfort. He remembered the flash of golden eyes in the Eraser's starry Void. When he did face that monster again—something in Arthur knew that it was inevitable—would he be able to defeat it? Would he be able to make its original form shine through before it erased him, piece by piece, layer by layer, skin from muscle from bone?

Arthur tried chuckling his fear away. "No pressure, right?"

"No, Arthur," Amelia said. "*Lots* of pressure."

Arthur adjusted BW, who suddenly felt much heavier in his arms.

"Anyway, I cannot take the lady now," Amelia said, gazing back into the darkness of the observatory. "I'm working on something. Ask that ferret, whatshername."

"Audrey," Arthur said. "No one's seen her. I think she might still be in the Manor."

"Right . . ." Amelia's expression went blank a moment, then snapped into focus. "Inside." She spun around, leaving the door open. "*Now*."

Arthur stepped into the observatory, cradling BW against his chest. It was cool and dark and smelled like a museum. A massive telescope jutted from the middle of the floor through a rectangular slot in the domed ceiling. Giant sheets of parchment, purchased from Mrs. Platypus near the river, hung on the octagonal walls, filled with sketches of what appeared to be Fae weather patterns painted over fantastical maps.

Amelia cleared a stack of rolled parchments from a chair. "*Sit*."

Arthur sat.

The acrobat shuffled through stacks of papers. "I don't know how you got the imagination you have, Arthur, but it's remarkable. You created a fake heaven with your obituaries. And then you dashed off a new DappleWood as if it was *nothing*."

Arthur felt a knot in his throat. "I got my imagination from my mom."

Amelia ignored this, continuing to fish among the sea of papers. "If you can create entire pocket-worlds with your well-intentioned lies, what other stories of yours have manifested in the Fae?"

"You mean"—Arthur shifted BW from one knee to the other—"I might have *more* creations out there?"

"Not might," Amelia said, finding the paper she was looking for.

Arthur blinked in shock. Did this mean that every fanciful

thing he had ever spoken aloud was running around the Fae like—he looked into BW's nebula eyes—his *children*?

Amelia laid the page in front of Arthur. It was blank. She found a pen and traded it for the baby, lifting the weight of the world from Arthur's lap. But he didn't feel more comfortable. The blank page before him made him nauseous.

"Am I supposed to remember every lie I've ever told?"

"Just one," Amelia said, taking the chair beside him. "When you first stumbled into the Throne Room, filthy and skinny with your pants full of our stolen gold, you told us such a preposterous lie, I've never forgotten it."

Arthur tried to remember, but it felt as if lifetimes had passed since then. And that was the thing about lies. They never stuck in your memory.

"You told us," Amelia continued, "that you had broken into the Manor because your *pet ferret* had scampered inside."

Arthur felt a rush of revelation. "*Audrey?*"

Amelia nodded. "The ferret is one of your creations."

Arthur grimaced, uncomfortable with the idea that anyone, even a talking rodent, was *his*.

"So many things make sense now," he said, shaking his head in amazement. "I sort of . . . *changed* her a couple times. When I needed her to rescue me from dragon prison, she developed the ability to pick locks."

"You were adding to her story," Amelia said. She pointed toward the observatory's window. "When you summoned the original Dapplewood to escape the Order, your imaginary pet ferret must have appeared there as a natural fit."

Arthur laughed to himself. "She definitely inherited my more stubborn qualities."

Amelia leaned in and tapped the blank page. "You said yourself the ferret is still in the Manor."

The smile left Arthur's lips.

"If you're able to change her," Amelia continued, "*control* her, she could be a powerful ally for the Wardens of Weirdwood. She could get the Manor *back*."

"But . . . Audrey is her own person. Er, *ferret*. I can't just force her to—"

"Yes, Arthur," Amelia interrupted, "you can. She's *your* creation. She lives because of you. And right now, she's in the perfect position to defeat our enemies. You have a chance to stop Wally and his brother before they do any more damage."

So it was true. Wally was Arthur's enemy now. But they had been friends once. Arthur couldn't forget that. And even if Audrey was *his* creation, she was his friend as well. He couldn't make one friend attack another.

Arthur threw down the pen. "I won't do it."

Amelia caught it before it rolled off the table. "The Eraser grows in power with every pocket-world it erases," she said, pressing the pen back into his hand. "We must do anything we can to stop it. *Anything*." She looked to the soft sunlight coming through the window. "Unless you'd rather see the entirety of the Fae—the DappleWood and all its citizens included—erased."

Arthur looked out the bright little window. He had promised his audience he would keep them safe.

"Wait," he said, "how can you tell what's happening in the Fae without the Manor?"

Amelia looked away from him. "I cast a spell on the telescope so it can gaze into other pocket-worlds."

Arthur frowned. He didn't know a lot about magic, but he didn't think that was how it worked.

"No more delaying, Arthur," Amelia snapped. "You have been impossibly selfish in the past. It's time to put that behind you and help the Wardens of Weirdwood."

Arthur looked from the blank page to BW, gurgling in Amelia's lap. Babysitting didn't seem so terrible anymore.

2
VILLAINS

Weirdwood Manor was on the move again.

Fantastic landscapes flashed past the windows, like a stage that couldn't decide where its play would be set. A bog haunted by automatons . . . a garden of singing, carnivorous flowers . . . an undersea candy metropolis infested with gummy sharks . . . And every so often a whiteness so blank, the Manor trembled as it passed.

Wally Cooper was not taking in the view. He was in the Emperors' Hall, hammering boards across a gaping hole in the floor. The Eraser had left the Manor in shambles, obliterating walls and disintegrating passages. Wally was no carpenter like Ludwig, but he was doing the best he could, patching gaps and clearing debris, boarding off missing hallways and replacing erased imp locks with fresh ones from Weston's training room.

The work kept Wally's mind off things. It helped him to not think about whether he'd made the right decision, stealing the Manor with his brother. It helped him ignore the quiet that flooded the halls.

Weirdwood Manor was as silent as a tomb. Wally missed the sounds of Ludwig's opera, Pyra's grunts, Weston's command whistle, and the clanging of swords as Sekhmet and her father trained in the courtyard. He had to keep reminding himself that the Wardens were not the protectors they claimed to be. They had locked up an innocent artist to stop the Faeborn in her paintings from wreaking havoc in the Real.

But the Wardens weren't the only ones Wally missed. He wished Arthur were there to tell him how he'd fix up the Manor much better than he, Cooper, ever could. He wished Breeth were possessing the floorboards, giggling while he hammered nails into the wood.

But Wally had made his choice. And now he had to live with it.

The hole in the floor covered, he wiped his forehead, collected his building supplies, and carefully stepped beneath the moony gaze of the Empress Archway. Without Lady Weirdwood around to control the magical hallways, the Manor had become more volatile than ever. But Wally had learned a few tricks. He leapt over writhing rugs along the Serpent Bridge, dodged stone arrows in Heart Hall, and tiptoed past the entrance to the Abyssment, now guarded by nothing more than a half-erased pile of armor.

Wally dropped the building supplies in Ludwig's workshop and grabbed a roll of twine. He headed through the plant wing, spiraling the sprout hallways, tightroping along the fluxing floorboards, and belly-crawling through a constricted passage before finally arriving at the War Room, whose metal walls glowed with weapons and artistic instruments.

In the center of the room, sitting on the waxen throne, was Wally's brother, Graham. Lady Weirdwood's caramel-colored snake lay coiled beneath the throne's shadow, blind eyes staring. It had barely moved since the old architect left the Manor.

"Here's that twine you wanted," Wally said, holding out the roll to his brother.

Graham didn't take it. His eyes were fixed on a large piece of flowery parchment, unraveled from the ceiling and lit by starbugs. The parchment showed an ever-changing map, the ink reorganizing itself to match the pocket-worlds that passed the window—a scraggly forest extended into city blocks, then spiked into choppy waves before smoothing into the rolling dunes of a desert. It was a Rift Detector.

"What do you see, Wally?" Graham asked.

Wally slipped the twine in his back pocket and stepped beside the waxen throne. As the fantastical terrains flowed along the shifting map, the occasional tear opened in the parchment before passing over the edge. The Manor was automatically traveling to these holes in the Veil like sap to a tree wound, but with no Wardens there to sew them up, it kept moving on to the next and the next.

"I see Rifts," Wally said.

Graham smiled. "More and more every day."

Wally suppressed a wince, lightly touching the burns he'd received on his palms from the flaming bull, the cuts on his arms from the scythe-clawed Corvidians.

Graham had stolen the Manor so they could tear down the Veil, melding the Real with the Fae and giving resources to the Fae-born and magic to humankind. Wally couldn't see how allowing every creature in the Fae to cross into the Real wouldn't descend into chaos.

"I'm not talking about the Rifts," Graham said. He watched the map until a blank space appeared in the ink. "*That*. What is that?"

"What do you mean?" Wally said. "It's the Eraser."

"The what?"

Wally blinked in shock. Graham hadn't foreseen the Eraser's actions. Just as he hadn't seen Breeth's. Did ghosts and nothingness somehow obscure the future?

Wally tried to remember how Lady Weirdwood had described the Eraser. "It's a *Void*, which is, um, the absence left behind by a beloved character that's been erased. When people miss that character, it creates a sort of black hole in the Fae, which sucks up everything it touches. Most Voids stay where they are until the Wardens come to solve it. But for some reason, this Void can move around. Almost like it's trying to find itself again. But the Wardens have no idea how to beat it. And it's been erasing pocket-worlds everywhere it goes."

"How *exciting*," Graham said. He looked at the Rift Detector's blank spots with admiration. "It's rare that the timeline presents something I never saw coming."

"Exciting? Graham, it's *horrifying*."

Graham grabbed the back of Wally's neck and gave it a light shake. "Don't worry, brother. The Eraser will not be a problem for us. Or the Fae at large."

"You sure about that?" Wally asked. A minute ago, his brother hadn't even known the Eraser existed.

Graham closed his eyes and got a serene look, as if lost in a dream. "I see the fall of the Veil. I see a *million* pocket-worlds converging into the Real. I see humans and Fae-born coming together to celebrate their differences and elevate each other's lives." He opened his eyes. "And there isn't a blank section in sight."

Wally bit his lip to keep from arguing. Every one of Graham's predictions had come true: the locked-up artist, the falling hospital, Huamei's death. What choice did Wally have but to trust that his brother's visions would continue to be accurate?

"How do we bring down the Veil, anyway?" he asked.

"*We* do not," Graham said. "You do."

"Yeah, you've said that," Wally said, shifting uncomfortably. "But *how* will I do it? And . . . why?"

Bringing down the border between the Real and imagined worlds felt as impossible as vacuuming every cloud out of the sky. And Wally couldn't envision bringing it down *himself*. Not when he was still unsure of the consequences.

"Don't worry about the details, brother," Graham said. "Otherwise, you won't enjoy the ride."

Wally fought the urge to seize his brother's shirt and *demand* an answer. He felt he was due some explanation after sacrificing his role as Novitiate and tricking his old trainer Sekhmet out of the Manor so his brother could steal it. Not to mention—his heart squeezed—leaving Breeth and Arthur behind. But Wally kept his hands to himself. When it came to talking about the future, Graham was tougher to crack than a clam encased in cement.

"Remember when Mom and Dad used to make us do chores?" Graham asked.

Wally put pressure on his temples, trying to keep up with the strange conversation. "Of course I do. You never finished yours, and I was so afraid we would get in trouble that I did them for you. It drove me crazy."

"You wasted a lot of needless energy," Graham said. "See, I never cleaned the parts that I knew our parents wouldn't notice. I peeked into the future and saw them returning home, content as lambs about the condition of the house."

A laugh burst out of Wally before he could stop it. "Maybe you predicted they wouldn't see the dirty parts because I ended up doing all the work!"

The brothers laughed together, and Wally felt his uncertainty fade. Mixed feelings about the Wardens and the Veil aside, it felt good to have Graham beside him. Wally no longer had to worry that his brother was going to receive experimental treatments in Greyridge or become lost in the Fae. Graham was home for him.

"So," Wally said, looking back to the Rift Detector, "where we headed?"

Graham didn't respond. He had that glazed look again, like his eyes were made of marbles. He was seeing the future.

"Graham?" Wally said. "What's happening?"

"In about thirty seconds," Graham said, "a talking ferret is going to sneak through that door. She'll attack me and then jump onto the throne where she'll try to steer the Manor back to the Wardens."

"Wait, what?" Wally said. "Audrey is here? She's going to *what*?" He couldn't imagine the sweet ferret attacking anyone.

"She's not herself," Graham said, eyes still glassy. "Arthur is controlling her with his writing."

"He's . . . ," Wally began but became too shocked for words. "How is he doing that without a dragon-bone Quill?"

The door burst open. *"Fangs to insurrectionists!"*

Audrey ran into the room on four paws and lunged at Graham, claws raised. Wally darted forward and just managed to catch her by the paw, the momentum bringing them both to the floor as Graham retreated to the far corner.

Audrey hissed and snapped at Wally's face as they rolled across the Throne Room. The ferret was maniacal. Feverish. Every bit of whiskery charm in her fuzzy face was gone. She gnashed her fangs, nearly catching Wally's eyelid, and he flinched back, letting her slip away. She had just managed to sit on the throne and shout, *"Dapple—!"* when Wally leapt up and tackled her, throne and all, to the floor.

Doing his best not to hurt the fragile ferret, he clasped Audrey's forepaws in one hand while grabbing the twine from his back pocket. But her paws were slippery, and one slid out of his grasp and slashed at his cheek, opening three cuts across his face. Wincing in pain, Wally managed to bind her wrists together as she continued to thrash like a wild animal.

Audrey narrowed her caramel eyes. "Surrender the Manor," she snarled, "and I'll let you off with the equivalent of a paper cut!"

Wally had met the ferret only briefly, but this didn't sound

like something she would say. He didn't know how Arthur had managed to control the ferret, but he wasn't surprised. The Wardens were not above abusing magic. And now they were having their Novitiates abuse it too.

Wally stared deep into the ferret's pupils. "How *dare* you, Arthur?"

With those words, Audrey suddenly relaxed. The tension left the ferret's limbs and she fell fast asleep.

Wally sat back and tried to catch his breath. "*That's* why you had me bring the twine?" he asked Graham. "So I could tie up my friend?"

His brother approached, giving the unconscious ferret a

sympathetic look. "She can't be allowed to roam the Manor, Wally."

Wally shook his head, beginning to untie Audrey's paws. "We don't lock up innocents. We're not like the Wardens."

Graham lightly touched his shoulder. "It's only until she learns how to shake Arthur's control over her."

Wally released the twine and rubbed his forehead in exasperation. Audrey hadn't done anything wrong. But he couldn't let Arthur use her to attack his brother again.

"I guess it isn't too bad in the Abyssment's first-floor cells," Wally said. "I'd need to get a proper bed from the Moon Tower and some food from the feasting hall . . ." He looked at Audrey's fluttering eyelids. "I still don't understand how Arthur did th—*whoa*."

The floor tilted, and Graham braced himself against the fallen throne. The Manor was landing somewhere. Wally looked to the window and saw a slate-gray sky. A familiar smell wafted down the corridors—fish and ash and ocean air.

His breath caught. "Are we in . . . ?"

Graham smiled.

Wally looked to Audrey, still sound asleep.

"She's not going anywhere," Graham said.

Wally leapt to his feet and sprinted out of the room. He ran down passages and cut around corners, through the Room of Currency, up and around the spiral hallway, past the Willow Room, and into the foyer where he and Arthur had broken in so long ago.

Wally stepped out of the Manor onto a bustling city street. He breathed deep the salty air.

"*Kingsport*." He exhaled the word.

He was in Fortune-Teller's Alley, the Manor currently occupying a shop space for rent. People were going about their day, getting their palms read and purchasing lucky trinkets. No dolls tottered along the cobbles. No ravens infested the skies. No tentacles slithered out of the drains. There wasn't a fake ghost in sight. It was just his city. And that was all.

Wally's jaw tightened. Then again, why would the Manor come here unless there was a—

"*Aaauuuggggggghhhhhh!*"

Someone screamed in the distance.

Wally froze, uncertain for a moment how to respond. As a thief, he would have run from trouble, not wanting to attract the attention of the Oakers. But as a Novitiate, he had been trained to run toward danger. What sort of person was he now?

Wally ran toward the scream, preparing for a fight. But as he drew closer, the scream rose to a higher pitch. It became a screech of . . . *delight*.

He rounded the corner and slowed to a stop. He was in the Ghastly Courtyard—the horrible place where the Oakers hanged condemned members of the Black Feathers. Wally expected to find killer nooses snaking after innocents, corpses sprung to life and terrorizing the living citizens . . .

Instead, he saw a Rift, no bigger than a doorway. The otherworldly light of Mirror Kingsport seeped into the colorless gray of the evening. Streaming out of the Rift were smokelike images—happy families, children opening birthday presents, smiling women arm in arm with dapper men in expensive, custom-made suits.

Wally had known some of these men. It didn't take him long to realize these were the hopes and dreams of the Black Feathers who had been executed there, their final thoughts drifting into the Courtyard where they could twirl freely.

Before the Rift stood a group of people, mouths covered, the final thoughts of the executed gleaming in their unblinking eyes. These were the hanged Black Feathers' loved ones—those who had lost their friends and fathers and brothers and sons much too soon, often without a chance to say goodbye. But now, these loved ones could step inside, even dance, in the final dreams of the executed.

On the other side of the Courtyard was a different kind of scene. The Oakers had heard about the ghostly visions and come to put a stop to the disturbance. But the moment Kingsport's officers saw the smoky images, they collapsed to their knees. Tears streamed down their faces as they begged the men they'd condemned for forgiveness.

The sight took Wally's breath away. He didn't know how long he stood there watching. But before he knew it, before he was ready, the light within the Rift brightened as dawn rose in the Mirror City, and the hopes of the lost Black Feathers faded.

The loved ones wiped their eyes, as if waking from a dream, and quietly returned home. The Oakers did the same, their usual sneers replaced by pale, slack expressions. One even left his oaken stick behind.

Wally looked at the Rift, its ragged edges flapping like ghostly drapes. If it grew any bigger, it might turn dangerous. And whether Wally was with the Wardens or his brother, he wanted to keep Kingsport safe. He whispered the Ward Sekhmet had taught him, and the Rift sealed like a closing eye. The Mirror light vanished, and Wally felt a pinch of regret.

He returned to Fortune-Teller's Alley and the space for rent. His brother was waiting for him in the Manor's entrance.

"The Wardens would call what you just saw a Daymare," Graham said.

Wally gazed back toward the Ghastly Courtyard. "It was beautiful."

"Of course it was," Graham said. "The Wardens tend to lump all Rifts, harmful and helpful, into the same category. Those in power have always remained in control by making things that could *help* us, like revolutions or the fall of the Veil, sound scary. Believe it or not, in the original Greek, *apocalypse* meant the unveiling of knowledge we haven't seen before."

Wally considered that a moment. Before losing his parents and joining the Black Feathers, he had thought thieves were evil. Before he'd met Breeth, he had thought ghosts were something to be feared. And just now, he had watched a nightmare turn into a dream before his very eyes. If the Wardens still had the Manor, they would have ended that beautiful scene in the Ghastly Courtyard before it could start.

"Everything you've heard about Rifts came from the Wardens, Wally," Graham said. "They treat the smallest leak between the worlds as a catastrophe. But the truth is that most holes in the Veil are advantageous. Eye-opening and soul-healing. The Wardens only send their Novitiates to the most dangerous Rifts so they can brainwash you into believing they're all that way."

Wally opened his hand and looked at the burn marks there. "What about the Fae-born zoo? You can't tell me those creatures weren't dangerous."

Graham chuckled. "Those Fae-born would have been harmless had they had remained in whatever part of the Real dreamt them up. You can't expect a tiger to be tame if you release it into a city."

Wally curled his fingers into a fist. He wasn't sure that was true.

"Now, brother," Graham said, putting an arm around Wally's shoulder, "imagine what you just saw spread across the *entire world*."

Wally tried to do just that. The idea wouldn't fit in his head.

His brother jostled his shoulder. "Where shall we go? Once the Veil has fallen and all this chaos is behind us?"

Wally blinked. "I hadn't thought about it."

"Well, you'd better start narrowing your options now," Graham said with a grin. "They'll be infinite."

Wally sighed and gazed around the street. He had the whole of creation, real and imagined, to choose from. But all he could think about were those spectral figures in the House of Spirits—the ones Arthur had assured him were not his parents.

"I want to see Mom and Dad again," he said.

"Sounds good to me," Graham said, and pulled him into a hug. "I won't even make you do my chores this time."

Wally laughed and squeezed his brother tight.

"Nearly at our yearny's end, my silvery sweet!" a grating voice said behind him.

"We'd better be, Rusty," a cracked and sugary voice answered. "If I have to sleep in another circus tent, I'll make you bite off your own pinkie!"

Wally slowly turned, the glow in his heart replaced by a curdling horror. The Order of Eldar was marching toward the Manor's entrance. His stomach churned when he saw Rustmouth's brown smile, which could chomp straight through steel. His nose ached when he heard Silver Tongue's voice, who with a single sip from her mercury flask could command anyone to do anything she desired. The sight of the rocky Astonishment made every bone in Wally's body feel brittle.

"Graham!" he said. "It's the Order. Quick, shut the door before they get inside!"

Graham didn't budge from the doorway. "That would be rude to our guests, Wally."

"*Guests?*" Wally said, his fear quickly replaced by fury. "You promised me we would never work with the Order!"

"Yes, I did," Graham said. "But I never said they wouldn't work *for* us."

Wally couldn't stop from shaking. How could he have forgotten that Graham had told the Order where Arthur was hiding? That his brother had manipulated him and his friends, putting them all in danger, just to get inside the Manor? Wally had wanted Graham to be good so badly that he had dismissed his brother's awful deeds.

"We must keep the Wardens out of the Manor, Wally," Graham said. "Are you going to do that all by yourself?"

"Little birdy!" Rustmouth said, striding up. "I see you've successfully hexterminated those Snoredens like the *shlockroaches* they are!" He saw Wally and grinned his brown grin. "And if isn't a *little* little birdy! Hatchling, really! Ha!" He slapped Wally on the back. "No blunder your face was so familiaratin'!"

Wally squeezed his fists so tight he thought his knuckles might break.

Graham raised his hand to greet the Order with his puppetless fingers. "Welcome to Weirdwood!"

"Much oblighted!" Rustmouth said, and entered the Manor, followed by Silver Tongue and the Astonishment, who tromped in, rubbing a crack in her forehead like a forlorn statue.

Graham kept the door open for Wally. "Coming?"

Wally felt like he was falling. Just minutes before, in front of that Rift and all its riches, he had come to see his brother's perspective clearly. Now he was less sure than ever. A part of him wanted to turn around, disappear into Kingsport, rejoin the Black Feathers, and wash his hands of the Manor, the Order, and this entire mess.

But if Graham's predictions were correct, Wally had nothing to fear. Not even from the evilest of villains. And if Graham was wrong and the Wardens were good after all, who else would stop Graham and the Order of Eldar . . . other than Wally?

Wally drew a deep breath, and he entered the Manor.

3
THE ERASED

In a little town . . .

    On a little lane . . .

      In a little cottage . . .

In a little bed . . .

Arthur Benton couldn't sleep.

He tossed and turned, fluffing the tiny pillow and shifting the tiny blankets. Audrey's home felt particularly drafty that night, and Arthur's body was racked with shivers and aches.

"*Rrg!*" he said, wrestling the blankets and punching the pillow. When the bed refused to cooperate, he flopped onto his back and gave up on sleep altogether. Arthur sighed. He knew it wasn't the tiny bed or the cold keeping him awake. It was guilt.

He pulled Audrey's diary from the nightstand and flipped to the last entry. It had been a day of sewing and deliveries for the ferret seamstress—mending a houndstooth jacket for the frog detective and presenting a new apron to Mrs. Chicken. Then, nothing. The following pages were as blank as the original Dapplewood . . . until tonight.

In the observatory that day, Amelia had instructed Arthur to return to Audrey's home and collect her diary so he could form an emotional connection with the ferret while controlling her actions in the Manor. Arthur had written his commands on the diary's blank pages.

He had tried to mix some adventure into the sentences. He'd wanted to play with Wally, remind him that they were friends, show him that he was acting like the bad guy. "*Fangs to insurrectionists!*" had seemed like a funny line at the time.

But then, Wally's own words had scrawled themselves across the page.

How dare you, Arthur?

The moment Arthur had read those words, he had hurled his pen across the room, regretting ever having picked it up. Graham had seen the ferret coming. Wally had even had twine ready. Arthur had controlled Audrey without her permission and made her and Wally think less of him. All for nothing.

Amelia had pressed Arthur to continue, arguing that Audrey was one little ferret compared to untold numbers of Fae-born that would be saved if the Wardens retrieved the Manor. Arthur had folded his hands in his armpits and refused to write another word, and Amelia had banished him from the observatory. As he left, he heard Amelia "speaking to herself" again.

"Did you just tear a Rift?"

Arthur didn't know what it meant, but it was clear Amelia was hiding something.

A tiny sigh drew Arthur's eyes to the crib beside his bed. BW's face glowed in the moonlight, her little snores light and quick. He knew the most important thing was getting the baby back into the Manor so she could return to her adult form, defeat the Eraser, mend the Veil, and restore the Balance between the Real and Fae . . .

But at what cost?

KNOCK KNOCK KNOCK!

Arthur sat straight up and blinked through the darkness. Audrey's cuckoo clock read three A.M. Who was visiting in the middle of the night?

KNOCK KNOCK KNOCK!

Arthur slid out of bed, shivering in the night air as he crept toward the curtained window beside the front door. He parted the curtains, then dropped them in fear.

There was nothing outside. The DappleWood was gone.

KNOCK KNOCK KNOCK KNOCK KNOCK!

Arthur backed away from the door. The Eraser was here. It had absorbed the little town and all its critter residents, even the Wardens and the staff. And now it had come for him.

"Arthur?" a voice said outside.

Amelia.

Arthur jerked forward and threw open the door, desperate

to get her inside before she was also erased. The acrobat ducked through the entrance with a waft of frozen wind, spilling white across the foyer. Arthur stuck his hand outside, and a bit of white landed in his palm and melted there. *Snow.* All down the lane, it piled high on the little roofs, doubling their height. The DappleWood hadn't been erased. It was buried in the deepest winter he had ever seen.

"When did winter start?" Arthur said, heart settling a bit.

"Tonight," Amelia said, removing her coat. "Obviously."

Arthur tensed when he saw she had a new whip coiled on her belt, a replacement for the one she'd lost while battling the Eraser.

"The seasons in a storybook town are quicker than most," Amelia continued, hanging her coat on the little rack. "As quick as a child deciding whether it wants a story set in spring or autumn on a given night." She looked at Arthur. "The creator's mood can also have an effect."

Arthur shivered and closed the door.

"So," he said. "What brings you here near the witching hour?"

Amelia swept around the house, checking windows and pulling curtains shut until only the faintest hint of snowy blue bled through. She checked on BW, fast asleep in her crib, before marching straight up to Arthur, eye narrowed. "Are you certain that was Garnett Lacroix you saw in the Eraser?"

Arthur remembered the starry swoop of the Gentleman Thief's hat, those golden eyes flashing in the nothingness. He nodded. "I'd recognize that guy's dashing good looks anywhere."

Amelia sighed and shook her head. "That doesn't make *sense*. When you retired Garnett with that dragon-bone Quill, you wrote him out of existence. This was not a story death, where a character could be resurrected with a clever twist. Death by dragon-bone Quill means complete elimination, even in people's imaginations."

Something clicked for Arthur then. After Lady Weirdwood had kicked him out of the Manor, he had returned to Market Square to tell new stories of the Gentleman Thief—one of the most famous characters in Kingsport. But the shoppers had had no idea who he was talking about. Now he understood why. Garnett Lacroix had been eradicated on both sides of the Veil.

"What you saw in the Eraser was impossible," Amelia continued. She studied Arthur, head to foot. "Unless . . ."

Arthur touched a hand to his chest. "He lives on in me?"

Amelia huffed. "*Nonsense.* You were in the Manor. It's immune to changes in the Real and the Fae. Garnett Lacroix 'lives on' in *everyone* in the Manor if you want to be drippy about it."

Arthur cleared his throat with embarrassment.

"Regardless." Amelia set a pen and notebook on the kitchen table.

"*No,*" Arthur said. "No, no, no. I refuse to control Audrey again. I don't care if you have to fire me as a Novitiate." He swallowed. "But also, please don't."

"This is something different," Amelia said, sitting in one of the little kitchen chairs. "You are going to try to bring Garnett Lacroix back from the dead."

Arthur slumped into the chair opposite. "I'm what?"

"If you really saw a flash of the Gentleman Thief, that means he still exists *somewhere*. And if the Void is searching for something to fill itself, then we are going to give it exactly what it wants. You are going to try and breathe life into the Gentleman Thief by writing a new story in this pocket-world where you hold influence. Maybe, just maybe, you'll be able to write over the Eraser like a blank page."

Something like hope shone through Arthur's fear. This felt much better than controlling Audrey. Still, something about it made him nervous. He remembered what he'd heard as he left the observatory. Amelia had been talking about tearing Rifts in the Veil.

"Amelia, you're not . . . secretly working for the Order, are you?"

Amelia's lips tightened. "If I were working for the Order, I probably would have let them into the Manor at the Great Elsewhere, now wouldn't I?"

"Yeah, I guess so. But . . . isn't this misusing magic?" He looked toward the bedroom and BW's crib. "What would Lady Weirdwood th—"

"*Shh!*" The acrobat clamped a hand over Arthur's mouth and stared at the crib, listening. When the baby's breath remained soft and steady, Amelia whispered, "Our lady is in no condition to give us her wisdom right now. And all my other ideas have fallen through." She touched her eye patch. "The . . . *elements* aren't being cooperative."

Arthur assumed the "elements" were those strange weather patterns he'd seen drawn over the maps in the observatory.

"Meanwhile," Amelia continued, "the Eraser is destroying everything in the Fae. Soon, it will create enough Rifts to drag the entire *Real* into Daymare. I hope I do not need to tell you how horrific that would be."

Arthur fell quiet as he imagined Kingsport overrun with the unspeakable monsters he'd seen in the Mirror City.

"Come," Amelia said, placing the pen in his hand. "Get writing before the Wardens wake."

Trembling, Arthur pressed the nib to the paper, but his hand refused to move. Every mistake he'd made on this adventure came flashing through his mind: writing *magical* before Kingsport, landing him and Wally in a dangerous mirror city; accidentally killing Liza's father; and worst of all, creating the Eraser by retiring his hero.

He dropped the pen before his heart could collapse in on itself. "I can't do it, Amelia. I'm sorry."

He could feel her staring at him as she rhythmically tapped her fingernails on the table. *Tap tap tap tap. Tap tap tap tap.*

"I didn't want to have to tell you this," she finally said. "But the Eraser has been revisiting its old stories, looking for something to fill its absence. It seems to have erased the Merry Rogues."

An emptiness opened in Arthur's chest. "No . . ." He couldn't imagine living in a world without Garnett or his Rogues.

Amelia scooted her chair closer. "*You* can stop this from happening, Arthur. With a few simple sentences, you can *save* the Fae and the Real and everyone in them."

Arthur frowned at the blank page and imagined Gus, Tuck, and Mim melting away, layer by layer, as Weston had. Then he imagined the same thing happening to everyone he'd ever met.

"Guess I'd better make this count," he said.

He scooted his chair in, picked up the pen, and without thinking, started to write.

Retirement did not suit Garnett Lacroix.
How could the man who saved a thousand orphans,
slew a thousand villains, and ~~smooched~~ swooned a
thousand damsels possibly sit still?
Having moseyed into the sunset with his friend and patron,
Alfred Moore, the Gentleman Thief found his mind wandering.
What orphans went unfed in the wide world? What adventures
went unventured? What evils lurked at the edge of all that was
known, bubbling and brewing and ready to ex—

BOOM!

There was an explosion outside, so loud it rattled Audrey's little house. BW woke with a gasp and started to wail as Amelia hurried to the window and threw open the curtain. A red glow cascaded across the winter clouds, casting a bloody light across the DappleWood.

Arthur slowly stood as his jaw began to shake. "I—I did just what you told me! I was writing about Garnett Lacroix! I—"

Shrrrrr!

A snarl, wet and grinding, spun Arthur around. Something was in Audrey's fireplace. Something spiny and hunched. It was *panting*.

Amelia uncoiled her whip and pointed to the notebook. "Get that outside!"

Arthur didn't need to be told twice. He snatched the notebook and ran out the front door as the sound of whipping and screeches filled the house behind him. He tromped through the snow, shivering with fear, until he reached the middle of the lane, where he turned back to see if Amelia was okay.

The sight took his breath away. He gazed up and up and up at a massive funnel of red and stretching faces, which poured like melting wax from a bloody swirl of clouds straight into Audrey's chimney. The funnel bent through the little house and out the front door, where it ended in the notebook in Arthur's hands.

SKREEEEKKKKKK!

With a final, guttural screech, the thing in Audrey's fireplace went silent and Amelia rushed outside, pulling on her coat. She seized the notebook from Arthur's hands, tossed it into the air, and struck her whip, creating a sonic boom that sent the notebook flying to the DappleWood's horizon.

The funnel of horrific faces went with it, now pouring into the heart of the forest.

"I was never here," Amelia said, and took off through the snow, vanishing among the flakes.

Arthur stood in shock until lights began to flicker up and

down the lane, sparkling the snowfall. The sounds had awoken the DappleWood citizens. He hurried back into Audrey's house and slammed the door behind him. BW continued to wail in her crib as Arthur collapsed to the floor, trying to catch his breath and wait for the feeling to return to his fingers and toes.

Finally, he had a gripping story worthy enough to tell his audience the next day.

And he didn't want any part of it.

4
SILVER AND RUST

"So there we was, beat to a pulpitude and adrifted in the spirit-infested pocket-world of a tykerant named Arthur Benton!"

Wally followed the Order through the Manor as they tromped down the passages, muddying the rugs and bumping the vases. An alarm was going off in Wally's head: *The Order is in the Manor! The Order is in the Manor!* He had to keep reminding himself that he wasn't a Novitiate anymore.

Rustmouth had propped up the Astonishment, whose cracked stone forehead seemed to have gotten the best of her while Silver Tongue followed behind, arms folded in a pout. Graham was nowhere in sight.

"The wincetant we plummeted through that cloud floor, I thought, 'It's all up for us!' Er, *down*, rather. Ha!" Rustmouth said, continuing to explain to no one in particular how they had managed to escape the Great Elsewhere. "I believed in my rustled heart that me, the Astonishment, and Silver Tongue would continue to fall forevermore as the winds stripped flesh and bone, rust and stone, till there was nothin' but a wisper of charm and gnashing good looks!"

"Rusty!" Silver Tongue shrieked. "When we gonna get me more of that silver stuff? I ain't got but the one swallow left!"

She shook her mercury flask, which sloshed, nearly empty. The sound reassured Wally, but he wished the flask was completely empty.

Rustmouth peered back at Silver Tongue, his brown smile drooping into a frown. "Apologies, my sweetly spoken spill of sugar. You know I'd sooner gargle vinegar than keep from you what's yorn." He hefted the Astonishment with a grunt, continuing to help her walk. "Once I've set our pal here to rocky rights, we'll open one of this Manor's rotational doorways right onto them Mercurial Mines."

"*Hmph!*" Silver Tongue said, scowling at the Astonishment. "You're always payin' her more attention than me."

"Only when she's got a fissured noggin, my liquid love."

Oh, Wally thought with a wince. Rustmouth and Silver Tongue were *lovers*. He imagined the man's brown lips kissing her blue ones, red saliva mixing with silver, and he nearly threw up right there on the floor.

"Say, Hatchling!" Rustmouth called back to Wally. "Where's this maniacal Manor's infirmary? My pal the Astonishment could use some firming."

Wally crossed his arms. "I'm not telling you a thing."

Silver Tongue spun around, stopping Wally in his tracks. She squinted her shark-black eyes and shook her flask in his face. "You wanna rethink that, hon?"

Wally rubbed the ache from his nose, which the woman had commanded him to break with his own fist. He sighed, pushed past her, and led the Order to the Healing Room. At least their destruction would be contained to one place.

The moment the Astonishment stepped into the room, she collapsed onto the nearest bed, shattering the wooden frame and laying it flat before instantly starting to snore.

While Rustmouth rattled through the medicine bottles and Silver Tongue continued to pout in the corner, Wally placed himself in the doorway like a guard. His brother might consider these people guests, but he was prepared to fight if they tried anything funny.

Rustmouth found some bandages and began gently wrapping the small crack on the Astonishment's head.

"Where was I? Right! We was plummeting through open sky, and where should we land but a familiaratin' space we'd tourerized not long before? It was mostly blanks and thinglessness, but I recognized a tree and a ladder, and a cobbly speck or two. Why, if it wasn't the fuzzity animal village we'd followed the Eraser into! We re-locatered ourselves to a half-erased barn, scaled it to a pub called the StormityCrow, exited into Kingsport, and the rest is mistory!"

Wally scowled. He wished the Order had remained lost forever in the Fae.

"*There!*" Rustmouth said, delicately tying the Astonishment's bandage with the tips of his fingers. "Fit as a fickle!"

The Astonishment sighed dustily like a rockslide come to rest. Wally didn't like that the strongest fighter he'd ever seen on either side of the Veil was being healed.

Silver Tongue didn't seem too pleased about it either. "*Hmph!*"

"Now, my silver spoonling," Rustmouth said, rubbing a vicious yellow bruise along his jawline. "If you wouldn't mind extrickating this spitiful little molar o' mine . . . That Arthur tried to defangle me with a flappin' pair o' pliers and now my jaw's aflamin'!"

He opened his rusted jaws in Silver Tongue's direction, and Wally noticed a tooth hanging loose in the man's brown gums.

"Pull your own tooth, you *beast*," Silver Tongue said. She flopped onto a bed and yanked the covers over herself.

Rustmouth closed his mouth in a frown and he rubbed at his bruise. He glanced at the Astonishment, passed out cold as a boulder, then gave Wally a hopeful look. Wally kept his arms crossed.

"*Rusty!*" Silver Tongue's arm shot out from beneath the blanket and shook her flask. "Refill!"

Wincing, Rustmouth took the flask. He tried to exit the Healing Room, but Wally blocked his way.

"Uh-uh," Wally said. "You're staying in here."

"Well now," Rustmouth said dangerously. "Seems someone fascists himself bigger than his britches."

Wally felt small in the shadow of the foul-mouthed man. He didn't have any magic to speak of. He didn't even have his gauntlets. Where was Graham when he needed him?

"You ain't still sore about that harmless little zoo we cobbled, is ya?" Rustmouth asked, nearly nose to nose with Wally. "It was just a smatter of business. Sorely you understand."

Wally stood his ground. "You stole innocent Fae-born, caged them, and sold tickets to make money off their suffering."

Rustmouth gave a half-pained smile. "Folks get by any ways they can, doesn't they?"

Wally's stance wavered. He'd had to do unspeakable things to survive his years in the Black Feathers. Things he wouldn't want held against him.

He stood a little taller. "You worked with Rose."

"You mean our adorigable little blacksmith?"

"She *murdered* my friend," Wally said. "Then she stole her body and possessed it."

"The woman was heartsick over her 'ceased son," Rustmouth said. He pressed a finger into Wally's chest. "How far would you go to see your lost loved ones again?"

I would bring down the Veil, Wally thought before he could stop himself.

"I wouldn't kill a kid," he said.

"That makes two of us!" Rustmouth said, grin returning. "Less'n Silver Tongue commandeered me to do it. Ha! I'm kidding, of course." He scratched his stubble. "Kind of."

Wally folded his arms tight, refusing to allow Rustmouth's rusted words to erode his will.

"You're working for the Eraser," he said.

"Ha!" The laugh must have brought a new wave of tooth pain, making Rustmouth wince. "Hear that, Silver? The Hatchling supposels we labor for His Blankness!"

"Mr. Raser?" Silver Tongue said from beneath the blanket. "I'm still mad at him. He erased that pretty lamp I wanted!"

Rustmouth raised an eyebrow at Wally. "See? The Eraser'd never join the Order, and we'd never have him. We was simply following that hollow hexcuse for a humanoid as it tore through the Fae like a bull through a china shop, taking madvantage of the Rifts in its wake. Not every dish gets smashered, y'know. Once the Eraser begun spoilin' pockety-worlds with wares what was valuating to us, we decided it bestish to part ways. By the end, we was running to save our own sins!"

A new fear opened in Wally. The Eraser, a walking black hole, was beholden to nothing and no one. Not even the Order. Did the Wardens know this? Was Rustmouth telling the truth?

Rustmouth placed a meaty hand on his shoulder. "We's partners, little Hatchling. You just ain't realitized it yet. Now, if you'll let me pass, I promise not to make any mixchief in your little Manor. We's just here to heal up"—he shook Silver Tongue's nearly empty flask—"and prepare to lay waste to some Wardys."

Wally scowled.

"And the Eraser, of course," Rustmouth said with a smile.

He moved to step past Wally, and Wally reluctantly let him go. As much as he wanted to keep the Manor safe, he couldn't keep an eye on the Order around the clock. Audrey was still locked up in the Abyssment. She had probably woken up by now.

***

After snagging some food from the feasting hall, Wally walked down a corridor of windows, which currently looked onto the starry expanse that existed between the pocket-worlds. In the distance, twining through the stars, was a train with a dragon head for an engine, blazing through the whole of creation.

Nearer by, Wally could see the protective bubble sheen Lady Weirdwood had cast over the Manor after having led the Eraser outside. He assumed it kept the Eraser from reentering Weirdwood and harming the Wardens. But now it was protecting the Order and Graham instead.

Wally sighed. "Sorry, Lady Weirdwood."

He stepped over the half-erased pile of armor and descended the staircase to the first floor of the Abyssment. Audrey was sitting up in the cell, fussing over stains on her apron. Wally had to remind himself it wasn't the sweet, innocent ferret he had locked up.

"Hi, Audrey."

She looked up, startled. "You're . . . *Wally*, right?"

Wally nodded, relieved to hear that the ferret's gentle accent had returned.

"What am I doing in here?" she asked, gazing around her cell with wide, caramel eyes. "One moment I was sniffing around this drafty old Manor for food, the next . . ."

Her voice faded when she saw the slashes across Wally's cheek—three thin lines. She stared down at her three claws and saw the blood crusting there. She looked lost.

Wally shifted uncomfortably. How was he supposed to tell her that she had attacked him and Graham? That her actions were not her own?

"You were, um, sleepwalking," he said. "We had to lock you up for your own protection."

Audrey didn't take her eyes off her claws. "That's what the Badgers with Badges always told Mr. Cottontail whenever he had a few too many blackberry juices."

Wally sat beside her, on the other side of the bars, and handed her the plate of cheese and bread. "Sorry about the food. I'm no Pyra."

Audrey attempted a smile. "Where I come from, we call this a *cupboard* banquet." She sank her teeth into the bread as if she hadn't eaten in weeks. "I apologize if I hurt you any. I never sleepwalked a day in my life before now. My family does have wild roots though. Highwayferrets and the like. But for the last several dozen generations, we Abbotts have been nothing but charm and hospitality. We're not the type to run around on *four paws*, so to speak."

"You didn't hurt me too bad," Wally said, touching the slashes. "You were just . . . surprised when I tried to wake you."

Audrey cradled her head. "It must be the stress of losing the Dapplewood and all my neighbors. It's awakening instincts I didn't realize I had."

"Oh!" Wally said. "I saw the Dapplewood citizens in the Real. They weren't erased."

Audrey's whole face lit up. "Are they all right?"

The last time Wally had seen them, they had been shackled in the House of Spirits. He wished he had thought to ask Rustmouth what had happened to them after that.

"I don't know," he said. "I'm sorry."

They sat in silence while Audrey finished the bread and cheese.

"It's probably none of my business," she said, dusting crumbs from her paws, "but may I ask why you and your brother stole this Manor?"

Wally's mouth fell open. "What makes you think . . . ?"

"Oh, come now." Audrey tapped the side of her muzzle. "It don't take an expert sniffer."

Wally sighed, trying to decide whether this information would be dangerous in Audrey's paws. But even if Arthur and the Wardens were somehow listening through the ferret's ears, it's not like this would come as a surprise. Besides, Wally could finally explain himself.

"We're . . . trying to bring down the Veil."

"The *what*, now?"

Wally did his best to capture his brother's intoxicating conviction as he told Audrey that the Veil was a border wall that kept free trade from happening between the Real and the Fae. That it gave the Wardens of Weirdwood control over all magic, which they hoarded from everyone else. That when the Veil fell, there would be a difficult period of transition. But once the nightmares were addressed, the dreams could come through and create a new, better balance between both worlds.

"*Well*," Audrey said once he was finished. "I think that is a terrible idea."

Wally winced. "I didn't explain it well," he said, pinching the bridge of his nose. "I'm not great with words. That was always Arthur's thing."

"It doesn't matter *how* you say it when the idea itself is corrupted," Audrey said.

Wally scratched the back of his neck. "There are a lot of pocket-worlds in the Fae that would benefit from trading with the Real. And the other way around."

He told her about the miracle he'd seen in the Ghastly Courtyard.

"But will that sort of thing happen *everywhere*?" Audrey asked. "Or is this just wishful thinking?"

Wally picked at his fingernails. "My brother can see into the future. He's never wrong about these things. At least . . . not so far."

"Well, that's all well and good for your brother," Audrey said. "But can he guarantee that the moment the Veil falls, folks like that awful Order won't come pouring into every innocent critter's town?"

Wally fell silent. The more specific the questions became, the tougher it was to answer them. The only way to verify his brother's claims was to wait for the Veil to collapse and see what happened.

"The Dapplewood would still be there if it weren't for broken borders," Audrey continued. "You tell me my neighbors are safe, but my beautiful hometown will *never* return. Every cloud, cart, and cobblestone was erased"—she snapped her claws—"like *that*."

She sniffed, and Wally looked up to find tears shimmering in her eyes. How could he have been so callous? He wanted to assure the sweet ferret that if the Veil fell, nothing terrible would ever happen again to any Fae-born, ever. But Wally still hadn't convinced himself that was true.

Audrey dabbed her eyes with the backs of her paws. "Seems to me that's something you should think about before you bring this whole Veil crashing down."

Wally suddenly felt childish for following his brother without considering every angle. For trying to argue for something he didn't understand. There had been so little time to think about anything in the last few months.

"Audrey, I need to tell you something."

Audrey folded her paws. "Go on, then."

Wally touched the slashes on his cheek. "What happened in the Throne Room wasn't your fault. You weren't sleepwalking. Arthur was controlling you. I don't know how he did it."

Audrey considered her apron, eyebrows furrowed. "*Well*," she finally said, smoothing her apron and eyebrows. "I'm gonna have to let that one percolate a while, aren't I?"

Wally wanted to tell her that he knew what it was like to be controlled. That no matter how much he tried, he would always end up doing what his brother predicted. He wanted to tell Audrey that if the Veil fell, Arthur might not have control over her anymore. That she would become her own ferret. But he didn't know if that was true, either.

Silence passed.

Snffff. Audrey tipped her nose and sniffed the air. *Snff snff snffffff!* "We're . . . *snff snff* . . . we're in the *DappleWood*." She whispered it. Like it was something precious she didn't want to scare away.

Wally looked to the staircase. "But . . . that's impossible."

He jogged up to the first floor and gazed out the nearest

window. It showed a haunted wood—an oppressive blue gloam crisscrossed with dead branches and flooded with a sinister mist. He jogged back down.

"You sure?" he asked Audrey. "The place we're in doesn't look very *dappled*. And the Dapplewood was erased."

Audrey shook her head. "I don't understand it either. All I know is that we are in my hometown right now. I can smell it from here. Sure as shadows."

Wally bit his lip. He'd known Kingsport by its smell.

But there were other reasons he thought the ferret was mistaken. Graham had told him to grab the twine so he could prevent Audrey from sailing the Manor to the Dapplewood. Why would his brother do that if the Manor was headed there anyway? Unless Graham hadn't seen this coming. Or worse, Arthur was using his writing to mess with the ferret's senses, making her smell things that weren't there so she would escape, and he could control her again to get the Manor back.

Audrey clasped the cell bars. "Wally? You can let me out, right? I'm so close to home." She gazed up the staircase with shining eyes. "I've been dragged through dragon cities and meltin' manors and all sorts of unfortunate places. I shouldn't be locked up in this grimy cell. I should be with my neighbors, sewin' buttons and lettin' out Mr. Pig's pants waist." Audrey reached a paw through the bars and squeezed Wally's hand. "Please. Let me go."

Wally stared into the ferret's caramel eyes. Audrey hadn't asked to be on this adventure. She was the most innocent of them all. He had condemned the Wardens for locking up an innocent artist, and he was a hypocrite for doing the same.

Besides, Audrey was speaking with her natural accent and not Arthur's affected one.

"Okay, Audrey," Wally said, gazing up the staircase. "I'll get you out of here. But only if you let me come with you."

✳✳✳

Wally and Audrey snuck through the Manor, creeping on toes and claws. Though he felt guilty for doing so, he couldn't stop glancing at the ferret's face to make sure she wasn't wearing an Arthurish expression.

"Stop lookin' at me like that," Audrey whispered. "If I start blabbing about what a hotshot I am, you'll know Arthur's taken over. Till then, eyes to yourself."

Wally nodded and did just that.

With every step, he pushed through fear and guilt. He had never worked against his brother like this. And Graham's future-seeing abilities meant anything might stop them at any point. Still, Wally was determined to escape. Why couldn't he go live in the Dapplewood and never worry about the Manor and the Veil and the Wardens and Order ever again? Why couldn't he live a simple life?

BOOM! BOOM! BOOM!

A pounding reverberated down the hall, stopping Wally and Audrey in their tracks. The Astonishment seemed to have recovered and was sealing one of Weirdwood's entryways, pounding nails with her fists so deep they left craters in the wood. Had Graham instructed the Astonishment to stop Wally and Audrey from sneaking out?

Audrey poked a claw into Wally's side. "Don't tell me you and your brother are working with the people who kidnapped my neighbors."

Wally held a finger to his lips and led the ferret around the corner. "Now you know why I want to leave with you."

The anger left Audrey's face.

"Come on," Wally said. "I think I know a way out."

But every exit had been nailed shut with rocky fists. And Sekhmet had demonstrated that the windows were made from shatterproof Fae material.

The pit in Wally's stomach deepened. How were they supposed to escape?

"How about the roof?" Audrey said. "Where me and Arthur landed when we first came here?"

Wally considered. "It's really high."

Audrey looked to the nearest tree-haunted window and gave her claws a wiggle. "Not to brag, but I can descend a tree as safe as a falling feather. I can help you too."

Wally nodded and guided her down several passageways toward the roof's zigzag staircase. They had picked up the pace for the last stretch when another, screechier sound stopped them in their tracks.

"*Rusty!* Where's my mercury? I'm thirsty, and I wanna bag myself a Wardy!"

"Patience, my petty! I'll fetch some just as soon as I

demolish off these jabbers! Snackin' on swords and munchin' on maces and pickin' my teethses with pickaxes, am I!"

Rustmouth and Silver Tongue were in the armory. Wally could hear shards of metal crumbling to the floor as Rustmouth devoured the Wardens' weapons one by one.

Of course, the armory was directly between Wally and Audrey and the zigzag stairs. He was about to suggest that he go first and use his talents as a sneak thief to make sure the coast was clear. But Audrey was already down on four paws, scampering past the door, as smooth as an oily shadow. She stood up straight and waved for him to follow.

Wally held his breath, went flat against the wall, quickly stepped past the door, and—

"Hatchling!" Rustmouth bellowed.

Wally spun, quickly leaning against the doorframe, blocking Audrey from view as the man came stomping over. He secretly waved his hand, hoping to make the ferret hide in the shadows beneath the stairs.

"Glad I catched ya," Rustmouth said, reaching the door.

He held a dagger in his hand. Wally eyed it warily. Was that a snack? Or a way to stop him from leaving?

"Say," Rustmouth whispered, reaching into his pocket and flashing a nervous glance back at Silver Tongue. He drew out her flask. "You wouldn't mind gliding this here creakity Manor to them Mercurial Mines, would ya? My blue-lipped beauty's been skrieking my eardrums some'm shredful, and I can't seem to get this place to *mine* its *Manors*, if you catch my meaning. We's Grahamshackled."

Wally fought the urge to tell Rustmouth that he would never lift a finger to help his "blue-lipped beauty."

"I don't think Graham will let us go anywhere until we defeat the Wardens," he said.

Rustmouth cocked his jaw, giving Wally a suspicious look. "Why, Hatchling, I half expectered you to tell me to stick this flask where the sun don't shimmy." He grinned. "We're not becoming . . . *palatables*, is we?"

Wally's mind went blank. He instantly regretted behaving differently than he had in the Healing Room. Before he could think up an excuse, Audrey stepped into the doorway.

Rustmouth's eyebrows rose. "And who's this feralized female?"

"Who you callin' feral?" Audrey said in a voice as sweet as syrup. She offered her paw. "I'm Audrey. You must be one of the folks who kidnapped my entire village."

Wally's blood ran with ice. He widened his eyes at the ferret, desperately trying to signal that this was no time for a confrontation. Not when they were this close to the exit.

"*Kitnap?*" Rustmouth's hand jerked from Audrey's paw to his chest. "I'd never scheme of it! Truth be tolled, I couldn't stand to stand by while innocentities was nearased." He bowed his head in humility. "When the Eraser deliminated your dappled town, we took them crittles with us to proserve them!"

Audrey folded her arms. "I hear you shackled their throats and were gonna stick them in a zoo."

"A *zoo*? What do you take us for? Them crittles can prattle and toddle on two paws! We was going to find a new home for your fuzzified folklins, but then they was up and kitnapped— for *real* this time—by that Arthur devil. As far as the shackles, *you* just try and keep frightened crittles from skittering into the bustly city where they'd be killeded or *worse*."

Audrey studied the man's onyx eyes, as if searching for lies. Wally had no idea what to think.

"Where'd ya get that shiner?" Audrey asked, nodding to the bruise on Rustmouth's cheek.

Rustmouth touched his jaw. "A near mishap with some flyer pliers what tried to rob me of my shamesake." He frowned at Wally. "Some's too selfish to help a man in needles."

"I can help with that!" Audrey said. She reached into her apron pocket and pulled out a spool of thread. "Heaven knows I've pulled a tooth or two. I had six younger siblings and a hundred and eighty-four baby fangs between them."

Rustmouth grinned. "Why, if you ain't a downy angel!"

To Wally's shock, the man handed him the dagger and knelt, coming nose to nose with the ferret.

"Tell me," Audrey said, biting free a stretch of thread, "how's a soul get chompers like those?"

"When I was but a bittle one, my buddy and me found some rust blossoms sprouching through a Rift in my home-town. We didn't see no harm in givin' 'em a snorfle." He got a shine in his shark-black eyes. "I survived, but my buddy rusted straight through."

Wally felt a pang in his heart for the strange man. But he quickly shrugged it away. He didn't know whether to trust this story. But he was impressed at how quickly Audrey had gotten

Rustmouth to open up. The ferret was using her deft claws to make a little noose at the thread's end.

Rustmouth sniffed and straightened himself. "Among the Order of Eldarlies, I got off measly. The Astonishment once quirked for a freak show. *Strongest Woman in the World*, was she madvertised. The owner trickled her into a pocket-world fulla gorgons, knowin' whatever crumbled out would come *stranged*, sell more tickets. Didn't care that the Astonishment's wife and kiddles would become terrorfied of her."

The Astonishment's pounding continued to echo down the corridor behind them. The sound wasn't so terrible to Wally now. He hadn't considered that Rustmouth's and the rest of the Order's existence might be a nightmare. That they were just regular people who'd had horrific accidents with Fae products and were now desperate to escape the pain.

"We's been smirching the wide pocket-worlds for curifiers for our maladies ever since," Rustmouth continued. "When you require resources to tender crackled stone, flailing lungs, and disintagreetin' chompers, you'll resort to just about any-think. Me and the lady-likes gotta keep hustling, rust-le up enough loot to buy fissure-cal therapy for the Astonishment, dentishry for me, and more mercury for my Silvey." He gave Wally a pathetic smile. "Tain't a breezy life, but at least we have each other."

Wally's thoughts returned to the Veil. With stronger border protections, dangerous Fae substances wouldn't have been able to find their way into the Real. The Wardens could have saved the Order's lives.

"Aaaaaand set," Audrey said, finishing the loops at either

end of the thread. "Say '*ahh*,'" she told Rustmouth, "and don't squirmify." She snorted. "Wouldja hear that? I'm catchin' your way of speakin'!"

Rustmouth grinned and cranked open his bear-trap teeth, which stretched with strands of orange spit. Wally feared for Audrey's paws as she reached inside to delicately tie the string around his back molar. She tied the opposite end to the armory's door handle.

"*There*," Audrey said. "Wally?"

Wally blinked. "You want *me* to slam it?"

"No," Audrey said. "I want you to *run!*"

She seized his wrist and yanked him down the hall toward the staircase.

Rustmouth grunted in surprise. "Shilvuh Tung!" he mumbled, trying to untie the string from his tooth with one hand and holding out the flask with the other.

"Cover your ears!" Wally shouted.

Audrey pinched hers shut while Wally stuffed his fingers in his, hoping to make it outside before Silver Tongue could guzzle her mercury.

Rustmouth's raging became muffled behind them, and Wally's legs remained under his control as they ran up the zigzag stairs and onto the roof, slamming shut the door behind them. Wally found some loose shingles and, using a trick he'd learned as a thief, wedged them beneath the door to keep it from opening.

But there was only silence on the other side. No approaching footsteps. Wally pressed his ear to the door.

"Ah, let 'em fly," Rustmouth said. "The little birdy said

our victoreal was assuretainty, and he ain't once mispronoun-sticated yet."

"Good," Silver Tongue said with a sniff. "Didn't wanna waste my last sip on those snivelers anyway."

"Come on," Wally whispered to Audrey.

They hurried to the roof's edge and located a sturdy branch near enough to grab on to.

Audrey rested a paw on his shoulder. "You sure you wanna do this?"

He took her paw and squeezed. "Not at all."

They leapt and grabbed hold of the branch, and then he and the ferret slowly descended into the haunted wood, away from Graham's control.

5
THE IN BETWEENS

Rrrrrrrippppppppp!

"Hello? Wardens? Wally? Anyone? *Eek!* Ha ha. Sorry. You scared me! Woof, you're ugly, aren't ya? And naked. Okay, byyyyyeeee!"

Whooooossssshhhhhhhhhhhhh

Infect! Mesmerize! Control!
"Hey! Spores! What'd I say about talk like that?"

Rrrrrrrippppppppp!

"How 'bout here? Anyone? Nope. Nothing. Yeeshk. *Really* nothing. *Brrrr.* Come on, spores. We gotta find Wally so we can help him fix this. Hey! Big blue eyeball! I found another erased pocket-world. I also tore two more Rifts. Sorry 'bout that."

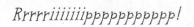

Rrrrriiiiiiipppppppppppp!

"Hiya! Any talking animals live around here? Augh! *Rude!* No need to chuck spears at my face! I'm going, I'm going! I like your beards though!"

Whooooosssshhhhhhhhhhhhhh

Infect! Mesmerize! Control!
"*Spores!* Behave yourselves!"

6

THE DAPPLEWOOD HORROR

Boom Boom Boom!

"Arthur! Arthur, wake up!"

Arthur sat up in bed. Someone was knocking on Audrey's front door again.

"Get to the edge of town! Now!"

The voice fell into place. Cadence.

Before Arthur could throw off the covers, he heard the drummer run down the lane. He rubbed his face, trying to get his eyes to focus. He hadn't slept a wink, worried about what was happening in the DappleWood forest. Worried about the dead thing in Audrey's fireplace. Worried about what he and Amelia had done.

An eerie sound drew his attention to Audrey's little window where a bare branch scraped the glass. Arthur got up and looked outside. The brief winter had ended, but the seasons seemed to have rolled *backward*. Autumn swept across the DappleWood. The air stank of rotting apples. The sky was a haunted hue. A crisp wind bent the branches and plucked leaves, as red as blood and as yellow as dead skin, twirling them down the lane toward a dark purple horizon.

Arthur shivered. He yanked on his pants, picked up sleeping BW, snagged a few blank pages from Audrey's desk just in case, and hurried out of the house toward the edge of town.

Beyond the little homes and cobbled streets, the DappleWood's fields had grown fallow. Overnight, the grass had yellowed, the fences crumbled, and scarecrows and pumpkins had sprouted up like weeds. Most disturbing, the small wood in the distance had grown to impossible heights—a branchy, expanding darkness that slowly consumed the dark-gray sky. The funnel of faces was gone, but the wood's shadowed edge seemed to be growing closer to the town, like it was *reaching* toward it.

Weirdwood's Wardens and staff had gathered before the Wet Beak, the DappleWood's pub. As Arthur headed toward them, he passed Mrs. Chicken, who clucked about the sour weather. "My eggs will crack with frost at this rate," she said, hauling open the trapdoor to her tavern's underground storage. Arthur caught a glimpse of the chicken's eggs, keeping warm beneath the soil.

He reached the circle of Wardens, and Ludwig took BW from his arms. The baby giggled as the giant bounced her in his hand, as small as a ball in a catcher's mitt. Nearby, Pyra loaded up Mr. Squirrel's pumpkin cart with lumpy burlap sacks and every weaponish tool that could be found in Mr. Mole's blacksmith tent—a pitchfork, a hoe, a scythe—all to replace the weapons Rustmouth had eaten in the previous battle. High overhead, Willa fluttered with her kites, keeping an eye on the forest's shadowy border. Only Sekhmet seemed to be missing.

Arthur peered over Cadence's shoulder and found Amelia and the Wardens were studying one of Ahura's maps, whose moving ink showed the quaint homes of the little village and the shuddering forest. It wasn't Arthur's imagination. The ink was spreading toward the little painted town like a disease.

"It appeared late last night," Ahura said, pointing to a small tear in the heart of the painted wood.

Inky shapes crawled out of the tear, infesting the forest. The shapes were blurry and indistinct, but no less horrific for that. Arthur tried not to throw up. He had managed to bring the storybook town back from erasure, but now he and Amelia had infected it with some sort of horror story. Arthur tried to catch the acrobat's eye, but she remained focused on the map.

"What are these?" Amelia asked, pointing to the monster blotches and sounding innocent as anything.

"We don't know," Linus said, flipping through a large tome. "Nothing in Weston's Fae-born catalogue resembles anything like them."

Ludwig sniffed nearby.

"Whatever they are," Ahura said, "we need to sew up this Rift before they swarm the town."

The Wardens gazed toward the trees, whose limbs stretched longer with every passing moment.

"There is some good news," Ahura said. "Unless Wally and Graham have figured out how to override the Manor's natural movements, it should flow toward this Rift soon. If we can get past these shapes, we might have a chance at getting the Manor back."

Arthur felt a tremor of hope.

"We're not asking the most important question," Cadence said with metal in his voice. "What opened the Rift?" His eyes traveled around the Wardens' faces. "Someone in this town has been abusing magic, and we know it wasn't the DappleWood citizens. I don't want to go into battle with someone who might have *betrayed* us."

Arthur's throat tensed. What would the Wardens do if they discovered it was he who had transformed the DappleWood? Fortunately, he had a tactic for remaining calm in guilty moments. He moved his eyes from face to face, and wondered, *Which of these people abused magic?* Was it Linus? Ahura? Amelia? Arthur couldn't help but notice that the acrobat's eye also moved from face to face without flinching.

"We don't have time to worry about that now, Cadence," Ahura said. "The Manor will leave once it senses another Rift in the Veil, so we'll have a short window to get inside. We should get moving."

"Fine," Cadence said. "But don't go blaming me when one of our own attacks us."

He helped Pyra finish loading the cart while Amelia waved Willa down from the sky, and Ahura put some finishing touches on her map.

"Arthur?" Linus said.

Arthur flinched, believing he'd been found out.

But then Linus pointed behind him, and Arthur saw the DappleWood's townsfolk gathered at the field's edge. They wrung their paws and fluffed their feathers, gazing at the wood with fearful eyes.

"The last thing we need is a panicked village," Linus said. "Could you distract them like you do with your performances?"

Arthur cleared his throat. "Of course."

He took a moment to compose himself, put on a winning smile, then approached the townsfolk, sweeping behind them to turn their attention away from the unsettling forest.

"Morning, everyone!" he said, as if they were back in the amphitheater. "I know what you're thinking. Who ordered Halloween in early spring? But fear not, this is a *temporary* redecorating. Fields must go fallow before they can burst with greenery."

Arthur didn't feel convinced by his own words, but he kept his smile as bright as a summer's day.

A turtle mother pulled her son close and slowly raised her hand. "Are we safe, Arthur?"

"Are you kidding?" Arthur asked. "You're as safe as . . ."

His voice trailed off when he spotted Sekhmet walking up to the Wardens. She held something wrapped in a blanket. A bloody blanket. She unraveled it, dumping the corpse of a spined creature on the ground. Arthur's heart went cold. It was the thing from Audrey's fireplace.

"Of course we're safe!" a squirrel scout finished for Arthur. "Arthur'll take care of that spookity forest! Just like he did Alfred Moore and the Order and the Eraser! Won't ya, Arthur?"

"Um," Arthur said, trying to put together what the squirrel had just said. Sekhmet must have done a sweep of everyone's quarters, searching for evidence of misuse of magic. Why hadn't he burned that creature's corpse? He swallowed and ruffled the squirrel's ears. "You know I will! Heh heh."

"How will you take care of it?" asked Mr. Mole.

"Yes," said the lizard librarian. "Can you really put thingsss back to rightsss?"

Arthur didn't hear her. He had his eye on the Wardens as they questioned Sekhmet, who pointed toward Audrey's house. One by one, the Wardens turned their heads until they were all frowning at Arthur.

"Arthur!" Linus called. "Could we speak to you a moment?"

Arthur smiled at the townsfolk. "Now, if you would all return to your homes and enjoy the haunted view from your windows, the Wardens and I will have this spookity wood business sorted in no time."

The critters returned to their respective homes, and Arthur shut his eyes for a moment. At least his adoring fans wouldn't learn what he'd done to their town.

He headed toward the Wardens, who continued to frown at him, Amelia included. As Arthur approached, Sekhmet drew her sword, igniting it with the lava light of the magma manacles, ready to lock him up. But Linus raised a hand toward his daughter as if telling her to wait.

Arthur kept his pace, not wanting to appear guilty. He tried to think of an excuse, but nothing sounded plausible. He was as good as magma manacled.

A few steps before he reached the Wardens, one of the sacks on the pumpkin cart sat up. The sacking fell away, revealing Breeth. She held something silver.

"*Knife!*" Arthur shouted.

But Breeth was already leaping off the cart and burying

the knife in Linus's back. Sekhmet screamed. Ahura caught her husband as he fell. Amelia cracked her whip, wrapping it around Breeth and binding her in place.

Arthur stood there, numb, while the Wardens sprang into action. Cadence pulled the knife from Linus's back while Sekhmet placed pressure on her father's wound, and Ahura wrapped it with her scarf. Arthur didn't know what to do. So he listened as Amelia questioned Breeth, who grunted and struggled against the whip.

"Who are you?" Amelia demanded.

Breeth spit at the acrobat's feet. "Whoddaya think?"

Amelia's eye went wide. "Rose."

Of course, Arthur thought. It was so obvious. That's why Breeth wasn't funny like Wally always said she was. That's why she'd been hanging around Mr. Mole's tent. The ghost of Weirdwood's blacksmith hadn't been looking to farm at all. She'd wanted to forge a weapon.

Arthur looked from the bloody knife on the ground to Linus, gasping like a beached fish in the late October light. "Why would you do this?"

Rose only huffed.

Amelia gave her whip a jerk, making Rose grunt in pain. "She wants the Veil to fall so she can see her son in the afterlife."

Arthur scowled. "I know a thing or two about the afterlife now." He looked Rose right in the eye. "I can promise you you'll never reach it. Not until the day you die."

Hurt flashed across Rose's face. She recovered with a sniff. "Takin' magic from the Wardens'll be its own reward."

The words made Arthur want to retrieve the Manor and take down the Order more than ever.

Near the cart, the staff gently lifted Linus onto a stretcher they had made out of rake handles and butterfly netting. The DappleWood's doctor had nothing but storybook medicine—thermometers, head bandages, bowls of stew—so it was agreed that Pyra would stay behind and tend to Linus with her potions, made from ingredients found around the town.

Sekhmet and Ahura watched, tears in their eyes, as the staff carried Linus away.

Sekhmet sniffed. "I want to stay with Dad."

"Me too," Ahura said, squeezing her daughter close. "But you know he would want us to fight."

Sekhmet wiped her tears away, and she and her mother loaded the last of the supplies onto the pumpkin cart.

Arthur couldn't help but think of the times the Black Feathers had left their own injured gang members behind to finish the job. But this was different. Arthur was now squarely on the side of the good guys. The fate of the Veil was at stake.

Cadence stepped up to Amelia, wiping blood from his hands. "Linus will be okay, I think." He nodded to Rose. "What do we do with her?"

Amelia unwound her whip from the girl's arms. "Bring her to the Badgers with Badges. Tell them not to let her out of their sight under any circumstances."

Cadence took Rose by the arm and led her away.

"Tell them to keep her in the greenhouse!" Amelia called after. "Tell them she likes plants!"

She and Arthur watched until the girl was out of sight.

"Why the greenhouse?" Arthur asked.

"A better question, Arthur," Amelia snapped, pointing her whip handle toward the dead creature, "is why that *thing* was in your fireplace."

Arthur coughed in surprise. He'd nearly forgotten he was still on the hook. Why would Amelia bring this up again after the rest of the Wardens had been distracted away from it? Unless . . . she was setting him up for a plausible excuse.

"I have no idea," he said, finding it much easier to lie without everyone staring at him. "It wasn't there when I woke up this morning. Maybe Rose had something to do with it?"

Amelia stared down the lane as if considering. "The black-smith does possess weapon magic," she said loud enough so Sekhmet and her mother could hear. "Perhaps she sliced open a small Rift, hoping to return to the Order." She nodded to the horror's corpse. "This thing must have escaped whatever pocket-world she opened, and Rose slew it and then stuck it in your fireplace to frame you."

"That . . . makes sense," Arthur said.

Amelia flashed him the subtlest of winks, and Arthur felt relief wash over him. They had gotten away with it. Now if only he could get rid of this guilt.

"It's good to hear you had nothing to do with that crea-ture," Amelia said. "You're our ace in the sleeve if our attempts to get into the Manor fail. Your connection to Wally Cooper, as well as your ability to add to the DappleWood's story and control certain *vermin*, might be our only hope."

Arthur smiled. His magic would help the Wardens on this adventure. And that, more than anything that had happened in the past, was the most important thing. "Just consider me your one-stop Wally and ferret shop."

"The Manor has arrived!" Ahura said. She held up her map and pointed to a splotch of orange that had appeared deep in the wood, in the knot of a painted, gnarled tree. It glowed with Weirdwood's light. "Let's move!"

Arthur stepped up onto the cart and sat on an upside-down apple crate. The cart groaned and leaned as Ludwig climbed in beside him, holding BW. The baby was calm and burbling, but the giant shook like a tree in a hurricane.

"We'll keep you safe, Ludwig," Ahura reassured him from the side of the cart.

Ludwig nodded, but his giant cheeks continued to quiver.

Ahura took BW from Ludwig's giant hands and set her in Arthur's lap. "Arthur, you're on babysitting duty. With Lady Weirdwood in her current state, Ludwig is the only one who can open the Manor's front entrance by communicating with the wood. The rest of us will handle the Order and whatever horrors await us in that forest." She looked deep into Arthur's eyes. "Whatever happens, you must get the lady into the Manor."

"I will," Arthur said, cradling BW close. "I'm sorry about Linus."

Ahura looked away. "Save the emotions till we get the Manor back."

Arthur sighed and considered the baby. "I can't seem to lose you, can I?"

She responded with a spit bubble.

Amelia climbed onto the driver's bench and took the

reins. She clicked her tongue—*nck-nck!*—and the horses set off at a trot, jerking the cart forward. The Wardens made a circle around the cart, their best fighter missing.

As they rolled toward the mouth of the Impossible Wood, Arthur gazed back toward the twinkling lights of the DappleWood, slowly shrinking on the Halloween horizon. He couldn't shake the feeling that he'd forgotten something.

***

The trees wrapped them in darkness. The shadows stretched as deep as lakes. The cart rattled along the rooted ground, around vast trunks and fallen pinecones as big as boulders. The forest's branches stretched so high and the canopy bristled so thick, the sky itself seemed to be made of leaves. The only light to guide them was the slender flame of Sekhmet's sword.

Arthur held BW close, grateful for the circle of Wardens that surrounded them. Sekhmet and Ahura walked on either side of the cart, sword and map at the ready, while Cadence trailed behind and Willa fluttered overhead, keeping an eye out for those strange inky shapes.

"How ya doing, Ludwig?" Arthur asked.

The giant shrugged.

As soon as they had entered the forest, Ludwig had stopped trembling, so the cart had, as well. Arthur wondered if it comforted the plant giant to be among his own kind. He was jealous. The Impossible Wood grew denser and deeper with each passing hour. Every so often he heard something like panting in the distance, and the air held a tinge of melting metal. He couldn't help but wonder if the horrors he and Amelia had summoned had claws and teeth of steel.

"We're going to win, right?" Arthur said to the Wardens. "With all our magical abilities—fire and maps and kites and rhythms and origami, um, not to mention my own writing—we'll get the Order out of the Manor no problem. Right?"

"We will not have your writing, I'm afraid," Amelia said. "Writing spells don't work once we're inside the Manor. It's a neutral zone. Dreams in the Real might create pocket-worlds in the Fae and vice versa, but the Manor is in between, so it remains unaffected."

"Well, that's terrible news," Arthur said. He remembered all the times he had tried to impress Lady Weirdwood with his storytelling spells. "No wonder I couldn't give those Abyssment Scarabs gingivitis."

Ahura glanced straight up. "Has anyone seen Willa?"

"*Whoa-oa!*" Amelia said, pulling on the reins and bringing the cart to a rickety stop.

They all gazed into the dark branches above. Willa had vanished, like a moth in the night.

"She was with us a moment ago," Amelia whispered.

BW started to whimper.

"*Shh, shh, shh,*" Arthur said, bouncing her on his knee.

He and the Wardens stared into the vast depths between the trees, searching for answers. The Impossible Wood kept its secrets.

"Ludwig?" Ahura said. "See if you can track her."

Ludwig reached into his pocket and pulled out his squares

of paper. He tried to fold them into butterflies, but his trembles had returned with a vengeance.

"Cadence?" Amelia said. "Do you see something?"

Behind the cart, Cadence stared into the mist, drumsticks lowered at his sides.

"*Cadence*," Amelia snapped.

Cadence dropped his drumsticks and took off at a sprint, his albino skin fading into the night.

Arthur watched him go with wide eyes. "Why did he just take off like that?"

Ahura unfolded her map, and Arthur peered over the cart's edge to get a look. There was the cart in the middle of the painted wood, Ahura's and Sekhmet's figures on either side. But Willa's figure had vanished completely. And Cadence's was fading like invisible ink.

"I'm going after him," Sekhmet said, her sword blazing brighter.

"*No*," Ahura said, catching her daughter's wrist. "You have to stay here and guard Lady Weirdwood. I'm not a fighter."

She grabbed a pitchfork from the back of the cart and took a step toward the darkness.

"*The map*," Amelia said.

"Right." Ahura turned and handed it up to her. Then she walked into the night.

Sekhmet stepped to the back of the cart, the flame of her sword barely keeping the shadows at bay. The only sound was the huffing of the frightened horses and BW's whimpers. Arthur sympathized. He'd felt much better when there had been a full ring of Wardens surrounding them.

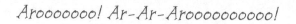

Then the howls began. They filled the forest, echoing off the trees and filling the spaces between, so it was impossible to tell where they were coming from. Shaking, Arthur covered BW's ears, wishing he could cover his own.

"Get in the cart, Sekhmet," Amelia hissed, uncoiling her whip.

Sekhmet stared into the darkness. "But . . . my mom."

"Now!" Amelia snapped.

Sekhmet pursed her lips, then leapt up beside Arthur.

"*Ya!*" Amelia screamed, cracking her whip.

The horses burst to life, jerking the cart forward. Arthur held on to BW, tight.

The forest became a rattled blur as the cart jostled and bumped over massive roots, tipping them dangerously from side to side. The acrobat cracked the whip again and again, trying to escape the howls, which boiled and yipped behind them. A big bump made BW briefly fly out of Arthur's arms, but Sekhmet caught the baby and thrust her back into his lap.

"You have to *hold on!*" she cried over the howling wind, the shrieking wheels, the screaming baby. "This mission is doomed without her!"

"I'm trying!" Arthur screamed back. "I'm a writer, not a *dad*. My arms are weak!"

Another bump split the board between Arthur's feet, and he had to leap to Ludwig's other side to prevent himself and the baby from falling to the rushing ground.

"*Amelia!*" Sekhmet screamed.

Amelia's eye remained fixed ahead as she continued to crack the whip—"Ya! *Ya!*"—making them go faster. And *faster*.

"Amelia, we have to slow down!" Sekhmet screamed louder. "If we hit another root, this cart will fall apart!"

Amelia didn't turn around. Her hair writhed like fire as she cracked the whip again and again.

With a grunt of frustration, Sekhmet stepped to the front of the cart and grabbed Amelia's shoulder. The acrobat's head finally rotated. But it did so slowly . . . *unnaturally*. Amelia's face was no longer her own. Her nose and mouth stretched into a toothy snout, distorting her eye patch and leaving a puckered emptiness behind. Her

remaining eye glowed as yellow as the moon. Amelia wore a wolf's face.

Ludwig saw the creature and scrambled to the back of the cart, nearly tipping it backward. Arthur and Sekhmet scrambled with him.

The reins fell from Amelia's clawlike fingers. She stepped one forepaw into the cart, then another, as the rest of her bones jerked and broke and rearranged themselves beneath her skin. Her shoulders hunched and her spine crackled lengthwise as a tail stabbed from the base of her back. Instead of sprouting fur, Amelia's flesh peeled away from her muscles, as if her skin were turning inside out.

The skinless wolf snarled, and the horses shrieked in fear and galloped faster. Arthur looked behind the cart at the rushing ground. If Amelia came any closer, the cart was going to tip backward. BW felt slippery in his grip.

"We have to stop the horses before this thing flips over!" Arthur cried.

"Funny," Sekhmet said, "I was more worried about getting eaten!"

She spotted a pitchfork rattling by the wheel well, hooked it with her foot, and flicked it up, catching it with her left hand. "Sorry, Amelia!" Sekhmet cried, and plunged the pitchfork into the creature's paw, impaling it into the bottom of the cart.

The skinless wolf howled in agony, splitting Arthur's ears and startling BW into brief silence. The horses galloped faster.

The wolf took the pitchfork's handle in its jaws, trying to wrench it free.

"We have to jump!" Sekhmet screamed.

Arthur nodded warily. It was either that or end up in Amelia's wolf belly. He prepared himself to jump, but then a papery flutter caught his eye on the driver's bench.

"The map!" he said, passing BW to Ludwig.

"Arthur!" Sekhmet said. "You'll be eaten!"

He smirked his trembling lips. "I never knew you cared."

He tried slipping past the wolf, but it released the pitchfork and snapped at him, its skinless lips snarled in warning. He spotted the badly broken floorboard and prised up a large splinter. He lunged forward and jammed the splinter vertically into the wolf's closing jaws, locking them open before reaching through its legs and snagging the map.

Arthur rolled backward, and he, Sekhmet, Ludwig, and BW tumbled off the cart, bumping and rolling painfully across the forest floor as the cart rolled off into the night.

In the distance, the horses screamed as if being devoured.

***

Arthur was awake. He blinked, trying to get his eyes to focus, and found a sky of leaves. He sat up and checked himself over. He was bruised and beaten, and his head felt split like a melon, but there was no blood.

A wailing turned him around. He found Sekhmet's flaming sword planted handle first in the forest floor, acting as a torch. Sekhmet was nearby, bandaging a nasty-looking wound on her leg while Ludwig cradled BW, trying to soothe her. The baby's little voice had run ragged with sobs. When they'd leapt from the rushing cart, the giant plant man must have kept her protected with his soft, massive form.

"Here," Arthur said, reaching for her. "She's used to me now."

The giant hesitated a moment, then handed the baby over. BW stopped crying immediately.

"We should get moving," Sekhmet said, grunting as she struggled to her feet. She located her mother's map on the ground and unfolded it, studying the stretch of wood between where their group stood and the gnarled old tree that held the Manor's glowing entrance. "We've got a walk ahead of us, and I don't want whatever transformed the others catching up."

"How are we supposed to take back the Manor now?" Arthur said. "You're the only Warden left."

Sekhmet folded the map and plucked up her flaming sword. "We have everything we need to get inside. Ludwig can open the door, I can fight the Order, and you can get BW through the entrance."

Arthur felt overwhelmed with the idea of sneaking a baby past the Order of Eldar, a man who could see the future, and his best friend.

"Hey," Sekhmet said. "What happened to that unshakable confidence? We could use some of that right now."

I lost it when I realized almost everything I did hurt someone, Arthur thought.

But he straightened his shoulders and put on a heroic air. "What's an adventure without impossible odds?"

Sekhmet smirked. "Better." She took a few experimental steps, limping with each one.

Arthur hoisted BW's sling around his back and offered Sekhmet his arm.

"I'll make it," she said, and limped ahead.

Ludwig followed, silent as the trees.

As they walked into the deepening wood, the air thickened with mist and the branches became more twisted and strange. It grew so quiet, even BW didn't dare cry. Arthur used the time to retrace the events that had brought them into this nightmare, hoping to keep himself and the others from becoming wolfified.

It had begun when he and Amelia had attempted to bring Garnett Lacroix back from the dead, trying to summon the Gentleman Thief through the Void that was the Eraser. Instead, they had unleashed a horror on the DappleWood. But why? Had they accidentally brought something else back from the dead instead?

Arthur imagined the skinless wolves crawling through the Eraser's silhouette, dragging their slavering tongues from some eldritch land. He wondered if the Fae shared an afterlife with the Real. Or did imaginary characters have their own place where story ideas went once forgotten or scribbled out by their authors . . .

"Oh," Arthur said, coming to a dead stop. "Oh no."

"What is it?" Sekhmet said, looking back at him.

Arthur hesitated. He had once read an interview with Valerie Lucas, speaking as Alfred Moore, in which she talked about some of the more disturbing ideas her editors had made her cut from the books. One of those ideas was the *Nowherewolves*.

When Arthur and Amelia had tried to resurrect the Gentleman Thief, they must have brought back something lurking at the edges of his adventures instead—nightmare ideas that never made it to the page. It was no wonder these creatures didn't appear in Weston's Fae-born catalogue. The skinless wolves had never existed in a pocket-world. They had returned from the story grave.

"Arthur?" Sekhmet said, waiting for an answer.

Arthur gave her a wary look. Usually when he figured out a tricky puzzle, he felt elated, bursting with excitement to share how he'd finally cracked the solution. But he couldn't tell Sekhmet how he knew about the origin of these creatures without admitting that he was partially responsible for this nightmare. Worse, he didn't know how to defeat these Fae-born because Valerie Lucas had never written them into a published story. For all Arthur knew, the Nowherewolves were immortal. His skin prickled with fear at the thought.

This reminded him of another detail from Valerie Lucas's interview. The author had been quoted as saying, *Fear makes all monsters more terrifying.*

"What if those wolves prey on fear?" Arthur asked, gazing back toward the spot where they'd fallen off the cart. "Like, y'know, *werewolves*. Only instead of biting you, they transform you by making you afraid."

Sekhmet narrowed her eyes at Arthur. "What makes you think that?"

Arthur averted his gaze, hoping she couldn't see the lie in

his eyes. "The trick of overcoming fear to defeat a monster is as old as storytelling. It's a cliché."

No wonder Valerie Lucas had cut it, Arthur thought. The author's solutions were always much cleverer than that.

Sekhmet shook her head. "The Wardens are the bravest people on either side of the Veil. How are *we* the only three who didn't transform?"

Arthur shrugged. "You're pretty confident in your fighting skills—as you should be—and Ludwig and I were safe in the middle." He pointed a thumb at the giant, whose terrified expression was as tough as bark. "See?"

Sekhmet nodded to the baby in Arthur's arms. "What about BW? She was definitely terrified."

"No offense to BW," Arthur said, "but *lots* of things scare her. She's a baby. Besides, I don't think she saw the wolves. I hid her eyes."

Sekhmet crossed her arms. "Amelia always said you would never be able to solve anything that wasn't about Garnett Lacroix."

Arthur fought a wince. Sekhmet had no idea that was exactly what he was doing.

He forced a smile. "'Bout time I prove her wrong."

Sekhmet unfolded her arms and they walked on, listening to the silence for panting breath.

"We just have to be bigger than our fear," Arthur said, walking a little taller. "Like when you run into a certain type of bear. You throw your hands over your head and scream, and they run away, believing you're bigger than you actually are."

"I've never met a Fae-born as gullible as a bear," Sekhmet said.

"Maybe you just didn't scream loud enough," Arthur said.

He refused to let her dampen his growing bravery. He reminded himself of the many horrifying Fae-born he'd survived before this. Compared to the monster hospital, the Abyssment, and the Great Elsewhere, this Impossible Wood was almost *quaint*.

Arthur's fear smoothed away, and he walked with more confidence. Soon, he felt a tingling in his chest, not unlike when he wrote a spell. The tingling became a shiver of excitement. The shivers grew bristly.

Arthur was feeling braver and braver with every step.

He had this.

This was easy.

7
THE HOWLING

Wally and Audrey walked through the towering wood, circling trunks as wide as city blocks and passing under bridge-sized roots. Their strides felt so small and insignificant, Wally wondered if they would ever find their way out of there.

"Cheer up, buttercup," Audrey said, poking his cheek with a claw. "It's only a forest."

"Sure," Wally said. He gazed up the nearest tree, trying to find its top in the gloomy darkness. "Does the Dapplewood always look like this?"

"Well, now that you mention it, *no*," Audrey said. "It's usually much smaller. And cuter. But I can smell the goodness in it. We critters tend to think of things in scents more than anything, and I can assure you there ain't a threat in sniffin' range. Speakin' of which . . ." She sniffed in a few directions, then pointed her nose toward a vast, misty dip in the forest floor. "Home's this way."

Wally stared warily into the dip. The mist flooded so thick they wouldn't be able to see any approaching danger. He studied the ferret's face, wondering if Arthur was currently controlling her, leading them into a trap.

"*Trust* me," Audrey said. "My nose is sharper than my sewing needles. I can practically smell Mrs. Chicken's maggot soup from here."

With nowhere else to go, Wally followed her down the leafy slope. The dip deepened, and the mist rose high above their heads until they could no longer see the massive trunks around them.

"So," Audrey said, "what's your plan when we get back to the Dapplewood? I can't picture you content sippin' maggot soup and tillin' a field till you're old and gray."

Wally sighed and kicked a pebble. The truth was he hadn't given it much thought. He'd just wanted to escape the situation his brother had put him in: forcing him to choose between the Wardens and the Order.

Graham kept assuring Wally that Wally would bring down the Veil. But what would happen if Wally refused to take part? His brother's predictions couldn't possibly come true if he removed himself from the equation completely . . . could they?

"I'll keep myself busy," Wally said. "What are you going to do when you get home?"

"Well, that's dodging the question if I've ever heard it," Audrey said, "but I won't push. *I* am going to live the quietest life imaginable. Spend time with family. Sew until my claws won't grow no more. If I never see another land again, it will be entirely too soon."

Wally smirked. The ferret had an uncanny way of cheering him up.

Audrey took Wally's arm in her fuzzy one. "You're good stuff, Wally. I don't know about that Arthur, but you I like. When we get back to my house, I'll make you a stew so savory and a pot of tea so sweet you'll blush all your troubles away."

Wally tilted his head, touching his cheek to the top of the ferret's fuzzy head. He found himself walking with more ease. Maybe Audrey was right. Maybe this forest was nothing more than a forest. Just a really big one. Maybe with the right choices life could be simple after all.

Something formed in the mist ahead.

A figure.

It seemed to be . . . floating.

Wally stopped walking. "Audrey?" he whispered. "What is that?"

Audrey saw the figure. "I don't know," she whispered, a touch of fear in her voice. She sniffed. "Smells like nothin' to me."

Wally touched her shoulder, signaling her to stay put, and crept forward, fists raised for a fight. The closer he got, the smaller the figure became and the higher it hung. It was *tiny* and dangled from a low branch. Wally stepped right under it, and he covered his mouth in shock.

It was Graham's devil puppet.

"Wally?" Audrey said, slinking up behind him. "What is it?"

He turned and stared into the ferret's sincere caramel eyes. The puppet could mean only one thing. Graham knew Wally would escape the Manor. He knew he would take Audrey with him. Wally's brother was still pulling his strings.

Wally didn't know how he would bring down the Veil. He

didn't know *why* he would do it. But if that was his destiny, no matter how much he fought against it, going to the Dapplewood could make Audrey's worst nightmares come true. The Rifts that opened around him could destroy the ferret's home again. This time for good.

"Audrey, you have to leave me here."

"Why?"

"Because if I come with you, I—*oof!*"

Something hit Wally so hard, the air was knocked out of him. His head slammed into the ground as a deafening snarl vibrated his bones. His eyes went wide with terror. His entire torso was in the jaws of a giant wolf. It was bigger than carriages. Bigger than nightmares. And it had no *skin*. With the merest clench of its teeth, it would chomp Wally's body in two.

But the wolf's fangs weren't sinking in. They rested against his sides like a threat. Wally peered around the creature's raw meat lips and saw its bright blue eyes, the strange expression on its face . . . It had left its throat exposed.

Wally carefully reached toward his belt, pulled out Rustmouth's knife, and raised it.

Behind him, Audrey sniffed. "Wally, *wait!*"

But Wally was already swinging his hand, burying the knife into the wolf's muscled flesh. The wolf released a scouring howl of pain. Wally had been aiming for its throat, but Audrey's voice had made him hesitate, so he struck its shoulder instead. He felt the sickening crunch of metal striking bone as he dragged the knife toward him, opening a bloody gash along the wolf's shoulder.

"Stop, stop, stop!" Audrey screamed.

Wally did stop. Right before the knife reached the wolf's jugular.

The fangs unclenched from his sides, and he leapt to his feet, checking himself for wounds. His shirt hadn't even been ripped. The wolf collapsed to the forest floor, blood oozing from its shoulder in a wide, black puddle. It panted in pain, blinking its foggy eyes. Then its tongue unrolled, spilling a swaddled lump onto the forest floor.

Wally picked it up and peeked inside. It was a *baby*. "What's happening?"

Audrey tore off her apron and moved toward the wolf.

"Wait!" Wally caught her paw. "Why are you helping it?"

Audrey yanked her paw back. "This isn't a wolf," she said, pressing her apron to the beast's bleeding wound with one paw while pulling out a needle and thread with the other.

"What is it?" Wally asked.

Before Audrey could answer, the wolf's bones made a cracking sound. It started to transform. Wally held the baby close and watched as the beast's tail, paws, ears, and muzzle shrank like melting ice. Its muscles inverted into hairless skin as its bones rearranged themselves into a familiar shape . . .

Arthur.

His shoulder was cut open.

And he was bleeding fast.

8
RIFTS

Arthur had wanted to surprise his friend. He'd been so excited to smell Wally in the mist he had broken into a lope to find him. The questions about why Wally had stolen the Manor could come later. For now, Arthur just wanted to embrace him.

But when Arthur had reached out, he didn't have hands, but *paws*. And those paws were knocking Wally down. When Arthur opened his mouth to speak, he found Wally between his teeth. It was only when he saw the fear on Wally's face that he knew something was terribly wrong. But before he could fix it, his best friend was driving a knife into his shoulder.

The pain was excruciating. A howling agony. The light had leaked from Arthur's eyes along with his blood from his shoulder. Fear flooded through him, shrinking his ears and teeth and *tail*—something he hadn't even realized he'd had.

Now he was floating in darkness, in and out of consciousness.

"I think I can sew him up," someone said above the surface. Her voice was pleasantly familiar and reminded Arthur of the books his mom used to read to him. "I'll pretend he's a dress, even though skin ain't exactly fabric."

"What about germs?" another familiar voice said.

"What's *germs*?"

"Right. I guess we're playing by DappleWood rules."

The pain in Arthur's shoulder spiked as someone jabbed him with something tiny and sharp. He tried to snarl in pain, but there was no snarl left in him.

"Will he be okay?" the second voice said.

"I hope so. You got him pretty good. Why didn't you listen when I said wait? I *told* you there was no danger nearby. No one ever trusts noses."

"I . . . I was trying to protect us."

The first voice sighed. "I suppose you can't be blamed."

Small gurgles bubbled.

"Whose baby is this? Why did Arthur have her in his mouth?"

"Don't look at me. I don't understand a thing about this."

A wave of nausea dragged Arthur into darkness.

***

He woke to the sound of giant feet stomping across the leaves.

"Ludwig!" the second voice said. "Arthur's hurt. Can you take this baby?"

The giant steps stomped away, and Arthur forced his eyes open with a gasp. He blinked, woozy and confused, as a misty light trickled through his lashes. He saw a face, blurry and distorted. It slowly wavered into focus. *Wally*.

"Still with us, Arthur?"

Arthur tried to sit up and woke a searing pain in his shoulder. "*Ow!* Ow ow ow ow ow."

Gentle claws laid him back down. "Stop your squirmin', Arthur."

He couldn't see whoever was speaking. It hurt too much to turn his head.

"What happened?" Wally asked. "Why were you a giant, skinless wolf?"

Arthur tried to piece together the events, his thoughts throbbing with his wound. He remembered a tumble off a cart. He remembered venturing through the Impossible Wood, instructing Sekhmet and Ludwig to be bigger than their fear. He remembered trying to make himself brave.

Then Sekhmet had started to snarl. And then Arthur was snarling. And then . . .

Arthur realized the real solution to the skinless wolves too late. Valerie Lucas had said that *Fear makes all monsters more terrifying.* He had thought that meant his own fear. Something to get on top of to make the monsters less scary. But now he understood that Lucas was talking about the *monsters'* fear. By trying to act braver than they felt, Arthur and the Wardens had transformed themselves into the very things they feared. Valerie Lucas's solution was as clever as always.

Arthur winced as he took his friend's blood-covered hand. "Fear is good, Wally. Hold on to it." He struggled to form the words, as if hauling them up from a deep well. "You . . . always were better than I was at letting yourself be afraid. That's a good thing. If you don't have fear . . . who knows what you'll turn into?"

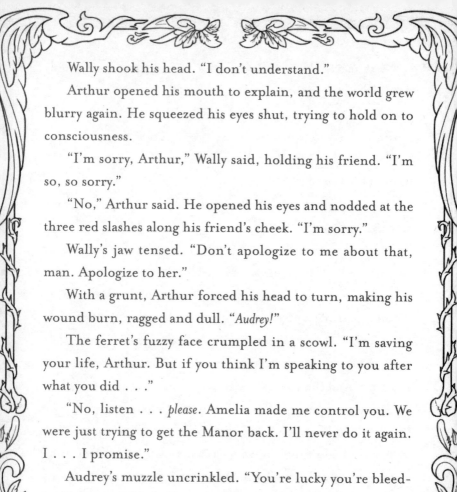

Wally shook his head. "I don't understand."

Arthur opened his mouth to explain, and the world grew blurry again. He squeezed his eyes shut, trying to hold on to consciousness.

"I'm sorry, Arthur," Wally said, holding his friend. "I'm so, so sorry."

"No," Arthur said. He opened his eyes and nodded at the three red slashes along his friend's cheek. "I'm sorry."

Wally's jaw tensed. "Don't apologize to me about that, man. Apologize to her."

With a grunt, Arthur forced his head to turn, making his wound burn, ragged and dull. "*Audrey!*"

The ferret's fuzzy face crumpled in a scowl. "I'm saving your life, Arthur. But if you think I'm speaking to you after what you did . . ."

"No, listen . . . *please*. Amelia made me control you. We were just trying to get the Manor back. I'll never do it again. I . . . I promise."

Audrey's muzzle uncrinkled. "You're lucky you're bleeding," she grumbled. "It makes it harder to be mad at you."

"How did you do it, Arthur?" Wally asked. "How did you control her?"

Arthur turned his head back and waited for a wave of shuddering cold to pass through him. He did his best to explain through winces and gasps how his stories came to life in the Fae. How he could channel others' memories and imaginations into entire pocket-worlds.

A dawning realization crossed Wally's face. "You made my parents' ghosts too."

Arthur swallowed. "It was an accident. It happened when you and I were in the hospital and I told you our parents were in a better place."

Wally sat quiet a moment. Then, he started patting Arthur's pockets. He found the blank diary pages.

Arthur was too weak to stop him. "Wh-what are you doing?"

"I'm not going to let you manipulate anyone anymore," Wally said, taking Arthur's pen as well. "Not their emotions and certainly not their bodies."

"I've done good things too!" Arthur turned his head again, blinking away a sweep of darkness. "Audrey, I'm the one who brought back the DappleWood. Your neighbors are safe and sound back in the village. This was all me."

Audrey stopped sewing, the anger smoothing from her whiskers. "That true?"

Arthur nodded. The sweet sound of her voice was enough to stop him from telling her that the skinless wolves and haunted wood were also his creations.

"Please, Wally," he said. "Let me keep those pages. I need them."

"I can't do that, Arthur," Wally said, pocketing the pages and pen. "You might use it to help the Wardens."

Arthur felt a pain, deeper than his wound. So it was true. Wally was his enemy now.

"Why'd you do it, Cooper?" Arthur asked. "Why did you steal the Manor?"

Wally stared at the forest floor. "I saw the Wardens for what they really are . . ." He proceeded to tell Arthur about finding the innocent painter locked up in the first floor of the Abyssment. About his brother's theories that the Veil was nothing but a border wall that kept both the Fae and the Real from thriving.

"But the Wardens are the *heroes*." Arthur strained to sit up. "They save people from—"

"Hold still now," Audrey said, pushing him back down.

Arthur winced as her needle dug back into his shoulder. He pushed past the pain. "Do you really think I would support a group that would lock someone up for no reason? We're not in the Black Feathers anymore, Cooper. I'm with the Wardens because they keep humans safe from raven children and tentacle monsters, and they keep Fae-born like Audrey from losing their homes."

"So, the solution is to lock up anyone with a good imagination?" Wally asked. "What if you're next?"

Arthur was speechless for a moment. The Wardens had protected him, even when he'd made a mess of things. Would they still do that if they knew that he had helped bring horrors to the DappleWood?

"I've read enough adventure stories to recognize heroes," Arthur said. "The Wardens fit the bill."

"You sure about that?" Wally asked, touching the slashes on his cheek.

Audrey pointed a bloody claw in Wally's face. "*You* need to stop asking him questions." Her claw swept to Arthur. "And *you* need to stop yammering while I try to keep your blood from watering these trees."

"Eehhhhhhh! Eh! Eh! Ehhhhhhhh!" Somewhere in the depths of the wood, a baby cried.

"BW!" Arthur sat bolt upright, and his shoulder screamed in pain. He tried to ignore it. His wound had made him temporarily forget his babysitting duties—the most important part of this mission.

"Keep still now," Audrey said, gently pushing Arthur's shoulders to get him to lie back down. "You're undoing my stitches!"

Arthur pushed back against the ferret's paws. He had to find the strength to stand and go find the baby.

"Who is BW?" Wally asked.

"Right, you don't know," Arthur said, still straining to sit up. "Lady Weirdwood turned into a baby."

"She *what*?" Wally said.

Arthur gasped in pain. "Too much to explain right now. I have to make sure she's okay. Lady Weirdwood is *my* responsibility."

"She's fine," Wally assured him, helping Audrey push him flat again. "Ludwig has her."

"Oh," Arthur said.

The fight went out of him and he let Audrey's paws guide him to the ground. So long as he knew the giant was taking care of BW, he could rest.

"Who else is here?" Wally asked. "Breeth?"

Arthur drew deep breaths. "We thought she was with us in the DappleWood, but it turns out Rose had possessed her body."

"Then where is Breeth?" Wally asked in rising panic.

Arthur opened his eyes. "I don't know."

Wally's head sank into his hands.

"Don't worry," Audrey said. "If anyone can take care of themselves, it's that spitfire of a ghost girl."

"Is her body safe at least?" Wally asked Arthur. "Breeth's ghost will have somewhere to return to?"

Arthur nodded. "Amelia locked Rose in the DappleWood's greenhouse. I don't know why."

"I can answer that one," Audrey said, still sewing. "Back in the Manor, Breeth asked me to watch over her body while she went and did whatever little ghost girls do. She told me to keep her body away from organic materials to stop Rose's ghost from slippin' in. So I built a box out of the room's windowpanes, which, by the way, *shattered* after the whole Manor shifted right under my paws. I'm guessing Amelia stuck the child in the glass greenhouse for the same reason—only this time to keep Rose's ghost from escapin'."

"Why didn't you tell me all this before?" Wally asked.

The ferret scowled. "I guess I was too busy being *imprisoned* by you and your brother."

Arthur tried to relax so Audrey could fix him, but thoughts kept tugging at his mind. Ludwig had been so quiet on the cart ride into the wood. He hadn't even trembled in fear. And there was that scent of melting metal, which Arthur had also smelled near the blacksmith tent when he'd caught Rose fishing around for weapons. That wasn't all. Back in the village, BW had loved being held by Ludwig. But once they boarded that cart, the baby had wailed around the giant, just like she had around Breeth, who it turned out wasn't Breeth at all . . .

Arthur shifted, trying to get comfortable, as he assured himself he had nothing to worry about. Rose was locked up in the DappleWood greenhouse. Amelia seemed to have been aware that the blacksmith's ghost had possessed Breeth, instructing the Badgers with Badges to lock the girl in the one building where Rose's spirit wouldn't be able to escape through the nonorganic glass walls. This, of course, was the first-draft greenhouse Arthur had created. The one with the ill-fitting windowpanes, which left just enough space for a ghost to . . .

Arthur sat bolt upright again. "That's not Ludwig!"

"*What* did I just say?" Audrey said, trying to push him back down.

Arthur strained against the ferret's paws and his own wooziness. "Rose is possessing him! She has BW! I have to go after her!"

Wally helped Audrey push Arthur onto his back. "You're hurt, man. Let me take care of it."

Arthur stared fire into his friend's eyes. "You're trying to stop me from getting Lady Weirdwood back into the Manor."

The expression on Wally's face told Arthur he wasn't wrong.

Arthur's head pounded. His shoulder throbbed. If this argument was going to turn into a fight, he had already lost.

"What are you going to do, Cooper?" Arthur said. "Keep me hostage, like the Wardens did that artist?"

The pressure Wally was placing on Arthur's chest lightened.

"Don't be my enemy, Wally," Arthur said. "Please."

SNRRRRLLLL

A snarl, as loud as engines, spun Wally and Audrey around. A massive, skinless wolf, lips curled like rancid meat, stared at them with bright green eyes.

Wally slowly rose to his feet. "Climb a tree, Audrey," he said, raising his fists.

"Don't gotta tell me twice," Audrey said, scrambling up the nearest one.

Wally and the wolf began to circle each other, eyes locked.

Arthur didn't want to see Wally hurt, but his friend had been trained to fight by Sekhmet herself. More important, Arthur had a mission to complete. And he couldn't have asked for a better distraction.

He huffed twice, trying to get on top of the pain, then forced himself upward, staggering to his feet. As the skinless wolf lunged at Wally, Arthur limped into the mist, hoping to find BW before Rose did something drastic.

***

The trees wobbled like black fire in Arthur's vision as he limped along Ludwig's giant footprints. He winced in waves of nauseous pain, holding his left arm to his side to keep it from jostling his shoulder. He'd been in enough fights to know this knife wound looked worse than it was. Were it not for Wally's hesitation and Audrey's stitches, Arthur might be in serious—

He stumbled and collapsed to his knees. He tried not to

retch as black spots formed in front of his eyes. Maybe Wally hadn't hesitated as much as he'd thought.

"*Come on*," Arthur told his legs, willing them to stand.

Rose was escaping with BW. The Wardens were going to lose the Manor, and the Veil would fall, endangering everyone Arthur loved . . . His legs didn't budge.

Arthur had power in the DappleWood. He could write materials to make a cast, maybe even summon one of Pyra's healing potions. But no. Thanks to Cooper, Arthur didn't have anything to write with.

Grunting in frustration, he tried to push to his feet, but he flopped to the ground instead. His eyelids grew heavy; his eyelashes blurred the wood. He fought against unconsciousness . . .

"*Ehhhhhhh! Ehhhhhhhhh!*"

Arthur's eyes shot open. BW was crying, not too far away. The sound gave him a burst of adrenaline that brought him to his feet. He staggered forward until he saw a light seeping through the dark, misty wood. He followed it to a glowing oval, like a cat's pupil, nestled in the knot of a twisted tree.

The Manor. He could smell the old wood and perfumes flowing from its halls.

Arthur hid himself behind the nearest trunk and watched as Ludwig, scowling with Rose's expression, tromped toward the entrance with the screaming baby. Rustmouth, the Astonishment, and Silver Tongue stepped out of the Manor to greet them.

Arthur's jaw clenched. Was Wally working with the Order?

"Would you spectacle this ickle one?" Rustmouth said, taking BW from the giant and holding her before his brown smile. "All that imagication, reducted to mere dribbles and nappies."

"Pee-yew!" Silver Tongue said, plugging her nose. "And I thought the old lady stank."

The Astonishment ran a rocky finger over the baby's tiny pink head.

"Get away from her!" Arthur said, limping out from behind the tree.

He didn't care about his safety right then. Only Lady Weirdwood's.

Rustmouth's face twitched with fear, then recovered in a wide grin when he saw Arthur's blood-soaked shirt. "Well now! If it ain't the little godling come a-limping to the rescue."

The Astonishment cracked her stone knuckles and took a heavy step toward Arthur. Rustmouth raised a hand to stop her, placing the other on his yellowed cheek. "Allow me, Astonishment. I owe this kiddle a touch of *accidentistry*."

Rustmouth strolled toward Arthur as though he had all the time in the world. As though he was *savoring* Arthur's fear.

Arthur wavered but stood his ground. "If you come any closer, I'll . . ."

"You'll what?" Rustmouth glanced around the wood. "Whatcha gonna attackle me with in this quaint little DapplyWood, eh? Cobblestones? Kitten snores?"

Arthur backed away. He had no plan. He had no pages. All he could do was keep the Order distracted until something, *anything* came along.

"See," Rustmouth said, taking another step, "my teeths is my *thrivelihood*. And your little lies plied one away from me. So I'm gonna take one of your valuabilities. You's an authorish Arthur, ain't ya? Let's see how well you scribble sans a finger or three."

The man chomped his rusted teeth in the air—*chomp chomp chomp*—causing Arthur to trip over his own feet and hit the ground hard. He pushed away from Rustmouth, fingers throbbing with his wound. Arthur's back hit the tree trunk, and he couldn't find the energy to move around it. He slunk down, tipping on the edge of unconsciousness as Rustmouth chomped closer and closer—*chomp chomp chomp*—the sound of his sickening teeth echoing through the trees.

Three steps before Rustmouth reached Arthur, a horrific howl filled the woods. The howl doubled, then tripled, punctuated with yips and snarls. Rustmouth slowly turned as three skinless wolves padded into sight. One was missing an eye—Amelia—but Arthur couldn't identify the other two. The Wardens were still above their fear.

"This chomplicates things," Rustmouth said, rubbing his scratchy chin. He grinned down at Arthur. "Lucky for me, I gots a snackling for them." He waved his arms in the air. "Come and get it, ya wolvies! Here's some tenderfied veal for ya, bloodied and shreddy to serve! You's can help me with the chewin'!"

The wolves padded closer, snarling their skinless lips. This was not the rescue Arthur had been hoping for. In their monster forms, the Wardens would devour Rustmouth *and* him without a second thought.

With Rustmouth's back turned, Arthur searched for an escape. He saw the tree bark inches from his nose, blank as a black canvas. He saw the blood seeping through his shirt. It wasn't paper and pen, but it would do. But what could he write? There was nothing in the DappleWood that could take down the Order or a pack of skinless wolves. It was all soft edges and lovely breezes.

Arthur's thoughts were a shadowy mush. If Wally hadn't stabbed him, he might be able to think of a solution. Instead, he was bleeding out, as helpless as . . . Linus.

Arthur lifted a trembling finger and swiped blood from his shoulder. He wrote on the bark.

AROOOOOOOOO!

A new howl descended over the wood. It echoed from somewhere far away but filled the forest nonetheless. Rustmouth spun around to see if a skinless wolf was sneaking up behind him and found Arthur smiling.

"What are you toothin' at?" Rustmouth asked.

Arthur nodded behind the man.

AROOOOOOOOO!
AROOOOOOOOO!
AROOOOOOOOO!

The wolves had dropped to their bellies and sides, writhing beneath some invisible force. Their muscles inverted into skin as their ears and muzzles shrank to normal size. Their bones snapped and shifted, so paws became fingers. Forelegs straightened into arms. Tails melted completely until only Amelia, Willa, and Ahura remained.

They were badly beat-up. Their weapons were lost. But the Wardens had returned.

Amelia stood straight, cracking her neck back into place. She pointed at Rustmouth. "Get away from him!"

Rustmouth blanched in shock, then retreated to the Manor's tree-knot entrance. "It's too late, Boredens! You've bungled your baby bunting and now we's got her trundled!"

Amelia crouched over Arthur and cradled his head. Her right hand, her whip hand, was bleeding from the pitchfork wound. "How did you bring us back, Arthur?"

Arthur nodded to the bark, and she squinted at the bloody words.

He had written instructions for Pyra's cauldron, currently filled with DappleWood ingredients that he could control, making them bubble and froth with words. The words told the chef to give her voice-enhancing potion to Linus and instruct him to howl in pain, making his voice travel all the way to the heart of the forest.

What better way to make skinless wolves afraid than to make them believe they might lose a loved one?

"Clever boy," Amelia whispered. She turned to the others. "Linus is safe!"

Ahura put a hand to her chest, and her face broke in relief.

Amelia continued. "One of us needs to return to the DappleWood and tell the townsfolk to *let themselves be afraid*. That's the only way they'll be spared this forest and its monsters."

Ahura took off through the trees at a sprint.

Amelia yanked a vine from a tree's trunk, coiling it into a whip with her uninjured hand. Willa raised her fingers toward the sky, and leaves tumbled from the branches to form kites with razor-sharp edges.

The two women, the only Wardens left, stood and faced the Order.

"Uh uh uh," Silver Tongue said, petting BW's bald little head. "I'd throw down those weapons if I was you."

Scowling, Willa squeezed her fists, and the leaf kites disintegrated. Amelia let the whip drop to the ground. She caught Arthur's attention and briefly glanced toward the forest canopy.

Arthur followed her gaze and found Audrey hunched on a branch that overhung the Manor's entrance, caramel eyes glittering in the mist. With a few words written in blood on bark he could make the ferret drop down and grab BW. He could get the Manor back. But Arthur had promised the sweet ferret he would never control her again.

He subtly shook his head at Amelia and mouthed, *I'm sorry.* Never had she scowled so horribly.

The Manor's entrance darkened, and Graham stepped out. He wore Lady Weirdwood's snake around his shoulders. He looked much healthier than he had the last time Arthur saw him. But he still held up his hand as if it wore a puppet.

"If you would be so kind," the hand told the Astonishment, "there's a pesky ferret directly above us that could pounce any moment."

The Astonishment looked up and spotted Audrey. She

wrapped her rocky arms around the trunk and jostled it until the ferret slipped from the branch and fell. Audrey hit the ground hard, striking her head. She did not get back up.

Arthur's heart broke. He watched the ferret's chest, making sure she was still breathing. He could feel Amelia's blue eye burning through him, telling him he had made a mistake. He didn't look at her.

Graham's hand turned to Willa and Amelia. "Wardens!" it said pleasantly. "Finally, we meet."

9
BW

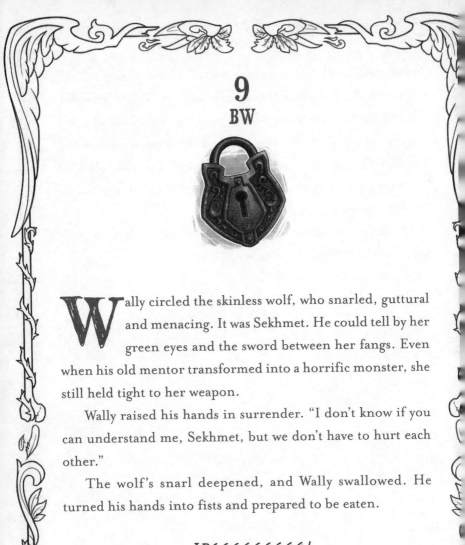

Wally circled the skinless wolf, who snarled, guttural and menacing. It was Sekhmet. He could tell by her green eyes and the sword between her fangs. Even when his old mentor transformed into a horrific monster, she still held tight to her weapon.

Wally raised his hands in surrender. "I don't know if you can understand me, Sekhmet, but we don't have to hurt each other."

The wolf's snarl deepened, and Wally swallowed. He turned his hands into fists and prepared to be eaten.

AROOOOOOOOO!

A new howl filled the wood. It seemed to emanate from the sky.

Sekhmet collapsed to her side in paw-twitching, lip-curling spasms. The sword fell from her teeth, and she started to shrink.

Wally didn't wait to see what happened next. He followed

Arthur's blood trail to the cat-eye glow of the Manor's tree-knot entrance, where he crouched in the mist and assessed the situation. The Order—Rustmouth, Silver Tongue, the Astonishment, and Ludwig/Rose—blocked the Manor's entrance. Willa and Amelia stood before them, weaponless. Arthur lay slumped against a nearby tree whose bark was covered in bloody words.

And in the middle of it all was Wally's brother, puppet hand raised.

"Please, Graham," Amelia said. "Give us Lady Weirdwood. You can take the Manor. But we cannot have our lady hurt."

Graham's hand sighed. "I'm afraid I can't do that. If the Manor is a puzzle, Lady Weirdwood is its missing piece. You'll pursue us to the ends of the Veil to get her back." The hand smiled at the baby, who sniffled in Ludwig/Rose's arms. "I'm going to hide her somewhere you'll never find. Somewhere she'll age at a regular pace and never even hear of magic." The hand gave her a tiny kiss on the head, then turned to Amelia. "Then the great tearing of the Veil will begin. The Fae and the Real will find a new Balance that gives magic to the people and resources to the Fae-born."

With that, Graham turned toward the Manor.

"Say buh-bye!" Silver Tongue shrieked, taking the baby's pudgy arm and waving it at Amelia and Willa.

Halfway to the entrance, Graham paused and turned to find Wally's eyes in the mist. His hand nodded toward the Manor. "Brother?"

Wally, caught, stepped into the open, directly between the opposing sides.

"Wally!" Amelia called. "We'll forgive you for taking the Manor. You can be a Novitiate again if you help us get it back!"

Wally gave her a helpless look. Amelia was clearly hoping he had some sort of power over his brother. That he could somehow talk Graham into giving up the Manor. But that wasn't how this worked.

"Brother," Graham said, lowering his puppet hand. "Have I ever steered you wrong?"

Wally stared into his brother's eyes. "I don't know, Graham. Have you?"

Graham smiled with their parents' smile. "You'll see. When this is all over, you'll see."

When Wally still didn't move, Amelia snatched up her vine whip and Willa raised her hands, reassembling her leaf kites in the air.

"Better to see Lady Weirdwood hurt than lose the Veil," Amelia said, twirling her whip.

The Astonishment cracked one fist into the other. Rustmouth grinned drippingly. Silver Tongue, giggling, took out her flask.

Before either side could make a move, a glow fell upon the forest. The Order and the Wardens fell silent as golden tendrils twined strangely around them, igniting coils throughout the mist. They rose and swirled around the branches, then lowered and circled the roots before making zigzags through the air. Almost like they were . . . *playing*.

"About *bloody* time," Amelia said.

The golden tendrils came together, uniting in a single, small cloud. The cloud seemed to notice Wally and arrowed straight toward him, making him stumble back, raising his hands to protect his face.

The moment before the cloud enveloped him, it formed a face and body and streaming hair. It threw up its hands, releasing an explosion of golden dust like fireworks.

"WAAAAAAAAALLLLLLLLLLYYYYYYYYYYYYYYYYY!!!"

Wally got to his feet and blinked. "*Breeth?*"

"Uh, *yeah! Duh!* Do you know any other girls who can spore up to you and do *this*?"

Breeth wrapped herself around him like a hazy coat.

"Hiya, Breeth," Wally said, hugging her back. Tears of happiness spilled down his cheeks.

Breeth unwound herself from his torso and used her sporey hands to cradle his cheeks and chin. "Let me look at

this face. This is the *best* face. I'd smooch it again if my lips weren't spores right now." She released him and swirled in a dusty, golden spiral. "Oh my gosh, I have *so much* to tell you!"

"Um, Breeth?" Wally said, trying to interrupt her.

But Breeth was bursting with an excitement that could not be contained. "Okay, so when did you see me last? Oh, right! I left my body and went and got spores from the Mycopath to save Arthur from getting eaten by a dragon! Ha ha. And that's only, like, chapter one!"

"Breeth—"

"Chapter *two* is that I thought I was gonna be lost forever in fake heaven. It was sooooooo boring. Like, sure, I had the spores to keep me company—like Lemon and Peabody and what I call the Gary division. *But*, and please don't tell them I said this"—she put a hand to her mouth to whisper—"they're not the best conversationalists."

"Breeth!" Wally said, fighting down a laugh. "I want to hear about all of this, but now really isn't the time."

He pointed behind her, and Breeth spun around to find everyone staring at her. With the spores lending her shape, this was the first time they had seen her in ghost form. Willa looked confused. Amelia looked pleased. The Order looked afraid. And Arthur had covered his nose and mouth to protect himself from the spores.

Finally, Graham wore an expression that Wally had never seen on him before: pure shock. His brother hadn't seen this coming.

Breeth curtsied her spores. "Evening, everybody!" With

the spores vibrating in her throat like vocal cords, they could *hear* her too.

Everyone was too shocked to respond.

"Sheesh," Breeth said, gazing at the standoff. "This looks *intense*. Good thing I learned a few tricks since you last saw me. The Order won't know what hit 'em"—she punched her sporey fist into her sporey hand—"until I tell them it was *me!*"

"Breeth, *wait*," Wally said.

She whirled. "What is it? I'm roarin' for some sporin'."

Wally bit his lip. He'd been gearing up to explain to Breeth why he'd stolen the Manor. But it seemed she had no idea he had.

Wally looked to the Wardens and the Order, who stood frozen, waiting to see what the all-powerful ghost girl would do. If Graham couldn't foresee the ghost girl's actions, did her presence mean Wally could make his own decision? One that didn't follow the Order *or* the Wardens?

Wally pointed to Lady Weirdwood in Ludwig/Rose's arms. "Can you bring me that baby?"

"*Psh*," Breeth said. "You're saying that like I've never saved a baby from *monsters* before. What's her name? Just so she doesn't freak out when she sees a ghost made out of mushroom spores."

"Um, that's Lady Weirdwood."

Breeth's eyes went wide.

"And that's Rose holding her."

"*What?*" Breeth's expression crumpled into anger. "Rose is *not* safe for babies."

She rocketed toward the entrance.

"*Inside!*" Graham commanded the Order with urgency. He ran toward the Manor's entrance, holding the snake tight to his chest.

"Unto the breach!" Amelia screamed, whirling her vine whip.

"*Breeth!*" Breeth screamed above her. "My name is *Breeth*!"

Wally watched with gritted teeth as Amelia and Willa charged the tree's entrance. Before Graham and the Order could retreat into the Manor, Ludwig began to struggle, like a tree infested with termites.

"*Gyyyeeeetttt out of my ffffffffriend, you ssssssstinky, murderous blacksmith!*" the giant bellowed.

Breeth was clearly inside, trying to kick Rose *out*. With a massive grunt, the giant hurled something toward the tree as if disposing of an invisible weight. The tree bark grew thorny, scowling with the blacksmith's face before melting into the Manor.

Ludwig grinned a Breethish grin and held BW aloft. "Got her! How long was that? Five seconds? Three?"

Amelia cracked her whip, wrapping it around the giant's wrist and jerking his arm down.

"What the?" Breeth said, yanking back on the whip with Ludwig's tree strength. "Amelia, it's *me*. Breeth. We're on the same team!"

Amelia continued to pull her whip. "Then give the baby to *me*!"

Breeth looked to Wally in confusion, giving the Astonishment just enough time to snatch BW from her/Ludwig's arms.

"Oh no you don't!" Breeth/Ludwig screamed.

Her spirit streamed out of the giant's ears and possessed the ground leaves, which leapt to life and slapped themselves over the Astonishment's eyes. The Astonishment reached up to claw the leaves away and Willa's kites swept in, swooping the baby from her grasp.

The kites tried to carry BW up to Willa, high in the branches, but they passed Rustmouth, who breathed his brown breath over them, making them darken and wilt. The kites crumbled, the baby fell, and Wally's heart fell with her. A moment before BW hit the ground, a waft of air buoyed her up, trailing her wedding-dress swaddling.

Sekhmet stepped out of the woods with her fiery sword, sending blasts of warmth that juggled the baby, like a giggling ball, out of the Order's reach. Graham fled inside the Manor while Ludwig collapsed to his knees and held his head, no longer haunted by ghosts. Rustmouth charged Sekhmet, jaws wide, but Amelia cracked her whip again, wrapping it around the man's neck and holding him back. Willa tried to overwhelm the Astonishment with her leaf kites while the stone woman punched them one by one out of the air. Silver Tongue, meanwhile, leaned against the Manor's entrance, yawning exaggeratedly and watching the fight with a smirk.

Wally felt strange just standing there. He wanted to help. But how? And who?

"I don't get it!" Breeth said as golden spores rose from the ground and connected into her shape. "Why did Amelia steal the baby from me? Did she think I was still Rose? Because my voice is *way* nicer than that lousy blacksmith's."

"I can't explain now, Breeth," Wally said, eyes still on the fight. "We have to get Lady Weirdwood."

He quickly untucked the back of his shirt as he whispered his plan to Breeth.

He hadn't quite finished when a voice shrieked through the battle. "Okay! Fight's all done now! Time for you to lose!" Silver Tongue stepped forward, lifting her flask to her lips and tilting it to drain the last few drops of mercury onto her tongue. She grinned a wicked grin at Sekhmet. *"Kill your own!"*

Sekhmet's arms jerked forward, as if her sword was pulling her to the center of the battle. As the pockets of warm air dissipated, BW took another tumble, but Willa swept down and caught her, carrying her to a high branch. The Astonishment punched at the tree, trying to knock Willa and the baby down.

"Ludwig, watch out!" Sekhmet shouted, a pained expression on her face. Her sword had pulled her straight toward the giant and was lifting her into the air, out of her control.

The giant looked up just as the sword came slicing down, cutting him in half. Ludwig got a horrified expression as his knees buckled and his top half rolled away like a felled tree. Sekhmet's arms didn't stop there. They continued to hack and hack at the plant giant as she sobbed all the while. Soon, Ludwig was nothing but sap and limbs.

"Ludwig!" Arthur screamed.

Everyone else fell into shocked silence.

"Have you all forgotten how plants work?" Amelia

shouted, grabbing one of Ludwig's arms and sticking it in the ground, fingers up. "He'll be fine!"

But now that Sekhmet had finished with the giant, she was going after Amelia, knocking her back with bursts of flame. Amelia cracked her whip again and again, trying to disarm her.

Wally felt numb. Silver Tongue setting Sekhmet on the Wardens was flat-out evil. He couldn't believe he'd ever trusted the Order of Eldar.

There came a breeze of wings as Willa swooped down and set the baby in his arms. "Order up!" she said, Breeth's spores wafting from her lips. "One baby. Lightly soiled."

"Breeth . . . ," Wally said, blinking, "you can possess *people* now?"

"That's chapter three!" Breeth said, grinning with Willa's teeth. She nodded to the Astonishment, who was still leaving fist-sized craters in the bark, unaware that the moth woman and baby were no longer in the tree. "Good thing that lady's got rocks for brains."

When Wally didn't respond, Breeth/Willa followed his gaze to Ludwig's remains.

"He'll grow back," she said, touching his shoulder. "I've been in his plant brain. It'll just be like having a friend go on a long vacation."

Wally nodded sadly and put his focus on the gurgling baby, swaddled in her wedding dress. He had her. The others were distracted. Now what was he supposed to do? He couldn't bring her to the DappleWood. The Wardens and Order would find her in no time. And Wally didn't want her growing up in Kingsport without parents.

Wh-ksh!

Amelia managed to get her whip around Sekhmet's waist, and with a jerk spun her in the opposite direction. Sekhmet spotted Audrey, still passed out on the ground, and her sword pulled her toward the ferret.

"No!" Wally screamed. "Audrey, *wake up*!"

The sweet ferret seamstress would not be able to regrow like Ludwig could.

Sekhmet slashed her sword, but the moment before its sharp edge met Audrey's throat, the unconscious ferret deftly rolled out of the way. Eyes still closed, she bounced onto her hindpaws and clasped Sekhmet's wrist, twisting until her hand released the weapon before pulling a spool of thread from her apron to bind Sekhmet's wrists.

Wally, tucking in the back of his shirt, looked in shock toward Arthur, who had written the words in blood on bark that saved Audrey's life.

Wh-KSH!

Wally flinched as Amelia's whip yanked the swaddled bundle from his arms. He lifted his hands in surrender and slowly backed away from the acrobat as Rustmouth and Silver Tongue rushed toward Amelia to try to get the baby. Even the Astonishment realized what was happening and joined them.

Wally didn't see what happened next. He was slipping through the tree-knot entrance into the Manor's foyer. He continued to the Willow Room, where he untucked the back of his shirt and pulled out the unswaddled BW.

"Well?" he asked the baby. "Now what do I do with you?"

Outside, the others realized they had been tricked.

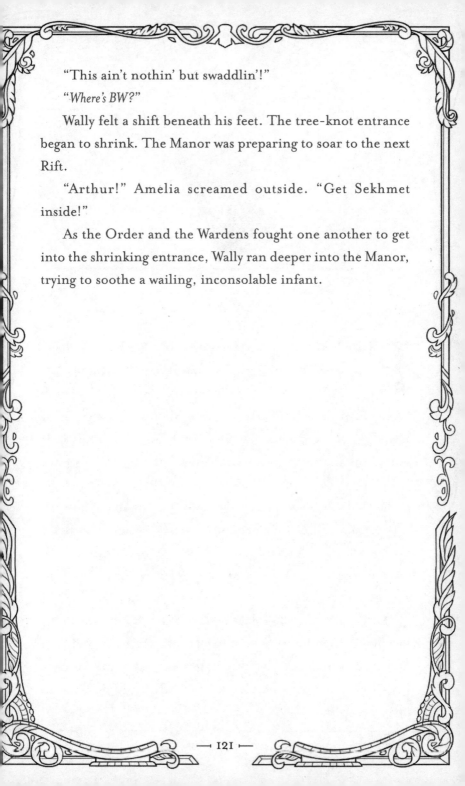

"This ain't nothin' but swaddlin'!"

"*Where's BW?*"

Wally felt a shift beneath his feet. The tree-knot entrance began to shrink. The Manor was preparing to soar to the next Rift.

"Arthur!" Amelia screamed outside. "Get Sekhmet inside!"

As the Order and the Wardens fought one another to get into the shrinking entrance, Wally ran deeper into the Manor, trying to soothe a wailing, inconsolable infant.

10
THE SPORE NETWORK

Many weeks earlier . . .

Fake heaven was the boringest thing that had ever happened to Breeth. And that was saying something.

After Arthur and the Weirdwood people had vanished through the Rift, leaving her all alone in the Great Elsewhere, Breeth was at the mercy of the weather. The winds wafted the spores she was possessing to and fro, swirling her low along the cloud bank before catapulting her high into the endless sky. She couldn't visit the rainy spirits walking through the storm cloud city. She couldn't even see where that pesky Order had gone to. And the Mycopath spores did not make good company, always talking about getting inside lungs to *infect this* and *control that*.

So Breeth spent her days being wafted about, stuck with her thoughts and nothing else. She wondered what Wally was up to. She wondered what that Rose ghost was doing with her body right then. She wondered how Ludwig was doing after losing his twin.

Would she ever see any of them again?

After a while, Breeth's thoughts turned to darker things. During the last adventure, she had been so busy saving Wally's and Arthur's lives that she had stopped thinking about her parents completely. Their spirits were still waiting for her somewhere, having been killed by the Wardens' ex-blacksmith Rose, who tried to use Breeth's spirit to access the afterlife and bring back her dead son.

Now Rose was making yet another attempt, stealing Breeth's body to infiltrate the Wardens. Breeth's spores bristled every time she thought about watching her body walk through that Rift without her, stranding her spirit in the Great Elsewhere. And to think Audrey had talked her into forgiving that no-good, surly-mouthed blacksmith. The second Breeth saw Rose again, she was going to spore right up her nostril and make her body sneeze so hard that Rose's spirit would go rocketing into the sky, never to return.

But for now, Breeth needed to distract herself. So she came up with a game. Whenever a rush of warm wind carried her high, high into the sky only to cool in the upper stratosphere before hurtling her back down like a roller coaster, she started making bets on which spore would win the race to the cloud bank. It was like rolling marbles down a dirt track and watching to see if the cat's eye, cleary, or plain blue would win.

But Breeth quickly realized she had a problem. There were a *lot* of spores. Not just a marble pouch's worth but hundreds upon hundreds of thousands of them. Millions maybe. How could she distinguish one from the others? How could she root for her favorite on the sweeping descent?

And so began the Great Spore Naming. Breeth named each based on its size and the tiny shape they made against the bright cloud light. After a while, she had quite a few memorized.

"Okay, let me try this again," she said. "Tucker, Ducky, Mouse, Couch, Bort, Tag, Fawn, Flip, Ace, *Welk*, Wriggle, Hoops, Antsy, Clover, Daffodil, Mulch, Gabby, Bachelor, Corncob, Felon, Slappy, *Cream-a-long*, Goose, Piggle, Cartwheel, Sprig, Helen, Wolfgang, Yeasty, Cat Spit, Musket, Toenails, Spigot, Ripple, Ice Box, Corduroy, *Doctor Socks*, Duncan, Maisy, Nemo, Wellington, Berserker, Pigskin, Bocce, Yum Yum, Periwinkle, Teflon, Cruddley, Tadpole, Wiglet, Sloth, Gluttony, Button, Spackle, Maggot, Smokey, Jim of Jims, Welt, Custardo, Simper, Flan, Thicket, Caboose, Runt, Chrysanthemum, *Regular* Mum, Aster, Wriggle-mortis, Diphthong, Spittle, Noggin, Canker, 'Fraidey, Sleet-y, Poley, Mr. Stain, Whisper, Hambone, Admiral Tumbleweeds, Quibble, Hubcap, Freckle, Soggy, Bangle, Bonker, Congo, Lunker, Pinkeye, *Ruffle*."

Breeth drew a deep breath—or whatever it was she took—and she continued.

"Bjorne the Balding, Baby FungFung, Batter of the North Wind, Winter Squash, Buttery Nugget, Pinecone Jones, Devil Dan, Ink Stain, *Bride* of Ink Stain, Tugboat, Puddle, Rollo, Kewpie, Veronica, Muffin, Biscuit, Skeeter, Midge, Madge, Mite, Ghast, Haint, Ghoul, Goulash, Tabouli, Ravioli, Wendell, Bixby, Aloysius, Putter, Lozenge, Pill, Packet, Poultice, *Gorgon*, Kruger, Luigi, Squeegee, Mop, Buckets, Bluebell, Bulgaria, Floss, Tinkle, Darla, Turtle, *Second* Darla, Oregano, Beaker, Quizlet, Sardine,

Bean-boy, Digger, Cecil, Ember, Owl-bat, Badger-bear, Mule-mole, Cat-gnat, Worm-germ, Tortoise Shell, Turkle Shell, Shekels, Cow Bell, Sheldon, Doodle, *Poodle*, Crab Cakes, Spongecake, Popsicle, Lemon, Baby Bubble, Dog Court, Bones Lawyer, Snack Judge, Butterball, Barnacle, Clavicle, Cinch, Pounce, Mr. Moonlight, Mr. Moonlight's Right-Hand Man, *Pretty Kitty Meow Meow*, Broomstick, Gloom, Gizzard, Wizard, Waffle, Chameleon, Double-Vision, Dung Beetle Stinkbug, Beetroot, Carrot Peeler, King Truffles, Truffle Pig, Stroganoff, Mushroom Cap, Scout, Shrimple, Skeeves, *Yumlin*, Fumblebee, Weeble, Wompo, Oats, Meeney, Miney, Morbius, Grub, Porquentine, This'll Be Thistleby, Derby, Bowler, Pustule, Buboe, Carbuncle, Timmy Rickets, Sigh-clops, Doughy, *Snogwight* and her Several Dwarves, Pockets, Clumpy, Strangle, Stick, Bangers, Lint, Marsha, Kegnog, Miss Wrinkles, Thrum-bundle, Corky, Snackbag, Bumpkin Spice, Cheese Booty, Piggle, Sky-brows, Dumpkins, Clot Sauce, Sluice, Creavey, Silage, *Feels*, the Slipper Twins, Danny Dry-rot, Picket, Moon Beetle, Cyril, Clovey, Nanny Dander, Scribble, Nuthatch, Blurb, Ingleberry, Dustbloom, Jelly Ear, *Sugar Bump*, Lumpkin, Startles, Rattle Catch, Photon, Pylon, Python, Pickle, Pucker, Pouchy, Fidgit, Rumple, Dimple, Fluff, Cabbage, Cud, Mudtrumpet, Gomer, the One Whose Name I Can Never Remember, Stewy, Splice, Toothache, Rag, Lyle, Piddle, Trickles, Trots, Bianca, Kelvin and His Sack-of-Cats, Plip, Snide, Flapjack, Arpeggio, Wallop, Tiny-mo, Wingey, Horror-cakes, Spotty, Clem, Rufus, Dinah, *Squidge*, Bunkum, Gibbet, Tripe, Burble, Conch, Bonnie Bunion,

Walter Wart, Lulu Lesion, Polly Polyp, Scarlet Marmot, Yuckles, Crag, Murmurer, Peabody, Petri, Poultry, Peter, Teeter, Ham Stew, Gumbo, Rumpus, Rangoon, Grumble, Bingo and Chop, Wrinkle, Cowlick, Little Tickle, Trinket, Trumpet, Crumpet, Grape-seed, Slobber, Scrubs, Flume, Ned, Bitty, *Pork Pie*, Gary 1, Gary 2, Garys 3 to 1,008, Mange, Knackers, Cram, Dregs, Mr. Moister, Ogler, Sploosh, Miss Meatfog, Flense, Barney Bonetongs, Creaky Beak, Echo and Ping, Mad Basil, Puffer, Clumps, Cleaver, Twaddle, Geezer, Chomps, Blimey, Placemat, *Twiggins*, Vespers, Munchkin, Wilmore, Snood, Skimpy, Wheedle, Nibbles and Flakes, Scourge, Puddin', Flip Flap, Fug, Garlic, *The Strangler*, Macho Man Pete, Tombstone, Charlie's Left Foot, Fern, Ooze, Shutter, Stoomples, Flank, Snarvle, Little Tommy Talcum, Mildred, Mr. Billows, Droopy Boots, Seepstress, Spurticus, Leech, Ghastle, Sleaze, Blintz, Drab Andy, Molt, Bluster, Mossy Locks, Plunk, Cosmo, Rankle, Dwindler, Pock, Plimple, Blott, Foamy, Wince, Teeters, Noodly Meat Sauce, and Mr. Mince."

Once Breeth had named this many spores, she realized she had barely covered those that composed her pinkie fingernail. So she gave up the whole effort and simply called them all . . . Breeth.

"Well, Breeth?" she said, gazing across the Great Elsewhere's cloudy expanse. "What the crap else can we do in this place?"

Infect! Mesmerize! Control! the spores responded.

Boredom set in again. This time with a vengeance.

Breeth breezed through the Great Elsewhere day and night,

dawn and dusk, while time tumbled along, interminable. She had nothing to do now but miss her friends, remember her parents, and hate Rose. And yet, Breeth couldn't seem to make her thoughts heavy enough to stop her spores from swirling.

∗∗∗

"Hello? Breeth?"

Breeth's spores jerked to attention. She'd been floating on the back of a choppy wind, trying to remember her parents' faces, when she heard what sounded like . . . a voice.

"Can you hear me?"

Breeth spun her spores in eddies, searching the Great Elsewhere for the source of the voice and trying not to get too excited. It sounded staticky and weird. Like leaves trying to speak. Was she imagining things?

"Breeth, please say something if you can hear me!"

The words were coming from . . . her stomach. The spores there vibrated like vocal cords, channeling a familiar voice.

"I'm here!" Breeth told her stomach. "Who are you? Have I finally lost my marbles? Er, spores?"

"It's Amelia, Breeth. I'm able to speak to you because the Mycopath took my eye many years ago, and I still have a connection to it."

Breeth was so excited she screamed for five minutes.

"Are you quite finished?" Amelia snapped.

"Has anyone ever told you your voice is the *prettiest thing*?" Breeth asked. "Prettier than breezes? Honestly, I could never hear wind again in my life and be just fine. How are you? Talk to me more." She continued to scream. "*Eeeeeeeeee!*"

"Breeth, if you would please be quiet, I would like to get you out of there and us out of here."

"Oh! Okay, yes, listening. Ready. Go. Wait. Hold on. *Eeeeee!* Okay. Now. Go."

"You're familiar with the Mycopath, yes?"

"You mean *Fun Gus*? Yeah! It let me borrow its spores! It's pretty nice when it's not eating Fae-born or oozing all over the floor."

Amelia's voice sighed. "I need you to think more scientifically, Breeth. The Mycopath grows by releasing spores that control the minds of whatever Fae-born breathe them in, convincing them to feed themselves to the psychopathic mushroom. That's why the Wardens locked it in the Abyssment. It is extremely dangerous."

Breeth lifted her hand and addressed her spores. "Meanies."

"Spores tend not to stay put," Amelia continued, "especially in drafty basements. Over the years, the Manor has traveled across the Fae, inadvertently releasing spore clouds into hundreds of pocket-worlds. In such low numbers, the spores are harmless, causing their victims to briefly wander in search of the Mycopath until the spores eventually clear out of their lungs. But the spores remain in those pocket-worlds. Breeth, I am going to have you take advantage of how far they have spread."

"Great! Fantastic! I have no idea what you're talking about, but keep talking. Never stop talking."

"The spores have a psychic connection to one another. This connection runs through the entirety of the Mycopath's spore network. That's how I'm speaking to you now. Make sense?"

"Not at all."

Breeth's stomach spores sighed with disgust. "I need you to

pay attention *to the words I'm saying. The fate of the Manor is at stake. If you can figure out how to stretch your spirit through the spore network into other pocket-worlds, you can escape the Great Elsewhere and come rescue the Wardens from the DappleWood.*"

"You mean I can actually get out of this place?"

"*Yes. But only if—*"

Breeth screamed for five more minutes. She was finally going to leave this awful cloud prison! She was going to see faces! Have *conversations*! She would find that Rose ghost, steal her body back, and then hug Wally so hard he would *squish*.

"*Please, Breeth,*" Amelia said. "*For once, I need you to control your-self. The longer this takes, the less chance we'll have of retrieving the Manor and the more pocket-worlds will be erased.*"

"You heard her, spores," Breeth said. "It's time to behave yourselves and stop distracting me."

"*Breeth, this is complicated, but . . . can you sense spores that aren't there?*"

Breeth studied the cloud bank far, far below. "You mean ones I dropped?"

"*Enough jokes, Breeth. I need you to* focus.*"

Breeth frowned. She thought she had been focusing.

"*I'm talking about spores in* other *pocket-worlds,*" Amelia contin-ued. "*Try to reach out to them.*"

Breeth strained. She reached. She expanded her spores out like a puffer fish and then sucked them back in again like magnets. Nothing happened.

"This is *impossible*! I'll be stuck here forever!"

"*You're not* relaxing,*" Amelia snapped. "*It should come naturally. Be* loose.*"

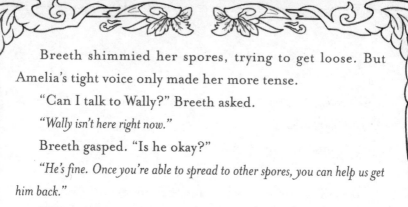

Breeth shimmied her spores, trying to get loose. But Amelia's tight voice only made her more tense.

"Can I talk to Wally?" Breeth asked.

"Wally isn't here right now."

Breeth gasped. "Is he okay?"

"He's fine. Once you're able to spread to other spores, you can help us get him back."

"How about that nice ferret lady? Is she there?"

Audrey had been the one who helped Breeth relax enough to temporarily die and leave her body behind in the first place.

"Audrey is stuck in the Manor," Amelia said. *"She's in danger. If you access the spore network, you just might be able to save her life."*

This made Breeth tenser than ever. She imagined the whiskery smile of her ferret friend as she tried to reach for those faraway spores. They remained out of her grasp.

Amelia made several suggestions, each less plausible than the last. Like telling Breeth to spread herself out like butter.

"Ugh!" Breeth's spores scattered in a burst of frustration. "This is worse than *reading*! I don't want to be bored anymore, but I don't want *homework*."

"Well then I give up, Breeth," Amelia said. *"Your lack of focus is going to keep you trapped in the Great Elsewhere forever and doom us all."*

Breeth fluttered her nonexistent lips. Amelia's sharp words made her feel guilty. And guilt always gave her a sort of glaze in her vision, like when she was reading. Her mind *really* didn't want to be there in that moment, so it went . . . elsewhere. She was never really sure where. Until now.

Breeth heard new noises. Felt new sensations. She shivered under a warm breeze that was not of the Great Elsewhere.

She could feel unfamiliar spores tingling just beyond her fingertips.

"*Breeth?*" Amelia said.

Breeth jerked back to herself. "*Shh!* I'm doing it!"

She let her eyes glaze over again. And quick as a light switch, she found herself in a new pocket-world. An expansive, underground place of darkness and carpets—incredibly soothing compared to the blinding cloud bank of the Great Elsewhere.

"Wow," she whispered.

If Breeth had tears, she would have wept then. She was finally free. Her celebration was quieter than she'd thought it would be.

"*Excellent work, Breeth,*" Amelia's voice said, vibrating Breeth's new belly spores. "*Now the real work begins. Find the DappleWood.*"

"Sure!" Breeth said. "I always wanted to see a whole town of Audreys!" She glanced around the dark pocket-world, hoping to spot a map with a *You Are Here* arrow on it. "Um . . . how do I find you exactly?"

"*I don't have time to hold your hand, Breeth,*" Amelia said. "*I have my own part to play in this rescue. This version of the DappleWood was created very recently, so the Manor hasn't brought any spores here yet. I'm hoping to solve that by nightfall.*"

"Exciting! How?"

"*Focus on finding us, Breeth. I must go. Someone is at the door.*"

"But—but . . . I like it when you talk in my stomach."

When Amelia didn't respond, Breeth let her eyes fade again, shimmering herself through several spore clouds in succession, like trying on new outfits. She found herself on a mountain made of mother-of-pearl. Then an orbital dune scape, with massive worms twining through the sand in infinity symbols. Then a place that was all purple, inhabited by creatures that had teeth for eyes and vice versa. Spores free-floated through these pocket-worlds, mindlessly searching for lungs to infect . . . until Breeth took command of them.

"Hallo, my pretties!"

As good as Breeth became at skipping from pocket-world to pocket-world, she couldn't seem to find the DappleWood. She shimmered into a castle with sword-fighting grasshoppers, through a cave of singing crystals, then over a swamp world filled with rusted robots. She arrived at a vast grassland dotted with the occasional bizarre tree and was about to shift to the next spore cloud when something snorfled her up.

"Whoa whoa *whoa!*"

Her spores were sucked up through tunnel-like nostrils into some sort of creature. And she wasn't just inside of it. She was *in control*. She had wide, stampy feet, big floppy ears, and . . . *eight* trunks.

"*Wheeeee!*" Breeth giggled, flailing about the strange elephant's many trunks.

When she had named her spores, she had been annoyed at their tininess. But now she realized they were the perfect size for slipping into a Fae-born's lungs and possessing it. She no longer had to work past the creature's frightened thoughts, like she had to with Ludwig and the mouse thing and the tentacle monster. The spores did all the work for her, just like they had with the dragon duchess. Now Breeth could possess anything or any*one* she wanted without even trying.

"Hope you don't mind," she told the elephant creature,

patting its head with its own trunks. "I promise I'm the best brain guest."

She dipped her many trunks into a muddy pool and slurped up a massive amount of water, which she sprayed over the rest of the herd in a rainbow shower. After months of cloudy boredom, she wanted to *play*. She noticed some spores still floating outside the strange elephant, and she had an idea. She took control of the external spores and soared them toward another strange elephant, which immediately snuffled them up. With a flick of her consciousness, Breeth managed to wave the other strange elephant's many trunks.

She squealed. She was in control of *two* strange elephants now. Like having one hand on two different toys. She decided the best use of this power would be to make the elephants floppily fence each other with their multiple trunks.

Shhhrrrrkkkkkk!

"*What was that?*" Breeth's belly spores buzzed to life with Amelia's voice.

"Um . . ." Breeth slipped her consciousness out of the strange elephants and possessed the spores that hadn't been snuffled. "Eek!" She squeaked in alarm. There, floating above the muddy pool, was a *hole* that looked onto a small town in the Real.

"Nothing!" Breeth told Amelia, gritting her sporey teeth as she tried to pinch the Rift shut. "That's just the sound I make when I get excited. *Ksshhtt.*"

"*Did you just tear a Rift?*"

Breeth stopped trying to pinch the hole shut and fell quiet with guilt.

Amelia sighed. "*I knew this was a risk. By possessing these Fae-born, you are technically misusing magic. That tears holes in the Veil.*"

Breeth was relieved, knowing she wasn't in trouble for tearing open reality. "*Wait!* I've been possessing all these spores! Shouldn't I have torn a Rift weeks ago?"

"*Spores aren't Fae-born,*" Amelia said, annoyed. "*They're not even organisms.*"

"Oh . . . ," Breeth said. "But—"

"*I don't have time to get into magical technicalities, Breeth. You haven't torn Rifts in the past because you've only ever possessed Fae-born in the Manor and Real. But this would be a good time to tell you that once you arrive in the DappleWood, we are never going to tell the Wardens how you found us. I'll do whatever I need to to get the Manor back, and that includes tearing a few Rifts along the way. Let's just try to keep the manipulation to a minimum, hm?*"

Breeth gasped. "Amelia, are you a little naughty?"

Amelia's voice grumbled. "*I don't have time for your humor, Breeth.*"

"But you have to have time for it!" Breeth cooed. "You *neeeeeed* me."

But Amelia had fallen silent again. Just like that. Had the Wardens caught her helping Breeth? Had something bad happened?

Worried about the acrobat and her other friends, Breeth began spore skipping through the pocket-worlds more quickly. But without Amelia's voice to guide her, she felt lost. The Fae stretched before her, as deep and wide as human imagination. Finding the DappleWood among the millions of pocket-worlds was like trying to find a needle in a haystack. Or like trying to find her highness Duchess Sporington IX after a particularly heavy gust blew Breeth's spores out of order.

Every so often, Breeth found herself in a blank land, possessing the last spores that whirled along the final breath of a dying pocket-world. The sight opened a bottomless loneliness inside her. But it also made her move faster, hoping to reach the DappleWood before the Eraser could.

The more pocket-worlds that passed—hundreds, thousands—the more hopeless things felt.

Until . . .

One day . . .

BOOM!

Something exploded in the distance. The sound rippled through the vast fabric of the pocket-worlds. Breeth followed the reverberations from spore cloud to spore cloud, traveling for hours, possibly days, until she reached a quaint little critter town that looked as haunted as Halloween.

"*Yesssssssss!*" Breeth said. She spun in a circle and found a massive funnel of melting purple faces pouring into the distant forest. She gulped. "Okay, maybe not so yes."

Breeth spored around the DappleWood, searching for Amelia and the others. Fuzzy noses peeked through the curtains as she passed. The critters had locked themselves in their little homes, clearly afraid of whatever evil had befallen their town.

Breeth came to the greenhouse and sensed something

familiar inside. She slipped through a crack in one of the windowpanes and found her body lying beside some pots and soil, as dead as the table it lay on.

"Hey there, me," she said. "Been a while."

She left her spores behind and put her body back on. She sat up and stretched her limbs and worked out her stiff jaw. She waited for the explosion of sensations she had felt the first time she had reinhabited herself. The flutters and goosebumps. The pops and twitches. The gurgly anticipation of sampling every food the DappleWood had to offer.

Breeth squirmed. Being back in her body felt *constraining*. Like putting on clothes she'd outgrown. She missed traveling through the air, feeling every wrinkle on the wind and riding the invisible roller coasters of the sky. She sloughed off her body like a wet bathing suit and whirled the spores back into her shape.

"*Whew!*" she said, giving them a wriggle. She felt the freedom of nakedness and none of the embarrassment. "Missed you all."

Leaving her body on the table, she squeezed her spores back outside and spotted Ahura limping into town. The mapmaker was headed toward a makeshift tent where Pyra spooned a potion into the injured Linus's mouth. Breeth wanted to sail right over and sweep them all up into a big sporey hug. But she remembered Amelia's warning not to tell the Wardens how she'd gotten there, and she headed in the opposite direction instead.

At the edge of town, she gazed toward the twisted wood, whose branches cracked higher up the horizon. Breeth was glad she'd left her body behind. This was clearly no place for mortals.

✻✻✻

By the time Breeth found Wally and the others, she had never been more ready for an adventure. Her spores shivered with excitement.

"Come on, Breeth," she told them. "Let's save this Manor."

11
THE BATTLE FOR WEIRDWOOD

Breeth swirled through the Manor like an ecstatic dolphin, diving in and out of walls and floorboards, splashing in and out of her spores. The boards crackled around her spirit as familiar as her own bones.

"Hi, slug painting! Hi, cupids! Hi, broken hallway! Hi, ya old pile of armor!"

It hurt her sporey heart to see how many hallways the Eraser had disintegrated. But once they kicked the Order out of there and Lady Weirdwood was back to her old-lady self, the architect would grow the Manor back to its full glory, sure as anything.

Breeth dove deep into the Abyssment, found the Mycopath—"Hiya, grumpy!"—swept a million more spores into herself, and then wafted them back up into the Manor like a polleny breeze. She felt like she had licked a battery. A *hundred* batteries. Her full power coursed through her—the ability to inhabit critters and humans as easily as she had once possessed plants and dead things.

She stuck her ghostly fingers into the floor and stretched

her senses throughout the Manor to get a sort of vibrational map of everyone's location. Arthur was in the Healing Room, applying salve to his wounded shoulder. That nasty woman Silver Tongue was wandering aimlessly. And the sweet ferret lady was snoozing softly in the front foyer. Only the forest wing trembled with battle. Breeth slipped back into her spores and wafted in that direction.

She found the Astonishment taking on Willa and her tin kites, which had come fresh from the War Room. The Astonishment deflected the slicing kites with her rocky fists, showering sparks onto the carpet. It was an even fight.

"For *now*," Breeth said wickedly.

She left her spores behind and possessed the floor, splitting the boards beneath the rock lady's feet like a giant wooden bear trap and holding her in place. The Astonishment grumbled in fear as the kites overwhelmed her, slicing chunks of rock from her arms.

"That's what you get for punching Weston!" Breeth yelled and then soared on.

Farther down the hall, she spotted Sekhmet pursuing some guy who looked a lot like Wally—*Oh! Graham!*—and was running with Lady Weirdwood's snake toward the Throne Room. This was a tricky one. Breeth wanted to help the Wardens, but she didn't want to hurt Wally's brother.

She was saved from deciding when Rustmouth stepped out of a side hall, blocking Sekhmet's way. Sekhmet retreated slowly, slashing her sword to keep the man back. But Rustmouth came toward her, unflinching, chomping his gross teeth at her blade every time she swung.

"Lemme jest *steel* a bite, eh?" he said, grinning. "I's been hangerin' for that second sword since tasting the sentimetals of the first!"

If Breeth had had blood, it would have curdled. The next time Rustmouth opened his brown teeth, she slipped her spores down his throat and into his lungs. A moment later, she blinked open his shark-black eyes and then jerked back on his muscles like reins, stopping him from pursuing Sekhmet.

Smack smack smack. Breeth licked rusted crumbles from her teeth and spit them onto the floor. "Blech!"

Sekhmet blinked at her, confused.

Breeth made Rustmouth bow to his opponent. "Madam, you are far too great a swordsman for my teeth. You have out dental-dueled me."

Sekhmet's confusion melted into relief. "Thanks, Breeth. Let me know if you find Wally."

She continued down the hall after Graham, and Breeth pressed Rustmouth's hand against the wall, slipping her ghostly fingers out into the wood to feel for nearby vibrations. She spun on Rustmouth's heel and tromped to the cupboard in the feasting hall where she found Wally trying to feed applesauce to a sobbing BW.

"Mac!" the baby cried, spitting out a gob of applesauce. "Mac! Mac! Mac!"

"Wouldja look at these lip-smacking morsels!" Breeth said rustily. "Er, *mortals* . . . morstels? How does that guy talk again?"

Wally frowned. "Let him go, Breeth."

"Aww. How'd you know it was me?"

—140—

Wally raised his eyebrows like it was obvious.

"Wally," Breeth said, plopping down beside him. "Listen very carefully." She pointed Rustmouth's well-chewed thumbnail at his own chest. "This guy tried to eat Ludwig's toes, Wally. His *toes*. You know what we do to bad guys like that?" She turned Rustmouth's hand into a fist and made the man punch himself in his own face. "Why are you hitting yourself? Why are you hitting yourself? Why—"

Wally caught Rustmouth's hand. "Breeth, you can't possess people."

"What about jerkwads, though?"

"How did you feel when *your* body was stolen?"

Breeth recoiled in horror. "Are you implying that I'm like that body thief, *Rose*?"

Wally gestured from Rustmouth's head to his feet.

"Ugh!" Breeth screwed up Rustmouth's face. "It isn't nearly as fun to beat people up when you sympathize with them! Thanks a lot!"

She laid Rustmouth down on the floor, lulled him to sleep, then swept some spores drifting in the hallway back into her shape.

"Mac!" the baby continued to wail. "*Maaa-ha-ha-haaaac!*"

"I don't know what she wants," Wally said. "I thought she was asking for a snack, but . . ." He tossed down the spoon. "If I can't make her quiet, we'll get caught before I figure out what to do with her."

Breeth ran her spore fingers along the baby's hair, tickling her head and soothing her cries. "Wally? Why don't you want the Wardens to have Lady Weirdwood back?"

Wally sighed. "It's complicated."

He tried to explain, and Breeth tried to understand. It *was* complicated. The Wardens clearly did *some* good, at least, protecting humans from Fae-born and vice versa. But Graham's vision of a Veil-less world sounded a lot more fun than boring old life. Everyone could meet the multi-trunked elephants.

"So, we don't know *which* side we're on," Breeth said, sighing spores.

"You don't need to be on my side, Breeth."

"I know. But I trust you."

Wally was good stuff through and through. Sure, he obeyed grown-ups too much and never played the things Breeth wanted to play. But when it came down to it, he would abandon his Novitiate duties to follow her down the pitch-black tunnels of the Mercury Mines to help get her body back.

Wally gave her a warm smile. "With you around, we might not need to choose a side."

He told her how his brother couldn't foresee ghosts.

Breeth's spores lit up. "I've always wanted to be a wild card! Then again, *woof*, that's a lot of pressure."

"Tell me about it," Wally said. "But we don't have to decide anything now. We just need to get Lady Weirdwood out of the Manor before she starts getting older . . ." He gazed into the baby's starry wet eyes. "Is it just me or does she look the exact same age as when we got here?"

There was a commotion down the hall. Scuffling footsteps.

"Go," Breeth said. "I'll keep the Order and the Wardens away from you."

Wally crept out of the feasting hall, holding the whimpering baby close. Breeth floated above him, spore eyes wide for movement. Wally turned toward the time wing, and Breeth saw what was causing the commotion.

Down the hall in the opposite direction, Amelia was tugging on her whip, its end wrapped around a translucent muscular figure, which grunted and struggled to escape. Anger rose in Breeth like lava. *Rose.* Amelia had managed to trap the blacksmith's spirit. But the acrobat was struggling to hold on to the whip's handle. Her right hand dripped blood.

Amelia noticed the ghost girl. "Breeth! Quick. Grab the demon lamb from the Abyssment!"

The spores in Breeth's chest rose and fell in an imitation of panicked breath. She knew what Amelia wanted to do, and she wasn't sure how to feel about it. Audrey had convinced Breeth to forgive the blacksmith for murdering her. But anger didn't turn off like a light switch. Sure, Rose might have been trying to see her son again, but that didn't make her a good person. Wally had said it himself. Possessing people was evil. And murdering little girls was eviler still. And hijacking their bodies a second time only to leave them to rot in the DappleWood . . .

"One demon lamb, coming right up!" Breeth shouted.

She dove her spirit straight down into the Abyssment, past the zombie ocean and monkey mummies and flying jackal heads, until she located the demon lamb, smoldering in the spot where Lady Weirdwood had contained it. Breeth possessed three of the flying jackal heads and used their teeth to pick up the demon lamb by its twisted horns, hauling it back up several floors to Amelia.

With one last grunt, Amelia jerked her whip, tugging Rose's spirit inside the demon lamb before wrapping the whip around its legs, binding the blacksmith inside. The lamb bucked and jerked and snorted, the spirit within desperate to escape.

Amelia stood up straight. "For killing a child," she said between strained breaths, "you will remain trapped in this lamb forever."

Amelia took the whip's handle and dragged the struggling demon lamb toward the Abyssment. Breeth watched them go. She'd finally had her revenge. Her killer was trapped in the very creature that killed her. She would never escape. A fitting end if there ever was one.

Breeth glanced up at the ceiling. A part of her had hoped

that Lady Weirdwood had been right. That once Breeth's murder had been avenged, an entrance would open to the afterlife, just as warm and pearly as it had been the last two times she'd seen it.

But the ceiling remained as wooden as always.

Breeth slowly floated down the hall, trying to feel as spry and splashy as she had a few minutes before. It took everything in her power not to think about Rose's son, waiting for his mom in the afterlife, just as Breeth's parents waited for their daughter.

12
MAC

Arthur limped out of the Healing Room, holding his arm. The wound in his shoulder was far from healed, but the Manor's magic salve had dimmed the roaring pain to a nauseating crackle. But he couldn't just lie in bed. He had to find BW. No baby cries echoed down the hall. Was she already aging back into herself? Would she be able to save them from this mess?

In the distance, the battle between the Order and the Wardens continued to rage—weapons clashing with stone and rusted teeth. Every so often, Breeth's spirit shuddered through the ceiling, cackling and reigniting Arthur's nerves. The ghost girl and all her power kind of terrified him. He wanted to get his hands on a notebook and pen to help fight, to track BW in a matter of seconds. But Amelia had told him his magic wouldn't work in the Manor.

Arthur spotted someone slumped against the wall ahead, their blood spreading across the rug.

"Sekhmet!" he said, crouching beside her. "What happened? Who did this to you?"

"Arthur . . . ," she said, hands pressed into her bleeding stomach. "You have to—" She winced, doubling over in pain.

She was hurt much worse than he had been.

"Don't talk," Arthur said, trying to calm the panic in his voice. "Let's get you to the Healing Room."

Bracing his injured shoulder, Arthur slid his healthy arm under hers, prepared to carry her every inch if he had to.

"*No*," Sekhmet said, stopping him.

Wincing, she leaned forward, revealing Lady Weirdwood's caramel-colored snake curled behind her. She tried lifting the serpent, but Arthur stayed her trembling hands.

"Don't worry about the snake right now," he said.

She squeezed his arm, smearing blood on his shirt and locking his eyes with hers. "You don't . . . understand. This . . ."

Her words failed, and her arm flopped to her side.

Arthur considered the snake, its tongue flicking down the hall as if it was searching for something. His head pounded. He couldn't think straight. But he did remember Ludwig's words about the fussy BW: "*Ze little vun misses her snake, no?*" And he remembered the rooftop battle when he'd watched Lady Weirdwood wrap the snake around her shoulders, quickly shedding her youth like it was a second skin.

"The Manor doesn't age Lady Weirdwood," he said in wonder. "The *snake* does."

Sekhmet's pained expression softened, and her eyes fluttered shut. He was right. The Wardens must have kept Lady Weirdwood's connection to the serpent a secret because it made the old architect as vulnerable as her pet.

Arthur hefted the snake into his lap and felt a strange dulling in his chest, the opposite sensation he felt when he cast magic. He ignored it. He had to get this snake to BW; otherwise she wouldn't grow up, and the Wardens would never take the Manor back.

Sekhmet's breath was growing shallow. The pool of blood beneath her was expanding. He hated to leave her, but BW was his top priority.

Arthur stood and adjusted the snake's weight on his healthy shoulder. "I'll come back for you. I promise."

He worked his way through the Manor, listening for BW's cries. It didn't take long.

"*Maaaaa-aaaaaaaac!*"

It was coming from the Judgment Passage. Arthur hurried that way as quickly as his throbbing shoulder and spinning head would allow.

The moment he stepped into the hallway, he found his friend stopped halfway down. Wally held BW. Arthur held the snake. Two parts of the Lady Weirdwood puzzle. The boys stood their ground, each waiting for the other to call the Order or the Wardens for help.

"How's your shoulder?" Wally asked.

Arthur gave it a roll. "Feels like it's been stabbed."

"*Mac!*" BW sobbed, reaching her tiny fingers toward the snake. "*Maa-haaaac!*"

Wincing, Arthur held out the pet. "She might feel better with her pet, you know. It soothes her."

Wally narrowed his eyes at the snake, suspicious. "That's what makes her grow up, isn't it?"

Arthur lowered the snake. So much for that plan. "How could you join the Order, Cooper? They're the *villains*."

"I *haven't* joined them," Wally said sharply. "I just left the Wardens. They've proven that they'll do whatever they can to remain in control of the Veil. No matter how despicable."

Arthur winced, expecting Wally and the baby to plummet through the floor for telling a lie in the Judgment Passage. But the floorboards did not open.

"I know which hall we're in, Arthur," Wally said, hitching the crying baby higher on his side. "I would never say something that put Lady Weirdwood in danger." He nodded to the snake. "Do you feel as confident?"

BW continued to sob as Arthur stared at his own feet. He would say what he believed to be true. If the floor swallowed him, so be it.

"I'm proud to be a Novitiate of Weirdwood. It's something to believe in. Something to fight for." He looked at the floorboards and drew a deep breath. "The Wardens *protect* the Veil, Wally. They protect the living things on both sides." The boards remained sturdy. He lifted his chin toward his friend. "It's like Garnett Lacroix—part gentleman, part thief. Yeah, sometimes the morals are hazy. We're forced to control Fae-born or temporarily lock up a threat. But we also save lives. Including an innocent ferret's."

Wally nodded. "That was a good thing you did, saving Audrey's life. But if Lady Weirdwood grows old and takes back the Manor, she and the Wardens will keep the Veil up, and everything will stay the same as it always has been."

Arthur adjusted the snake. "And what's wrong with that?"

"*Everything*," Wally said.

"Mac!" BW wailed. "Mac! Maaaaaaaac!"

"You and I got *lucky*, Arthur," Wally continued. "We just happened to stumble into a Manor that granted us magical lives and saved us from a life of thieving. But think of all our friends back in Kingsport, stealing for the Black Feathers to keep from starving. Think of *Harry*."

"I *am* thinking about them!" Arthur yelled. "I don't want them to be devoured by some terrifying creature sprung from Kingsport's worst nightmares!"

"That won't happen," Wally said quietly. He stared at his feet. "Graham can see the future." The floorboards held, and he looked back at Arthur. "Can you say the same about the Wardens?"

"*MAAAAAAACCCCCCC!*"

Arthur's jaw tightened. How could he argue with someone whose every prediction had come true? He needed a different angle.

"Wally, I created the Eraser when I retired Garnett Lacroix with that dragon-bone Quill. I'm responsible for the damage it's done. If we don't stop it, none of this will matter. Not the Wardens. Not the Order. Nothing." He held out his free hand for the baby. "I have to get Lady Weirdwood back to her old self. She might be the only one who knows how to defeat the Eraser."

Wally considered Arthur's eyes a moment, then squeezed the weeping baby close. "*We* created the Eraser, Arthur. And by my count your solutions have only ever made things worse."

There was a moment of silence, filled with BW's cries.

Then the Judgment Passage jostled, throwing both boys into the wall. For a moment, Arthur thought the floor had swallowed them both for lying. But the sinking sensation in his stomach told him that the Manor had arrived at the next Rift. He had to get BW away from Wally before he and his brother took her to some random pocket-world and the Wardens lost her forever.

But arguing was getting him nowhere. And without his magic, Arthur couldn't possibly beat Wally in a fight.

The ceiling rattled and spilled dust onto the carpet beside Wally. The dust popped up into a girl's shape.

"Wally!" Breeth said. "The Order's getting their butts handed to them thanks to your neighborhood ghost girl! Wanna go to the zigzag staircase and play xyloph—" She saw Arthur. "Oh. I'm interrupting something serious, huh?"

Arthur looked from Breeth to Wally. "What are you going to do, Cooper? Make your ghost friend attack me so you can get away with Lady Weirdwood? Let your brother toss an innocent baby into the Fae?"

"Wait." Breeth slapped her forehead. "Is *Arthur* the bad guy now? Is there a chart somewhere so I can keep track?"

"*MAAAAAAAAC!*"

"I won't ask Breeth to do anything," Wally told Arthur. "She can make her own choices."

"Unlike some of us," a voice said.

Wally looked behind him at a fuzzy figure standing in the doorway.

"I almost forgot!" Breeth said. "Look who I found waking up in the foyer!"

Arthur tried not to grimace as Audrey stepped beside Wally. It was three against one now. BW was as good as lost.

Audrey sniffed down the hall, as if trying to sense Arthur's intent. "You gonna control me again, Arthur? Make me snatch this infant outta Wally's hands or somethin'?"

Arthur swallowed. The ferret didn't realize that he'd saved her life from Sekhmet's sword. And she didn't know he couldn't control her in the Manor. In fact, not even Wally knew that.

Arthur adjusted the snake on his shoulder and raised his hands to show he had no writing implements. "Audrey, the only reason I controlled you was so the Wardens could get this Manor back and save your people from ever being kidnapped again."

Audrey's eyes remained narrowed, but Arthur couldn't help but notice that her ear twitched ever so slightly.

SHHHHHHCCCCCRRRRKKKKKKKK

There was a noise in the distance. Loud and horrific. A sound Arthur had wished he would never hear again. Reality was tearing like paper.

"The Eraser!" Amelia shouted down the hall. "It's here!"

"Graham," Wally whispered.

Sekhmet, Arthur thought.

Audrey hugged herself. "How did it get in the Manor?"

"On it," Breeth said. She closed her eyes and her spores drifted downward, as if her body were melting. The ceiling shuddered as the ghost girl went to investigate.

Wally turned to go find his brother as Arthur turned to get back to Sekhmet before she was erased. BW's wails turned Arthur back.

"*Wally*," he said, stopping his friend. He held out the snake. "Trade me."

Wally paused, hesitated.

"The Wardens are Lady Weirdwood's family," Arthur said. "Don't take her away from her family."

Wally looked at the weeping BW, considering. Then he took a step forward.

Arthur raised his hand to stop him. "We need an intermediary. Audrey?"

The ferret eyed him warily.

Arthur raised his hand again. "No tricks. I promise."

She took BW from Wally and padded down the hall. The baby was fascinated by the ferret's fuzzy face and kept grabbing at it with her pudgy fingers.

"Watch the whiskers, sugar," Audrey said. "I need those for steerin'."

As she continued down the hall, Arthur noticed she seemed to be *shrinking*. Her claws diminished like melting icicles, growing dull on her paws. He didn't understand, but this didn't seem to be a good time to bring it up.

The ferret reached Arthur and shuddered as he draped the snake around her aproned shoulders.

"If the Veil falls," he whispered, "every pocket-world will become vulnerable to humans. Every. Single. One."

Audrey's expression didn't change a whisker as she handed over BW, whose cries turned to sniffles the moment she was in Arthur's arms. The ferret returned to Wally as spores rose from the carpet and popped back into Breeth shape.

"The Manor landed next to a Rift created by the Eraser," she said, looking as terrified as Arthur felt. "It just . . . walked right in."

Wally looked to Arthur. They nodded once at each other, then headed in opposite directions. Arthur held BW close. He had resented being her babysitter back in the DappleWood, but now the baby's weight felt reassuring. He didn't know what he would do now, but at least the lady was safe.

Arthur moved through the Manor, listening down branching hallways, hoping to find one that wasn't filled with the sickening crunches of battle. He found an open passage and hurried down it, only to stop a few steps later when something flashed as bright as lightning.

When Arthur blinked open his eyes, the end of the hall was gone. Cut clean through. Its floor was now as jagged as a cliffs' edge and fell to a bottomless chasm of staticky white. The Eraser was cutting through Weirdwood as if it were made of butter, carving it to pieces. Chunks of the Manor floated through the nothingness—a stretch of hallway, half of the swamp room, a scattering of weapons and roots and artistic instruments.

Heart pounding, Arthur retreated before the Void spotted them with its eyes of nothingness. BW whimpered, and he pressed her face to his shoulder so she wouldn't see what was happening to her Manor.

"*Shh shh shh,*" Arthur said, stroking her head. "We'll get you back to normal. Even if I have to take several decades to raise you back to an old woman myself."

He came to another erased hallway and found that scattered throughout the nothingness were Rifts, ripping open in the Eraser's wake. Arthur recognized a couple—Mirror Kingsport and the Great Elsewhere—but others were unfamiliar, like the tangled tunnels of silvery liquid. It dawned on him that the Rifts he'd seen opening in the nothingness were whichever pocket-worlds the Manor doors had most recently opened to.

"Mac!" BW cried.

Arthur grimaced and quickly retreated from the open pit, hoping the Eraser hadn't heard.

"Mac!"

"We're going to get your snake back," he whispered. "But for now, we need to be *very quiet*, okay? There are bad things nearby."

"Mac! Mac! Mac!"

"I *know*. But if you keep making sound, we're both going to be erased, and then no one will be able to take care of your precious—"

"MAC! MAC! MAC! MAC! MAC!"

"Why, what's this?" a crumbling voice said behind them. "If it ain't some hinjured prey, whose helpless squeaklins beckoned the predator. And a magishun without a drip of blood to scrawl himself to savety."

Arthur turned around slowly and found Rustmouth filling the hall. Behind him, Silver Tongue laughed giddily, clapping as she stared at BW with her eyes of blackness. "We found her! We found her!" she chanted. "We win! We win!"

Rustmouth cracked his jaw. "Toss that wee grub over to yer old pal Rusty, and I swear by my gums not to munchle it. I'll just chuck her out a window into some sofity pocket-place where she'll be cradleweissed for all eterminity."

Arthur held BW close and stood his ground.

"Ah, come now," Rustmouth said, stepping closer. He gestured to the nothingness behind Arthur. "Ain't no recovering from this, eh? Your precocious Manor's in hissrepair. Your wittle architect's replaced blueprints and blue veins with naps and nappies. Heh heh."

"I can tell you how to get to the Mercury Mines," Arthur said.

Rustmouth shuffled to a stop. Silver Tongue peered over his shoulder and licked her cracked, blue lips. So, Arthur was right. The silvery tunnels he'd seen were where Silver Tongue got the mercury for her flask.

"You prevaricaterin' to us?" Rustmouth asked.

Arthur shook his head. "Cross my heart."

He stared into Rustmouth's sharklike eyes, and nodded toward the end of the truncated hall, where the Room of Fathers floated by. "Step into that room, and I'll tell you exactly where to go."

Rustmouth glanced back at Silver Tongue, who was already skipping down the hall, leaping off the broken edge into the passing room. He grunted in frustration, then joined her.

Once they had floated a ways from the hall, Arthur told them exactly where to go.

"Dam your ayes, little godling!" Rustmouth shouted. "I ever see your smugly ug again, I'll eat your hands!"

"Shut up talking to that kid, Rusty!" Silver Tongue screeched. "Find a way to steer us to that sweet stuff!"

The Room of Fathers drifted off into the nothingness, and Arthur breathed a little easier.

"Augh!"

Something sharp poked him in the back, spinning him around.

He found Audrey, holding out Lady Weirdwood's snake, her muzzle turned away. "Get this thing away before it eats me or vice versa."

"Audrey," Arthur said.

The ferret reached up and wrapped the snake around BW's neck like a bib. "Despite our differences in opinion on how to treat a lady ferret, you and I do see eye to eye on some things."

The snake coiled itself around the baby's neck as she giggled and popped her lips. "Mac, Mac, Mac."

Arthur ran his finger between the baby's throat and the snake's coils, making sure it wasn't strangling her. The snake's muscles were relaxed.

"What do we see eye to eye on?" Arthur said.

"We both want to keep the Veil right where it is, thank you very much," Audrey said, giving the baby's cheek a pinch. "Now that the Dapplewood's back, *thanks to you*, I don't want any more humans tromping through it." She frowned at the snake and released a shudder. "And if you don't realize just what a difficult decision that was for me, you don't know how much I despise serpents."

Arthur shook his head in wonder. "How did you get away from Wally and Breeth?"

"I told them all this jostling shook my bladder up something severe and I needed to find the little ferret's room," Audrey said. She shook her head and sighed. "If I've got any trickery in my whiskers, I probably get it from you, don't I?"

Arthur beamed. "I've never been prouder."

A bump snapped him back to the current danger. A tower with a weather vane bounced off the truncated hallway and spun off into the static. Weirdwood Manor's roof had collapsed.

Arthur made sure the snake was secure around BW's neck.

"We need to find somewhere safe where she can grow back into her old self."

Audrey stared into the nothingness and shivered. "Is there anywhere safe?"

"I guess we'll find out."

They quietly hurried down the hall, away from the tearing chaos of the Eraser, but they came to dead end after dead end. Hallways ended in nothingness. Debris was piled high on staircases. The Wardens were nowhere in sight.

They reached yet another broken hall and found Lady Weirdwood's wedding dress lying crumpled on the floor. Audrey slipped it around the child. "There now. Ain't that a mite more comfortable than slimy scales?"

They were about to turn back when a voice called out from the nothingness. "Arthur!"

He stepped to the floor's edge and found Amelia standing on the waxen throne, which floated through the staticky abyss.

"We got the snake!" Arthur cried. He shifted the baby in his arms, the pain in his shoulder sharp. "BW's already getting heavier!"

"Look around you, Arthur," Amelia responded, with more softness than he'd heard from her before. "It's over. The Manor is destroyed."

Arthur went numb. "But . . . Lady Weirdwood will be back to herself soon. She can fix this . . ."

Amelia closed her blue eye, as if pained. "Find an exit. Save yourselves."

A shape appeared behind her—a horror of a human silhouette pressing out of the static.

"Amelia, watch out!"

The acrobat spun and cracked her whip at the Eraser, who floated toward her, arms spread. Before Arthur could see what happened next, Amelia and the waxen throne floated out of sight.

Arthur stood in shock until the broken hallway started to bow and splinter under its own weight. He returned to Audrey, who worried her paws.

"Did she tell us to save ourselves? How are we supposed to do that?"

Arthur gazed around, hopeless. They were islanded. Every way led to a dead end. The Eraser's destruction had ensured they couldn't reach the Manor's exits or any of the opening Rifts. He wondered how the others were doing. The Wardens. Sekhmet. *Wally*. He couldn't reach them if he wanted to.

He felt woozy. Weak. If he carried BW any longer, he was going to pass out from pain. He bent to set the baby down on the floor . . . But she landed on her own two feet. BW wavered a moment, her snake compensating to balance her, and then she stayed upright.

"Mac, Mac, Mac."

"Looks like we got ourselves a toddler," Audrey said.

The sight of BW standing gave Arthur a touch of hope. Maybe the old architect would still know what to do. Maybe the Manor wasn't lost.

He stepped to the doorway of a room that was no longer there and gazed across the floating pieces of the Manor—

a strange, exploded, X-ray view. Far below he could see the Abyssment, its top peeled back like the lid of a can.

"I'll tell you how we get out of here, Audrey," Arthur said. "Same way Wally and I escaped this Manor the first time."

He headed toward the Manor's center. Audrey followed, leading BW as quickly as her tiny feet could patter. He leapt over a narrow chasm at the base of a staircase, then reached back for BW before the ferret made her own leap.

"There's a special mirror on the first floor of the Abyssment," Arthur said as they continued down the hall. "It allows you to step inside any book you place on its pedestal. We'll find a safe story and hide in there until the snake ages the lady back into her wise old self, and she can tell us what to do. Now all we need is a book . . ."

He reached another edge, peered over, and nearly collapsed to his knees. The Bookcropolis—that sprawling labyrinthine city of a library was gone. Every last page erased.

Arthur, refusing to let his hope die, squeezed his eyes shut. "There have to be more books in this Manor somewhere . . ."

Back in Kingsport, he never went anywhere without an adventure story in his pocket. Mostly of the Gentleman Thief variety. But ever since he and Wally had stepped into the Manor, Arthur had barely had time to sit down for a minute, let alone read a gripping tale. He'd been too busy living his own adventure . . .

Arthur's eyes leapt open. "*Thieves of Weirdwood.*"

Audrey quirked her head. "You mean you and Wally?"

"Kind of!" Arthur said, striding past her toward the staircase they'd just passed. "It's a copy of our first adventure that Lady Weirdwood gave me as a consolation prize for not becoming a Novitiate. I was devastated about it then and even sadder when I left the Manor and realized I'd accidentally left the book behind in my room. But now it's going to be our salvation! So long as my room hasn't been erased . . ."

He reached the base of the staircase and gazed up. The second floor was as black as pitch. Every candle snuffed out. The Eraser had been pursuing the Wardens along the main floor and hadn't ravaged the upper ones, but the halls had fallen as still as winter branches.

"I'll be right back," Arthur whispered to Audrey. He looked at Toddler Weirdwood, TW, who cooed and made nonsense words, making more complicated facial expressions as the constellations in her eyes burned more brightly. "Keep her safe."

The ferret took TW's hand.

Arthur crept up the stairs, feeling the walls to guide himself in the whisper of light coming from the first floor. He reached his room, went straight to the nightstand, and picked up the copy of *Thieves of Weirdwood*. Their last salvation.

SHHCCCRRRKKKK

Outside the room came that terrible sound, like wood and carpet disintegrating. Arthur slowly turned around, and his heart turned inside out.

The Eraser stood in the doorway—a blackness that burned darker than the nothingness behind it. It had erased the hall, severing the room from the Manor. It was just Arthur and the

Eraser now, drifting through the static. Its starry body pulsed as its eyes, jittering and chaotic, stared at the book in Arthur's hands.

Of course. The Eraser was still trying to find itself. First, it had tried to acquire the dragon-bone Quill, hoping to write itself back into existence. Next, it had returned to Garnett Lacroix's old adventures, hoping to fill the void within. Neither had worked. So now it was looking for the very last place where the Gentleman Thief existed. This copy of *Thieves of Weirdwood*.

But if the Eraser had erased the Merry Rogues, it would erase this book too.

The Eraser didn't move from the doorway. It seemed to be hesitating. Arthur remembered calling the Eraser by its true name, Garnett Lacroix, making its eyes flash golden and its head swoop into the Gentleman Thief's hat before it briefly became corporeal and fell through the clouds.

Arthur hoped the Eraser was still afraid of him.

"H-h-hello, Garnett," Arthur said, unable to control the tremble in his voice. Shaking, he held up the book. "Looking for this?"

The Eraser blurred toward him.

13
GHOSTS

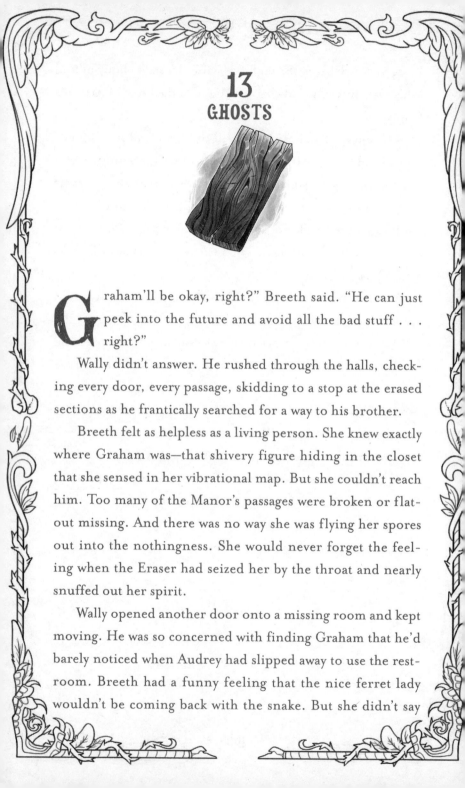

Graham'll be okay, right?" Breeth said. "He can just peek into the future and avoid all the bad stuff . . . right?"

Wally didn't answer. He rushed through the halls, checking every door, every passage, skidding to a stop at the erased sections as he frantically searched for a way to his brother.

Breeth felt as helpless as a living person. She knew exactly where Graham was—that shivery figure hiding in the closet that she sensed in her vibrational map. But she couldn't reach him. Too many of the Manor's passages were broken or flat-out missing. And there was no way she was flying her spores out into the nothingness. She would never forget the feeling when the Eraser had seized her by the throat and nearly snuffed out her spirit.

Wally opened another door onto a missing room and kept moving. He was so concerned with finding Graham that he'd barely noticed when Audrey had slipped away to use the restroom. Breeth had a funny feeling that the nice ferret lady wouldn't be coming back with the snake. But she didn't say anything to Wally. She owed Audrey for teaching her how to die.

Wally grunted in frustration when yet another passage led nowhere. Breeth was pretty frustrated herself. What use was being a ghost if she couldn't contort walls to save her friends? This was just like the time she had first put on her body and couldn't help them escape Lady Weirdwood's shifting passages . . .

"The Hall of Doors!" Breeth squeaked, remembering how they'd gotten around that time.

Wally pivoted and ran in that direction, and Breeth swept after him. They came to an Eraser-sized gap, but Breeth possessed a broken floorboard and slid it across, creating a bridge to the Hall of Doors. She released her spores and stuck her ghostly head through every door.

"Found it!" she said, opening a triangular green door for Wally.

She put her spores back on to follow him through, but he stood in her way. "Can you check on the others?"

"But . . . ," Breeth said, spores sagging. "What if you get erased?"

Wally looked away from her. "Like you said. Graham can see into the future. He'll keep me safe."

Breeth's spores sagged with worry. Even Wally didn't sound convinced.

"I'll be okay, Breeth," Wally said. "I promise."

"You better be," she said.

He closed the door in her face.

Breeth hugged her own spores. If she lost Wally, she didn't

know what she would do. But she couldn't just float there, worrying. She checked behind every door in the hall, searching for survivors. She tried to ignore that tiny part of her—a few heart spores worth—that worried about Rose in the Abyssment. No one deserved to be erased.

Not only did Breeth not find any Wardens, she didn't find much Manor. The Eraser had left vast streaks of emptiness behind, cutting through passages and rooms, now bowing and collapsing without structural support.

Breeth's spore heart disintegrated at the sight. This Manor had been her bones and skin for years. Seeing it fall apart like this felt like losing her own limbs. When Lady Weirdwood had been in charge, the Manor was a safe, cozy place, full of countless mysteries and wonders.

Breeth couldn't help but hope that the Wardens would win it back from the Order and Wally's brother. But how could she tell her best friend that she might disagree with him? Would she even get the chance?

"Rrg!"

Breeth heard a grunt behind a large black door and opened it to find Amelia hanging from her whip, whose end was wrapped around what remained of the waxen throne. The acrobat's eye frantically searched the surrounding area, looking for something, *anything*, to land on.

"Hold on, Amelia!" Breeth shouted.

Without thinking, she pushed her spores off the door-frame and drifted through the static. Halfway to Amelia, she shed the spores and possessed the wax of the throne. She stretched and contorted herself, trying to create a bridge to safety. But the more she stretched, the droopier the wax grew, so she ended up making a slide, which Amelia rode down into the feasting hall, which had a chunk taken out of its ceiling.

Breeth seeped out of the wax to join her . . . but she couldn't find her spores. The moment she had left them behind, they had drifted into the chasm where they were swallowed up by the static. Worse, the wooden floorboards that led to the Abyssment had been erased. Breeth was sporeless.

She frowned into the chasm and sniffed. She was going to miss the millions of little guys.

"Breeth."

Breeth turned and saw Amelia. Without the spores to lend her shape, the acrobat could no longer see or hear her. She was alone again.

"Look at your skin," Amelia said.

It was only then that Breeth noticed Amelia's eye was fixed right on hers.

Breeth held up her hand. It shone like blue glass.

"*Whoooooaaaaa*," she said, wriggling her fingers. "H-how?"

"The Rifts," Amelia said, gazing toward the distant holes that led to pocket-worlds. "Ghosts exist in a liminal space, so the tearing of the Veil reveals them."

"Right," Breeth said, still in awe of her new blue-glass self. "Libinal."

She held her hand up over a Rift and found that the light shone *through* her, giving her nothingness texture. These were *her* hands. Not paws. Not tentacles. Not spores or constricting bodies. She no longer had to possess anything organic. She was just . . . there.

"Amelia! I have *skin*! Do you know how many things you can do with *skin*? I'm really asking. It's been so long since I had it that I forgot."

"I'm very happy for you, Breeth," Amelia said, not sounding happy at all. She nodded toward the floating chunks of Manor. "If you consider having a shape worth all this destruction."

Breeth dropped her hand from the Rift's light, feeling a little selfish.

"I'm going to look for survivors," Amelia said. "I suggest you do the same."

The acrobat stepped off the edge of the feasting hall, twirling her whip toward another chunk of the Manor. The whirlwind sent a single spore wafting in from the nothingness. Breeth caught it and cradled it in her blue palms. It looked a lot like Mr. Moonlight's Right-Hand Man.

She pushed the spore through her glowing blue chest, tucked it inside her heart, and floated off to search for survivors. A short time later, a tiny squeak caught her ear. She *knew* that squeak. It stirred the single spore in her chest. She descended to the Hall of Portraits, where she had first met Wally. There, near the baseboards, she spotted a rodent whose fur also shone like blue glass. It was the mouse thing.

"Hi, you!" Breeth squealed. "I never got to apologize for getting you turned into porcelain and shattered! How are you? What's new? Are you still mad about that shattering thing? Wait, where are you going?"

The mouse thing hopped down the hall, and Breeth pursued it to a grand portrait of the dragon duchess. Breeth had passed this portrait thousands of times, but something about it was different now. The dragon painting's scales glowed blue—just like her and the mouse thing. And—she couldn't believe her ghost nose—it smelled of sea salt.

Breeth reached out and brushed the painting's scales with her fingertips, then jerked away when they began to writhe. She floated back, terrified, as a serpentine ghost uncoiled itself from the painting, revealing a tail, a long, scaled body, and a massive head with a blue mane that drifted like seaweed.

"Huamei," Breeth whispered.

Motherly memories stirred inside her. She had once possessed the dragon duchess to get her to spit out Arthur, gaining sympathy by waking memories of the duchess's son. In the process, Breeth had felt as if she was raising the dragon boy herself.

Huamei saw Breeth and snarled, crinkling his ghostly dragon eyes. Her motherly feelings evaporated as she noticed his coral-sharp claws, his broken seashell teeth.

"Please don't eat me," she said. "I have zero meat on my bones, and I just got skin for the first time in years."

The dragon sniffed at her, and his snarling relaxed. He lowered his muzzle, allowing the mouse thing to hop onto his nose, where it scampered up between his eyes and nestled in his seaweed mane.

"Is that your pet?" Breeth said. She blinked at the portrait. "Have you both been trapped in the Manor's walls since you died?"

Huamei looked from Breeth's glowing blue skin to his own, then gazed down the broken hall toward the Rifts at the edge of the blankness. He coiled his body and pushed off the edge, twining through the nothingness.

Breeth watched until the dragon boy's spirit vanished through a Rift that sloshed with seawater. With a shudder, she composed herself and continued her search for survivors. But she couldn't help but wonder: Were more ghosts locked away in the Manor's walls? What about elsewhere in the Real and the Fae? How many spirits were trapped in the many buildings and pocket-worlds of the Real and Fae?

Most important, how could Breeth find them?

14
STRINGS

Wally sprinted down the broken halls, trying to find the one that would take him to Graham. He leapt gaps and balanced along single floorboards that bridged one room to another. It was like traversing rooftops in Kingsport. Only here, one wrong step would send him tumbling into unending nothingness.

But Wally wasn't thinking about his fear of heights. An old panic swelled in his chest—something he hadn't felt since Graham was in the hospital. His brother was in trouble. When Wally had learned that Graham could see into the future, his brother had seemed immortal. But Breeth had proved that Graham didn't always get it right. Wally ran faster.

The journey grew more treacherous—steep, slanted hallways, upside-down staircases, a stretch where the stone cupids randomly shot their stone arrows through the air. The defense system reminded Wally of the bubble sheen that Lady Weirdwood had cast over Weirdwood. The one that had failed to keep the Eraser out.

He pressed through the last of the obstacles and made it to the storage closet, throwing open the door. Graham was inside, sitting among the shelves of quills and bottles of ink, head bowed between his legs.

The fear drained from Wally's body so quickly that he collapsed to his knees. "*Graham*. Thank God you're okay."

Graham did not look up.

"Hey." Wally touched his brother's shoulder. "The Manor's falling apart. This closet could break free any second. Where can we go to be safe?"

Graham lifted his head. "I should have listened to you, Wally." There were tears in his eyes.

"What?"

"You've spent your whole life listening to me," Graham said, wiping his cheeks. "I should have made your fear of the Eraser my own. That's the least I could've done."

Wally's chest went numb. The spark of certainty in his brother's eyes was gone. He sounded soft and vulnerable. Graham had always spoken with such calm confidence, waltzing right into danger, knowing nothing could hurt him. Wally barely recognized this new person.

Wally slunk down beside his brother. He had been relying on Graham to tell him what would happen next. What they should do. But for the first time, there was no plan. They were trapped in a Manor that was slowly but surely crumbling away into nothingness.

"It's funny," Graham said. "You once said you felt controlled by me. Strung along by my visions of the future. But the truth is, the future has been stringing me along since I was six years old, when I caught my first glimpse of it." He gave a sad smile. "You weren't the puppet, Wally. I was."

Wally blinked in disbelief. "But . . . what about the Veil? You told me I would bring it down. Is that still true?"

Graham closed his eyes, his forehead wrinkled in consternation. "The future is breaking up. Growing hazy. I can no longer tell you what was true and what I *hoped* to be true." He opened his eyes, jaw trembling. "I'm sorry I led you astray, Wally. If I had known it would end like this . . ."

Wally felt an overwhelming rush of emotions. He was angry with his brother for insisting that his fate was to bring down the Veil when Graham himself felt like nothing more than a mere puppet for the future.

But for the first time in their lives, Graham was talking to him like a brother.

"I kept my ghost friend a secret from you," Wally said, staring at his hands. "I realized you couldn't predict what she would do after she stopped the water tower from falling. I didn't tell you about her just in case you were wrong about all this. About the future. About the Veil. If everything fell apart, if you turned out to be evil, I wanted her around to help with any fallback plan. I'm so sorry."

"There's no need to apologize," Graham said. "It makes sense you didn't mention her. It must have made you feel like you had some control over something, at least."

Tears spilled down Wally's cheeks. "Graham . . . what now? Is the Veil still supposed to come down? Am I supposed to do it? The things you saw, they're still real, right? When this is all over, we can still see our parents?"

Graham's eyes went wide with horror. "Get out of here, Wally. Run. *Now*. Get to one of the Rifts."

Wally's entire body tensed. "Why? What are you seeing?"

"*Nothingness*," Graham whispered. "This entire floor. Gone. In a matter of seconds."

"I'm not leaving without you," Wally said.

His brother blinked the glaze from his eyes. He looked at Wally, and his brow softened. "I see a path forward." He got to his feet. "This way."

Wally followed Graham out of the closet as he cut a jagged path down the severed hallways and through chunks of rooms, away from the terrible tearing sounds. It was a relief to be able to trust his brother's instincts again. Even if Graham's predictions were spotty and filled with static, he could see a safer route across the Manor's remains.

Graham threw open the door to the Hermit Passage. "Through here!"

Wally stepped up and found nothing but blankness. The hall had been erased. Several yards below floated another room.

"This can't be the way," Wally said. "There's nothing here."

"Thank you for keeping me safe in Greyridge, Wally," Graham said. "Your efforts were needless, but it showed you loved me."

"Huh?" Wally turned around. "Why are you talking about that now?"

"It's time I be the big brother for once," Graham said.

He shoved Wally, sending him tipping over the edge, where

he fell several yards before landing with a thud on the floating room.

"Graham!" Wally screamed, pushing himself back to his feet. "What are you doing?"

Graham smiled down at him. "Don't let anyone ever pull your strings, brother."

"Graham, *no!*"

Wally watched, helpless, as his brother climbed from the hall to a slanted floor and onto a passing staircase, which he climbed to the second floor. Graham held up his puppetless hand and spoke to someone out of view. "Once upon a time, Garnett Lacroix, the world's preeminent Gentleman Thief, was feeling lonely."

A figure stepped into sight. A silhouette of starry nothingness. The Eraser, drawn by the story about its previous form.

Wally watched, heart pounding, as his brother leapt from the hall's broken end, falling several yards before catching the edge of a Rift. The Eraser blurred after, passing straight through Graham and unraveling his body—skin, muscle, skeleton—until there was nothing left. The Eraser's trajectory carried it into the haunted wood pocket-world, erasing the Rift behind it.

Wally's eyes remained frozen open in horror, unable to blink away the afterimage of Graham's final expression as he was erased. It was pure shock.

***

The Manor continued to splinter and crack as the static spread through its halls like a disease. Wally waited for it to consume him. His brother was gone. The reason he had started this adventure in the first place had been erased. What else was there to fight for?

He didn't even flinch when someone dropped from above, landing on the floating room with a thump.

"Whew!" Arthur said, picking himself up and rolling his shoulder with a wince. "You sure don't make it easy to save you, Cooper."

Wally didn't respond.

Arthur gave Wally's shoulder a shake. "I mean, what's an adventure without Wally Cooper?"

Wally had a vague sense that he'd been upset with Arthur, but he couldn't remember why now.

A great splintering sound spun Arthur around. Several yards away, a chunk of curved hallway broke from the Manor and went floating down. Clinging to the hall's edge was Audrey.

"Hang on, Audrey!" Arthur called. He looked to Wally. "Come on, Cooper. We gotta move before there's nothing left to leap to."

Wally's limbs felt made of concrete. He couldn't shake that image of Graham's final expression. "I can't do it, Arthur."

Arthur crouched beside him. "Wally, I *need* you." He nodded down to Audrey, still floating away. "The survivors need you. We broke into the Manor to feed ourselves and our loved ones, but we stayed because we wanted to protect the innocent and keep Kingsport safe. These last few weeks made me realize I can't do that without you."

Wally tried to remember that spark of pride he'd felt when he first became a Novitiate. A higher purpose beyond feeding himself or protecting his brother. But he felt nothing.

Everything he'd fought for—the Manor, his brother—had vanished in an instant.

"Your brother saved my life," Arthur said, placing his hands on Wally's shoulders. "I was *seconds* away from being erased when he started telling that Garnett story . . . Don't let his sacrifice be for nothing."

Wally pictured the spot where his brother had died. Leaving this place. Staying. It all felt the same to him.

Arthur offered his hand and Wally let himself be pulled to his feet. Together, they peered over the room's edge several yards down toward Audrey's bit of floating hallway, the eerie whiteness stretching infinitely beneath it.

"Ready?" Arthur asked.

Wally stared into the chasm. He didn't feel any fear. "If we miss, we'll fall forever into nothingness."

"Can't think of anyone I'd rather do that with," Arthur said.

The boys hooked arms. And they leapt.

15
WE R WOO M NOR

Breeth and her single spore floated through the noth-ingness, searching for survivors. It looked as if the Manor was exploding in slow motion around her. Debris spun in a thousand different directions. Yet all was as quiet as a graveyard.

Breeth had searched nearly every splintered piece when she spotted a floating chunk of curved hallway and soared to it. Inside, she found two rows of grandfather clocks. Huddled between them was Audrey and a girl of about six who had beautiful starlight eyes.

"Audrey!" Breeth said, zooming toward them. "You're okay! *Phew.* I don't wanna live in a world where nice ferret ladies get erased."

The little girl squeaked in fear and buried her face in the coils of the snake wrapped around her shoulders.

"Oops!" Breeth said. "Sorry. I'm Breeth. Probably the nicest ghost you'll ever meet." She put a hand to her mouth and whispered to Audrey, "When did you have a human child?"

Audrey hugged the girl close and whispered back, "This is Lady Weirdwood. Er, Kid Weirdwood now, I suppose. KW."

"*That's* Lady Weirdwood?" Breeth said.

The girl peeked out from behind her snake and blinked. Instead of being swaddled in the old architect's wedding dress, the little girl was wearing it. The sleeves, much too long for her little arms, flopped onto the floor. The starry glint that had been in the baby's eyes was expanding into a flowery web of colorful constellations—a microscopic galaxy.

"Um, Breeth?" Audrey said, pointing a claw. "Do we need to worry about that?"

High above, Wally and Arthur stood on top of a room, gazing over the edge toward the hall of grandfather clocks and looking ready to jump.

Breeth eyed the distance between the room and their hall. "They're not going to make it. They're going to *fall*."

The spore in her heart trembled. How could she save them? There was nothing to possess out there. And her blue-glass skin, while beautiful, was not made for catching.

A forked tongue flicked against her arm. The snake had uncoiled itself from KW's shoulders and stared toward Breeth with its milk-white eyes. As if it was offering itself. Breeth had once possessed this snake to rescue Wally from the storm cloud city. But it couldn't slither out into the *nothingness*.

Just then, Wally and Arthur jumped.

"Augh!" Breeth said. "Augh! Augh! Augh!"

She immediately possessed the snake, wriggled to the hall's end, wrapped her tail around a broken floorboard, and struck out. Arthur just managed to catch the floor's edge as

Wally snagged hold of Breeth's serpentine neck. There was a snap, but she tensed the snake's muscles, coiling her tail tight around the floorboard as Wally painstakingly climbed up her body like a rope.

The snake's tail started to slip. Wally wasn't going to make it. Audrey and Arthur reached out for Wally's arms, trying to help him climb up and over the edge to safety, but they couldn't quite reach. Breeth left the snake's body and possessed the broken floorboard, bowing its end to create a foothold for Wally to step up with. Arthur clasped Wally's hand.

"Audrey!" she screamed. "Quick! Grab the snake before—"

But Breeth was possessing wood instead of spores, so all Audrey heard was creaks.

The snake's tail uncoiled from the floorboard, and Breeth watched with knotted eyes as Mac, Lady Weirdwood's beloved pet, fell into the nothingness and vanished. KW started to wail.

Wally made it up and over the edge safely and then collapsed onto his back. He didn't get up.

"Wally?" Breeth said. "You okay?"

Wally wouldn't meet her eye.

"He just lost his brother, Breeth," Arthur said.

"Oh." She wrapped her blue-glass arms around her best friend.

"Wait, where's the baby?" Arthur said, panicked as he frantically searched the chunk of hallway. *Where's BW?*

"Um, Arthur?" Audrey said, and pointed to the six-year-old child. "She's more of a *KW* now."

The little girl had not stopped sobbing, burying her face behind folded arms and propped-up knees.

"Oh!" Arthur said. "Fantastic! Just another . . . seventy years or so, and she can start fixing this Manor! Wait. Where's her snake?"

KW wiped away a tear with the wedding dress's sleeve and pointed down into the nothingness.

"*What?*" Arthur yelled.

Breeth gritted her ghostly teeth. "I'm sorry! I didn't know how else to save you and Wally from falling!"

Arthur's face sank into his hands.

"If it's any consolation," Breeth said, "the snake didn't seem to mind. Almost like it was ready to—"

"Our entire mission," Arthur said, muffled through his hands, "was to age Lady Weirdwood back into an old lady so she could fix the Manor and save us all from the Eraser. The *only* way to do that was with that snake."

"I—I didn't know!" Breeth said. "No one tells me anything! M-Maybe she can still do stuff!" She hovered before the little girl. "When you were old, you could move the hallways around like they were your own limbs! Can you do that? Maybe, um, grow all these pieces back together with your mushroom magic?"

KW sniffed and wiped some snot from her chin.

"Okay," Breeth said. "Good start. Can you try a little harder?"

Arthur sighed. "Breeth, can you at least tell me how the other Wardens are doing?"

Breeth cradled her cheeks. "Amelia made it out. I don't know about the rest of them."

Arthur drew an angry breath. "Let me get this straight. The Wardens are missing or possibly dead. Ludwig is chopped to pieces and can't help us fix the Manor. I can't use my magic. And now Lady Weirdwood's snake is dead, so our all-powerful architect is basically stuck in kindergarten. Do I have all that right?"

No one answered. Wally and KW were still folded up in themselves, grieving a brother and a pet.

"Fine," Arthur said, clearly trying to push past his anger. "Let's figure this out, I guess. It's not like we can just sit here until the floor crumbles beneath us and we all fall to the same fate as that snake."

KW let out a whimper, and Audrey cradled her with her fuzzy arms.

Arthur didn't notice. He was too busy pacing the hall. "The only way out of here is to use the mirror in the Abyssment to escape into the only book left."

Arthur pulled a book out of his pocket. It was called *Thieves of Weirdwood*. Breeth didn't have to read this book, thank goodness. She had lived it.

"Wait," she said, holding her head so it wouldn't explode. "We're gonna enter our own adventure? Can we *do* that?"

"I don't know," Arthur said.

Audrey peered over the hall's edge at the Manor's erased foundation. "Is the basement still down there?"

"I don't know."

"Will the us that are in that story die of shock when they see, um, us?" Breeth asked.

"I don't know."

"What will we do inside that book?" Audrey asked. "And how do we get out?"

Arthur stared at the book a moment, lost in thought. His eyebrows slowly unfurrowed. "Garnett Lacroix isn't gone."

"Yeah, he is," Breeth said. "We saw him mosey off into the sunset with that scary author with the blood ink."

"We sure did!" Arthur said, excitedly flipping through the book's pages. He seemed *giddy*. Every trace of anger was gone.

"I hate to be a fussy ferret," Audrey said. "But are you about to hatch one of those schemes that's actually going to get us into more trouble than we're already in?"

"You're right, Audrey!" Arthur said, still flipping pages. "I do hatch schemes that get us into trouble! In fact, it was my actions that got us into this terrible situation when I retired the Gentleman Thief!"

"Now isn't the time for character growth, Arthur," Audrey said.

But nothing would wipe the grin from his face. He found the page he was looking for, bookmarked it with his finger, and beamed.

"Back in the Great Elsewhere, when I gazed into the Eraser's nothingness, I saw a flash of Garnett's golden eyes and a swoop of his signature hat. I *shouldn't* have been able to see that. Amelia said when I retired the Gentleman Thief, it eliminated all traces of him in the Fae or the Real. And yet, for just a moment, I saw him." He opened the book toward

Breeth and Audrey, pointing to the Gentleman Thief's name in ink. "See? The Gentleman Thief still exists *in this book*! After I retired Garnett with the dragon-bone Quill, our first experience in the Manor was no longer the latest Gentleman Thief adventure . . . it was the *first*. But it doesn't have to be! We can step into these pages and make it so the Eraser was never created!"

Breeth leaned in to Audrey. "Are you getting any of this?"

"I believe he's talking about time travel," Audrey said.

"Mm," Arthur said, rocking his head side to side in disagreement. "More like editing a story."

Audrey crossed her arms and scowled her whiskers. "You've read time travel stories, right? Going into the past to try to stop something from happening never turns out how the characters want it to. In fact, it tends to do the opposite."

"Good thing it's not time travel," Arthur said without a dip in confidence. "Like I said, we're just editing a story. We'll eliminate the Eraser from the present by . . ."

"Aha!" Audrey said.

Arthur winced. "I meant from *later* in the story. Do you have a better idea?"

"Y'know," Audrey said, turning out her apron pockets. "I plum forgot to pack one."

Arthur nodded down into the nothingness. "All we have to do is get this copy of *Thieves of Weirdwood* to the mirror in the Abyssment, step inside the story, and stop me from retiring Garnett Lacroix. I've cleaned up my mistakes before. But now we're going to fix my fixing of a mistake. We're going to erase the Eraser!"

Audrey raised a paw. "What if something goes wrong like it has *literally* every other time?"

Arthur steepled his fingers. "*If* for some reason we can't solve the problem—which we totally will, don't worry—then Cooper's story self will transform the whole hospital into marshmallow with the dragon-bone Quill. We'll have ourselves a little tumble and a soft, sugary landing before returning home through the Manor on the ground."

"The fall is fun!" Breeth said. "Once you realize your best friend isn't going to die."

Arthur went to the hall's edge and peered over. "Now, how do we get all the way down to the Abyssment?"

"I'm no scientist," Audrey said. "But would jumping work?"

Breeth and Arthur both gave her a look.

Audrey rolled her eyes. "Not to our deaths. I mean, jumping up and down in this broken piece of hallway to make it sink."

Arthur made an experimental small hop, and sure enough, the hallway sank a few inches.

"Perfect!" Arthur said. "We can use our weight to sail the hall down there! Steering might be a bit tricky . . ."

"If only you had a ghost girl around," Breeth said with a smirk.

She stretched her being through the floors, walls, and ceiling, and straining, angled the bit of hallway toward the Abyssment stairs. Audrey and Arthur took turns jumping and shifting their weight, gathering at one end or throwing their shoulders into a wall to help Breeth steer. The hall sank through the nothingness before touching down before the Abyssment stairs, miraculously still intact.

Audrey and Arthur helped KW and Wally to their feet, and they all descended to the mirror, connected by electric wires to a wooden stand. Arthur set the copy of *Thieves of Weirdwood* on the stand and flipped through the pages. The text of their first adventure flickered past while adjoining sensations poured from the mirror itself. The animal scents of Mirror Kingsport wafted through. Breezes and Corvidian feathers gusted across the floor. A tentacle whipped through and nearly snagged Audrey by the neck.

"Watch it!" she yelled.

"Sorry," Arthur said, quickly turning the page and severing the tentacle. "Not here . . . Not here . . . We can't save Valerie Lucas, otherwise we'll have to battle that tentacle monster . . ." He reached the book's ending and stopped flipping. "Here. We'll go in here."

Breeth gazed through the mirror, down a spooky, gray hallway, which bobbed up and down. The monster hospital. Its bat wings flapped strangely through the sky.

"Breeth?" Arthur said. "Can you can possess Alfred Moore to relieve him of the dragon-bone Quill?"

Breeth turned to Wally, who hadn't even looked up from his feet.

"Don't worry," Arthur told her. "You'll only possess him for a brief time, and the mad author's been hurting people, so it's morally sound."

Breeth thought a moment, then nodded.

Audrey worried her paws. "How will we get back home?"

"Once we get the dragon-bone Quill, we can write portals to wherever we want!" Arthur said. "We'll come back here, the Manor will be back to its old creaky self, and we'll all laugh about it over pumpkin soup in the feasting hall. Audrey, we'll get you back to the DappleWood, and then the rest of us will sit down and solve the whole Veil disagreement like civilized folks."

Everyone was quiet. But it was a hopeful kind of quiet. Tears still shone on Wally's and KW's cheeks.

The ferret helped the little girl make a giant step over the mirror's frame, then offered her paw to Arthur. They both stepped into the monster hospital, whose grayness seemed to leach the color from their clothes.

"So, Cooper," Arthur said from the other side of the mirror. "Ready for one last adventure?"

Wally finally looked up at his friend. "I'm sorry, Arthur. We agree on what needs to happen. We just don't agree on how."

Arthur's smile melted as Wally reached toward the stand and shut the copy of *Thieves of Weirdwood*.

"No!" Arthur said.

His hand darted out just as the mirror flickered like static and then vanished in a flash of silver.

The last time Arthur had been in the monster hospital, he had been terrified for his life. Now he was furious.

"Calls himself my friend," he said, pacing the stone hallway. "Where does he think he's going to go anyway? The Manor's been erased! It's not like he can sail it anywhere!"

He was so caught up in his anger with Wally, he barely noticed that KW had collapsed in a corner and covered her face.

Audrey crouched and gave the girl's little knee a squeeze. "Don't let this drafty old hospital scare you. In your old age, you're one of the bravest people I've ever seen. I once watched you duel a dragon and *win*."

KW peeked through her fingers with her constellation eyes. "I gotta fight a dragon?"

Audrey shook her head. "That is not what I meant. Your dragon-fighting days are far behind you. Er . . . ahead of you."

KW quickly covered her face again.

With a grunt, Audrey stood and peered through a narrow

stone window at the great flapping wings and the thousand-foot drop. She poked a claw into Arthur's side. "Why are you always bringing us to places in the sky?" She whisper-hissed to keep KW from hearing. "You told us we'd be safe, Arthur!"

Arthur didn't stop pacing. "Why don't you ask Cooper why he didn't send Breeth with us! She's the one that keeps us from dying more often than not!"

Audrey gritted her fangs and flexed her claws. "I need somethin' to keep my paws occupied, otherwise I am going to scratch your face to *ribbons*." She looked at KW's drooping wedding dress and clicked her tongue. "This will not do for adventures. Highly impractical."

She took a pair of scissors from her apron and began trimming the dress's hem.

"You know what?" Arthur stopped pacing and faced the gray stone hallway. "If Wally doesn't want to be the hero, I'll do it alone. Won't he be embarrassed when I'm praised by everyone for vanquishing the Eraser and saving the *world*?"

Arthur caught his breath and finally allowed the surroundings to seep into his senses. The monster hospital looked the same as it had last time. Dark and undulating with the occasional *whoosh* of cold wind blasting down the hallway. Only . . . something felt different. The hall seemed *grayer* than he remembered. The wind felt stiffer. Sure, the place was named *Grey*ridge, and it had transformed into a screeching bat-winged monster. But had it really been this *bleak*?

Arthur blinked through the low light at Audrey, still trimming KW's dress so it landed above the child's ankle. He noticed that the ferret's black and brown fur was now gray and *darker* gray. KW's eyes were as colorless as the stars seen through the narrow window. The blue was gone.

"Is it just me," Arthur said, "or is there no color?"

Audrey looked down at her light gray dress and made a frustrated sound. "This had better not be ruined. It belonged to my grandmother!" She tried swiping the gray away, saw the gray fur on her paw, and gasped. "I got this fur from her as well!"

KW held up her colorless hand and, frowning, gave it a shake, as if trying to make the color come back.

Arthur studied his own gray hand, wondering what it could possibly mean. "Maybe this is just the way story pocket-worlds look. They're made of white pages and black ink, after all. I'm sure we'll return to normal once we complete this second draft and give it a better ending."

He strode down the hallway while Audrey led a whimpering KW behind. "Come on, sugar. Let's go find out where our colors went."

"This will be easy," Arthur tried to reassure them. "All we need to do is stop Wally and myself from approaching Alfred Moore and using the dragon-bone Quill to retire Garnett." He cleared his throat. "And find another way to talk Moore out of writing monsters into Kingsport."

"You sure we can do all that?" Audrey asked.

"Of course we can!" Arthur said. "Of course I'm sure!" He grinned back at her, trying to forget the horrors that lay ahead—the flaming eyeballs, were-gators, sewage snails, and, most challenging of all, convincing Moore to retire *without* his beloved Gentleman Thief. "If we can just reach the second floor of this monster hospital, this story will take care of its—"

Vvt! Vvt! Vvvvvvvvvt!

A sharp drilling sound echoed through the hospital. Arthur, Audrey, and KW peered around the next corner and found Wally and the tentacle monster battling the mad hospital's questionable cures. A swarm of electric drills jabbed at their heads, trying to put holes in them, while a flock of straitjackets clamped themselves around Wally's limbs and the monster's tentacles.

Arthur blinked. The scene was in *color*. Green metal and slimy purple tentacles.

KW whimpered and Audrey quickly covered her eyes with a paw. "It's just a show, sweetie. Like a play." She looked to Arthur and whispered, "You need to save Wally before he gets drilled to bits!"

"Watch," Arthur whispered, confident in his friend.

He hadn't been in the hospital for this fight, but he had found Wally in one piece once he arrived. Sure enough, Wally and the tentacle monster worked together to banish the hospital's questionable cures.

"Nice, Cooper," Arthur whispered.

Audrey's muzzle wrinkled. "Why's Wally helping that giant squid?"

"That's Breeth," Arthur said.

Audrey shook her head. "I do not know how y'all keep track of this."

Wally and the tentacle monster continued down the hallway toward them. With each step their color spread through the hall like watercolor paint, shimmering the yellow moss between the blue stone cracks. Behind them, the darkness fell back to gray.

"I think I get it," Arthur whispered. He nodded to Wally in the hallway of color. "That's the story. Where the adventure happened." He gestured to the gray hallway he, Audrey, and KW were crouching in. "We're not in the story. We're off the page. That's why we're all gray."

Audrey covered KW's ears. "Why do I get the feeling we're about to get a lot more *colorful*?"

Arthur nodded. "Let me talk to Wally. He'll be shocked enough seeing me here. Let alone a ferret and a little Lady Weirdwood."

He straightened his collar, reminded himself that this was not the Wally who would abandon him in a maniacal hospital (not yet, anyway), and stepped into the hall, right in front of his friend.

"Don't freak out, Cooper," he said, hands raised. "I know I'm supposed to be way back on the ground controlling Garnett, but, boy, do I have a crazy story to tell you."

Wally didn't even look at him. His eyes swept back and forth, passing over Arthur like he was just another shadow as they searched for the hospital's next danger.

"Cooper?" Arthur said, waving his hands in front of Wally's face. "*Hey!* Cooper!"

Wally didn't slow down. His chest struck Arthur's—"*Oof!*"—moving Arthur backward down the hall. Arthur stepped to the side and caught Wally by the wrist, trying to stop him. But Wally's arm continued to swing forward like a mallet made of concrete, ripping itself out of Arthur's hands.

Arthur quickly stepped ahead of Wally and pushed against his chest. "*Rrrr!*"

It didn't slow him an inch. Wally was as firm as a walking statue.

"Help me!" Arthur called.

Audrey took KW's hand in her paw. "Think you can help me stop that guy from walking?"

The little girl shook her head vehemently, eyes locked on the tentacle monster still slithering down the hall.

"*Audrey, please!*" Arthur shouted, straining.

Audrey huffed and scooped up KW, who immediately buried her face in the ferret's fuzzy shoulder.

"Remember, sugar," Audrey said. "It's all a play and can't hurt you . . . I hope."

She was just able to step in front of Breeth before her tentacles blocked the hall. She took hold of Wally's arm with her free paw and pulled back as hard as she could, skidding her paws as Arthur pressed from the other side, desperately trying to slow him down. When Wally's shirt didn't so much as ruffle, they gave up, exhausted, and shuffled between Wally and Breeth, who moved down the hall like rolling boulders.

The two were still in color while Arthur, Audrey, and KW were in gray.

"*All right*," Arthur said, catching his breath. "This might be harder than I thought."

"It's that pesky time travel," Audrey said, hefting KW in her arms and shaking her head. "I tried to warn ya. The past is set in stone."

"For the last time, it's a *story*," Arthur said. "And it only *seems* to be set in stone. See, this happens on every adventure.

We enter a situation that feels completely hopeless and impossible to escape and spells death for everyone involved . . . But that's when we figure out the perfect *solution*."

He considered the pieces around them—the hospital and its medicinal horrors, Wally and Breeth and the unstoppable story—waiting for that tingling rush of epiphany.

"Maybe we just need more power," Arthur said. "Audrey, how do you feel about me writing you some sharper teeth and longer claws, making you so strong you can tear the dragonbone Quill right out of Moore's hand?"

"Absolutely not," Audrey said, shaking her head. "No more canoodling in my noodle."

Arthur sighed in defeat. "I guess I don't have anything to write with anyway. The tentacle monster's slime is as solid as dried sap."

He was getting more and more nervous. They had to figure something out before Wally reached the second floor and started the process that would create the Eraser.

Just then, Wally stopped walking. He and the tentacle monster had caught up with Alfred Moore, who madly scribbled in his notebook. Coils of blue reflected against the damp walls as a goblin made of pure electricity manifested in the hall. It spotted Breeth with its jittering eyes and struck like a bolt of lightning, sizzling her tentacles.

KW covered her ears while Audrey petted the child's hair and watched the tentacle monster jerk and smoke. "Poor Breeth."

"Wait for it . . . ," Arthur said.

There was a splintering sound in the distance and a triumphant "Ha *ha!*" A minute later, Garnett Lacroix came strolling up behind tentacle Breeth.

"Oho! Hello there, massive tentacle butt! How do I get around you?"

Arthur winced at his own Gentleman Thief impression. At this point in the story, he'd been in the Stormcrow's cellar, using the dragon-bone Quill to write as Garnett Lacroix, who easily saved the tentacle monster from being electrocuted.

"Hey, Garnett!" Arthur shouted. "Hey, Arthur!"

Nothing. Arthur couldn't even communicate with himself.

"*Rrg!* How are we supposed to change this stupid story if no one can see or hear us and we can't even *move* anything?"

"I haven't the faintest notion of how any of this works," Audrey said, "but don't we need to get *out of here*? Didn't you say this building was going to"—she placed her paws over KW's ears and whispered—"fall out of the sky?"

"Well, yeah," Arthur said, "but Wally turns it into marshmallow at the last moment. If he survived, we can too."

"Um, I'm not sure if you've noticed, but"—Audrey poked a claw into a nearby squishy tentacle and didn't make a dent—"even marshmallow will be as hard as moon rocks to us."

Fear caught Arthur by the throat. "Oh. Right . . ."

The electric goblin sorted, Wally, Garnett, and Breeth continued forward, shuffling Arthur, Audrey, and KW to the hospital's winding staircase. Arthur's nervousness was growing into outright terror. He had to solve this *fast*.

"Sorry, sugar," Audrey said, setting KW down with a huff.

"This old ferret's arms have turned to noodles. You're gonna have to take these stairs yourself."

KW whimpered, refusing to let go of the ferret's neck.

Audrey winced. "Maybe Uncle Arthur will carry you."

"I'm trying to solve our problem!" Arthur said.

The ferret scowled at him. "If this child is anyone's responsibility, she's yours. I never even met the old woman."

"*Fine*," Arthur said. "But I promise my skills are better used elsewhere. And if she gets snot on me . . ." He picked up KW with a grunt. She was much heavier than he had expected. "*Oof.* Couldn't we at least have aged her into a teenager before her snake died?"

The little girl's sobs shuddered. "*Ma-hac!*"

"Sorry!" Arthur said. "Sore subject. Sorry."

They climbed the winding staircase, which soon became infinite, the marble steps unbuilding themselves below to rebuild above. Arthur and Audrey hustled to keep up with the colorful story so they wouldn't get spit out into open sky. Once Wally and Garnett solved this final staircase puzzle, they would reach Alfred Moore on the top floor, and they would trigger the series of events that would create the Eraser. And then they would all fall a thousand feet.

"*Think!*" Arthur said, lifting his leaden feet up the next step . . . and the next. His breath came in huffs. His heartbeat pulsed in his eyes. It wasn't easy, brainstorming while carrying a large child up an infinite staircase. "What will make us integrate with the story?"

"Don't look at me," Audrey said. "I don't *do* adventures."

Arthur adjusted KW with an exhausted grunt. "What if we

pretend we're part of the adventure! Audience participation! *Ahem*." He tried and failed to catch his breath. "Oh no! What are we going to do? These bricks are coming right out from under our feet!"

Arthur looked to Garnett, who hadn't so much as blinked. Audrey and KW remained in gray.

"So much for that idea," Audrey said.

"Madam?" Garnett was saying to the tentacle monster. "Could you lend us one of your long appendages and tickle this flapping monstrosity?"

Breeth slid her tentacles through a barred window into the armpits of the giant bat wings. The staircase began to tremble with silent giggles, throwing Arthur off-balance.

"Augh!"

With KW in his arms he couldn't brace himself against the wall, and he stumbled back toward the vanishing steps. Audrey lunged forward, just managing to catch his arm as he stepped into open air.

The ferret strained, pulling back with everything she had. "I'm not sure I can hold on!"

"Sure you can!" Arthur said, trying to regain his footing on the last stone step, currently loosening itself from the staircase. "I made you stronger back at the dragon prison! Just—"

Audrey's paws slipped, she tumbled forward, and the ferret, Arthur, and KW all fell screaming out of the hospital and into the open sky.

17
OUTLANDISH LANDSCAPES

oments after Wally and Breeth stepped onto the cobbled streets of Kingsport, the oval mirror blipped out behind them. Wally stared at the blank brick wall, hoping everyone—the Wardens, the staff, and the Order—made it out safe.

Breeth floated beside him, maintained by a single gray spore in her heart. "So, um, did we just leave Arthur and Audrey and tiny Lady Weirdwood in a bat hospital all alone?"

"They'll be okay," Wally said. "They have a tentacle monster on their side."

"Oh yeah!" Breeth said. "I miss that guy sometimes." She gazed into Kingsport's overcast sky and sighed. "I guess we're stuck here now."

"Only until the Manor shows up in Hazelrigg," Wally said. "We can use its mirror to go wherever we want."

"*Rrrrright*," Breeth said. "The thing we *just* did."

Wally took in the day—the gray horizon, the crashing waves, the roiling clouds—as hazy and ominous as he remembered. This was the morning his and Arthur's adventures had begun. After shutting the copy of *Thieves of Weirdwood*, Wally had flipped to the very beginning of the book, stepping through the mirror and into a part of the story when his life was still simple—stealing for the Black Feathers to pay Graham's hospital bills.

Wally had felt so uncomfortable back then, trying to survive as a lowly thief. Fighting for rank. Stealing to eat. Finding safe places to sleep when bad things were happening in the tenements. As awful as his life had been, at least it had been predictable. When traveling with Weirdwood Manor, the challenges were always new. Each adventure stranger and more deadly than the last. Wally missed knowing exactly how things worked, no matter how scary it all felt. Even Kingsport's ash-polluted air smelled kind of sweet.

Wally headed down the alley toward Center Street, Breeth floating beside him.

"Soooo, what are we doing here again?" she asked.

"We're going to talk to my brother. But this time I won't let him speak in riddles. He's going to tell me everything he knows."

Wally considered taking a path to Greyridge that didn't pass any of the Black Feathers' hideouts, but he knew how to fight now. Sekhmet had taught him. And he had Breeth, who could handle absolutely anything this city could throw at them. They were unstoppable now.

"*Ow!* What the—? Ouch! You stupid—! Ow!"

Wally looked up to find Breeth knocking into a shop front over and over again. She was trying to seep into the wood, but it wasn't working. Her ghost kept bouncing off the shop like bread dough. The slats squished her face flat. A signpost impaled her eye.

"Wally, I can't—*ouch!* I can't—*ow!* Why won't it let me—*rrg!*"

Wally stared around the street. Kingsport days were almost always gray. But never *this* gray. The horizon was leached of color. The weeds sprouting through a crack near his feet were as colorless as the granite. He crouched and delicately touched one of the leaves. It did not bend, instead slicing into his fingertip, as sharp as a knifepoint. The drop of blood was as colorless as the ocean.

"You can't change the story," he whispered.

"I can change anything!" Breeth said above. "I've been *training*."

She tried to possess several more objects, but none would let her spirit inside.

Wally fell back and covered his face. If flowers were as sharp as knives, and Breeth couldn't possess so much as a wooden beam, then what would a monster hospital do to Arthur, Audrey, and KW? What about the fall when the marshmallow was as solid as diamond? He winced, imagining his friends plummeting from the sky and being impaled on grass as stiff as nails.

He uncovered his face and breathed slowly, reminding himself that the fall wouldn't happen until the end of the adventure he was currently in. He had time to think of something.

"Come on," he said, hurrying down Center Street. "Maybe Graham will have some answers."

"Wait," Breeth said, floating to catch up. "If your brother can't even see you . . ."

Wally didn't slow his pace. "Maybe he'll have predicted me coming in his visions."

They reached Paradise Lane and dodged around the carts and horses, which could crush them as flat as paper. None of the citizens so much as glanced in his and Breeth's direction. Their path through the city seemed as set as clockwork.

"Ugh!" Breeth said. "I almost forgot how boring it is to go down the street like the *living*."

Once they reached the other side of Paradise Lane, the journey grew smoother. Smoother, in fact, than any other Wally had taken through his city. He could walk out in the open without fear of the Oakers trying to arrest him or Black Feathers collecting their due. And if they ran into the other big threat—Alfred Moore's doll—it couldn't turn him into porcelain.

As they passed through Market Square, Wally spotted one of the younger Black Feathers named Sam. Sam was crouched in an alley, eyeing a mark. He didn't look well. His arms were skinny. His face was gaunt. His shirt and pants were riddled with holes. But Sam still had a fire in his eyes. That hunger the Black Feathers instilled in its thieves to keep them fighting, even when they were starving. Especially then.

Wally watched as Sam tried to pickpocket the mark. He watched as his friend was caught and dragged to the nearest Oaker. And he watched as that Oaker beat Sam within an inch of his life. That's all Wally could do—watch, heartbroken and helpless, as his friend's gray blood dripped on the concrete.

Breeth laid her blue-glass hand on his shoulder. "If I could possess that Oaker, I'd make him beat himself up. And then I'd steal a food cart from Market Square and roll it here so all the hungry kids could eat."

"I know you would, Breeth," Wally said sadly, and turned away.

As they continued toward the coast, he thought about what Lady Weirdwood once told him about inequality in the Real: *If any of Kingsport's wealthier citizens went a day without bread, they'd throw a brick through the first pastry shop window they saw. And yet they're disgusted when the poor do it. It boggles the mind.* If the old architect knew about this imbalance, why would she want to keep the Veil up? And would bringing the Veil down really improve Sam's life? Or would it make it more complicated and dangerous like Wally's? Wally wished he'd known enough about the magical world back then to ask the old architect these questions.

Wally and Breeth reached the coast and climbed the craggy pathway to Greyridge. It was visiting hours, so they walked straight through the front gate and past the receptionist's desk, which would soon be destroyed by tentacles. Wally wished he could warn the hospital workers of the horrors that were coming for them and the patients.

He reached the hall to the west wing and got a sting in his eyes. "Hey, um, Breeth? Do you mind . . . ?"

"Nope!" she said. "I'll go say hi to my old friend Valerie. Even though she can't say hi back."

Breeth floated off down the hospital's east wing.

A voice caught Wally's ear. It was his own voice. He followed it to the doctor's office and peeked through the cracked-open door. His eyes went wide. The office was in *color*. As were the doctor and Wally's past self.

"*Graham Cooper*," the doctor said, studying his brother's file. "Ah, yes. Our resident artist. Though I prefer paintings of flowers myself. Or a bowl of fruit. None of your brother's *outlandish landscapes*. How about you?"

"Yes, sir," Wally's past self said.

The present Wally winced. He would never call this doctor *sir* now. The man had so little respect for human life. That wasn't all that had changed about Wally Cooper. His past self had a youth about his eyes that had been hardened when training with Sekhmet, darkened when he'd seen his parents' Faeborn ghosts. Wally was barely a few months older now, but he hardly recognized himself.

The doctor began describing the experiments the hospital would perform on Graham if Wally was unable to pay his brother's bills. Wally wished he could tell his past self that the experiments would never happen. That Graham would be free within a few days. That Wally didn't have to keep stealing to support him.

"Have the back payment by Friday," the doctor said. "Otherwise we'll take care of your brother the way the hospital sees fit."

Wally stepped back as his past self left the office toward the hospital's exit, bleeding color into the walls like dyed garments passing through water.

It was funny. Wally had always blamed Arthur for dragging him into this magical adventure. But Wally had been desperate for money. Arthur never would have brought him to Weirdwood Manor had he not put Arthur up to it. Everything that happened was his fault. Well, the hospital's fault, anyway.

Wally continued past the doctor's office and reached the stretch of inmates' cells. He came to the fourth one on the left and peeked through the barred window. Graham was inside, painting on the bricks and smiling to himself. He, the paint, and his cell's walls were all in gray tones.

"Hi, Graham," Wally said, a tremor in his voice.

Graham was caught in a burst of excitement and scooped more goopy black moss from the cell's corner to smear across his picture. Wally's eye twitched. His brother couldn't hear him. He hadn't predicted Wally's coming. The story could not be changed.

"I'm lost, Graham," Wally said. "The Manor is gone. The Wardens are missing. Arthur, Audrey, and Lady Weirdwood are falling. And you're—" His throat constricted, stopping him from finishing the thought.

Graham kept painting.

Wally clasped the bars, desperate to make his brother hear him. "Something is coming, Graham! Something *bad*. The Eraser is going to erase your visions of the future, and then it's going to erase *you*!" He tried shaking the cell door, but it remained stiff as stone. "You have to tell me how to stop it!"

Graham just painted.

Wally's head fell against the bars, eyes stinging. "You told me we could do what I wanted when the Veil fell. You told me we could hang out with our parents . . ." He sniffed and caught a tear with his knuckle. "I guess you're with our real parents now."

Wally wished he could tell Graham to remain in his cell, that the future was not going to go the way he believed. But the only time Wally had seen his brother truly happy was in the Fae. He had seen Graham freed from this cell and walking through his literal dreams. He wouldn't take that away from his brother for anything.

"I need you to tell me what to do," Wally whispered, jaw trembling. "Everything you predicted came true. Every last thing until . . ." He composed himself and continued. "You said I was going to bring down the Veil. But you never told me *how*. You couldn't even foresee your own death. And now . . . now I don't know what's right anymore."

Graham worked on his painting.

Wally blinked away his tears. He had seen this painting every time he visited the hospital. He'd always thought Graham, in his madness, had accidentally painted their city backward, adding unsettling, nonexistent details. But now Wally realized the painting was a map of Mirror Kingsport.

Wally searched it for answers, hoping his brother had painted some sort of clue for what to do next, knowing that a future version of his little brother would someday peek through the bars of this cell.

But it was just a painting of the Mirror city. Nothing more.

Wally wasn't ready to leave yet. He wanted to take in the sight of his still-living brother for as long as he could. Even if Graham was grayed out. Even if he couldn't hear him. So, for the first time, Wally stood there and watched his brother paint. He was soothed by the sound of Graham's finger smearing mold against the dusty rock.

In the past, Graham's artwork had made Wally uncomfortable. It had seemed like proof that his brother wasn't right in his head, evidence that the doctors were right to lock him up. Of course, Graham hadn't been mad at all. He could just see what existed on the other side of the Veil. Funny how a piece of art could look like insanity one moment and like the creation of a world the next.

"I wish I'd understood, Graham," Wally said, tears rolling down his cheeks. "Your work is beautiful."

Graham froze. He stopped painting, his hand hovering a few inches from his art.

Wally's breath caught. Had his brother . . . heard him?

He watched in shock as Graham's color returned. The stains on his clothes sickened yellow while a rich brown bloomed across his skin. His hand shifted directions, rising

to the top of the painting, Mirror Kingsport's sky, where he made three quick swipes followed by a wide smear beneath.

Wally started to breathe again. "Graham? Can you . . . hear me?"

But the color was already fading from his brother's clothes and skin. Graham, gray again, blinked, as if waking from a sort of trance. He looked at his fingers, now paintless, and shuffled to the corner to collect more mold.

Wally swallowed his disappointment. He studied the addition to the top of his brother's painting. The three little figures reminded him of Arthur, Audrey, and KW, currently plummeting through the Mirror sky. But what was the smear beneath them? Wings? *A storm cloud?* Or was it his friends' deaths, swooping in to collect their souls?

"Are you trying to tell me something?" Wally asked his brother.

Graham painted in silence.

"Okay," Wally said. "Okay." He pressed his hand against the door. "Goodbye, Graham. I love you."

✳✳✳

Wally found Breeth floating near Greyridge's exit.

"Turns out Valerie and I don't have much in common unless we're both ghosts," Breeth said. "Right now, she just *reads* in her cell all day. Blech. How was your brother?"

Wally told her what had happened. How Wally's appreciation for his brother's artwork seemed to have briefly changed Graham's actions. That Wally could've sworn the three falling figures his brother had painted were Arthur, Audrey, and a young Lady Weirdwood. But he couldn't figure out what the black cloud had been.

"Maybe it was a bird," Breeth said.

Wally shook his head. "It was too big to be a bird."

"Maybe it was a big bird."

They exited the hospital and found a skyline waking in bright grays. Wally squinted toward Arthur's favorite reading rooftop, whose bricks shone red in the morning light—the only color in the city.

"My past self is headed to see Arthur right now."

"Let's go make fun of them!" Breeth said.

Wally smiled, then shrugged. They had nothing else to do until the Manor arrived in Hazelrigg.

The two descended the craggy cliffs and entered the city. Wally had never felt so vulnerable. Stealing the Manor had seemed like the right thing to do when his brother was there to assure him that they were headed toward a brighter future. But the moment Graham died, that future had wilted. Suddenly, Wally had no guidance. Nothing was inevitable. And he was afraid he'd ruined everything.

He and Breeth crossed Fortune-Teller's Alley, Breeth allowing herself to be knocked like a pinball by every pass-erby and crushed by every wagon wheel, distorting her ghost in more and more extreme ways.

"Wally, you *gotta* try this! Oh, wait . . . You'll die, huh? Never mind."

How could Wally undo the damage he'd done? How could he save Arthur, Audrey, and KW from falling to their deaths? How could he return the Wardens to their proper place? And was that even the right thing to do? Had he just seen a prophecy in his brother's painting? A way to save his friends? If so, how did he follow it? Should he abandon the mission to bring down the Veil? The one thing his brother had spent his entire life fighting for?

Wally had no answers to these questions. And he was terrified.

Fear is good. Hold on to it.

Arthur had said those words to him back in the Impossible Wood. They had stirred something in Wally, though he wasn't sure why. He had always seen fear as something that held you back. Never as something positive.

So, Wally tried embracing his fear. If he was being honest, a part of him felt relieved to no longer be controlled by his brother's vision of the future. Wally's puppet strings had finally been cut. It was a freedom he hadn't wanted in the moment. It made him feel like he was falling. That he would never stop.

But, Wally realized, *he could choose where he fell to now.*

"Wait," Wally said, stopping in the middle of the alley.

"Oh, come on," Breeth said. "Arthur and old you won't be able to hear us when we make fun of them! And what if we do that color trick and make them *kiiiiissssssss*?"

"I've got a better idea," Wally said. "Follow me."

18
OFF THE PAGE

rthur didn't see what saved their lives.

One moment he was free-falling, twirling through the sky, bracing for certain death. The next he was being cradled by something soft and feathery. Like an angel's wing that lightly laid him on the gray, cobbled ground. Audrey and KW were there beside him, both unharmed.

Arthur leapt up and squinted toward the stars, just able to catch a huge silhouette that flapped across the backward constellations. "What *was* that?"

"Don't ask me," Audrey said, standing and straightening her apron. "I was too busy screaming for my life."

The winged silhouette dissolved into the evening. Arthur felt a squeeze of recognition. But that was *impossible*. She hadn't been a bird this far back in the story. How would she have traveled here?

"Hush hush," Audrey said, rubbing KW's back, trying to soothe the child's panicked breaths. "That was a scary fall. But look! We're okay!"

KW continued to sob, facedown on the ground.

Audrey flashed Arthur a look. "Any way we could leave this horrifying place before this poor thing cries herself to pieces?"

"That's the hundred-dollar question," Arthur said, gazing around the backward city.

It was late, so few of the Mirror City citizens were out on the streets. Those who were acted strangely. Some stood perfectly still, staring at their hind paws or the cobblestones. Others spun in circles like broken toys. A newt kept running its cart of flies into a wall again and again. *Bang! Bang! Bang!*

Audrey tilted her head. "What's wrong with them? No one in the Dapplewood ever behaved like *this*."

Arthur didn't know what to tell her until—*Reeeeekkkkkkkkk!*— a shriek drew his attention to the sky where the monster hospital swooped its great bat wings across the moon. It was still in color.

"We're *off* the page," Arthur whispered. "The story is still happening way up there"—he looked at the Mirror creatures, moving like automatons—"so this part doesn't have the details filled in."

"And what does that mean exactly?" Audrey asked.

Arthur sighed, uncertain. One thing he did know: With its beastly citizens and strange physics, the Mirror City had been one of the most dangerous places he'd ever set foot. But now he, Audrey, and KW were as invisible as the wind. And the colorful story wasn't going to interrupt them anytime soon.

"Let's head to the Manor," he said. "If anyone is able to

communicate with us or free us from this grayness, it's Lady Weirdwood."

KW's breath was still shuddering from the fall.

"The old version, that is," Arthur said.

***

On the way to the Manor, they passed the Ghastly Courtyard, and Arthur spotted the skeletal Merry Rogues, standing around the sling that had launched Wally, Breeth's tentacle monster, and Garnett Lacroix to the monster hospital.

Audrey quickly covered KW's eyes.

"Catapult?" skeleton Gus said in a monotone. "More like *Mana*pult."

"More like *Slimy Monster*pult," said skeleton Mim blandly.

"More like . . . ," skeleton Tuck began but then drifted off and stared blankly into space.

Arthur winced at the first-draft puns, feeling a mixture of heartbreak and relief. The Merry Rogues had been erased, but something of them lived on in this story. Even if they were just bones and half-baked jokes.

They reached the entrance to the Manor and slipped inside. The first thing Arthur noticed was the lack of smell. The magical hallways couldn't emit their intoxicating incense, and the doorways couldn't waft their wild, Fae-born scents. It was unsettlingly quiet. Nothing moved. Even the floorboards refused to creak beneath their feet.

Audrey shuddered. "Feels like walking through a tomb."

"Yeah," Arthur agreed, "but a harmless one, at least." With

the Manor all in gray, they wouldn't trigger any of its traps. He gazed down the quiet halls. "Now we just need to find, well"—he nodded to KW—"*you.*"

They walked through the Manor, peeking into rooms.

"*Tiiiiiired,*" KW whimpered, dragging her feet like they were bricks. "My legs *h-h-hurt.*"

Arthur gritted his teeth. It was like they'd brought along an anchor that wouldn't stop crying. "Um, can you get her to move . . . *faster?*" he asked Audrey. "If the story returns to the Manor before we find Lady Weirdwood, we're going to get smashed flat by a stomping Ludwig."

Audrey huffed. "Just because you invented me doesn't mean I'm your personal nanny."

"I never said it did! Didn't you have like a thousand little siblings or something?"

"Ferret babies take care of themselves!" Audrey hissed. "Human children are"—she mouthed the word—"*impossible.* Why don't *you* carry her?"

"Because when *I* hold her, bad things happen," Arthur said, checking another room. "Like we *fall out of the sky.* I need to focus on getting us out of here."

Audrey scoffed. "How could I argue when you've done such a fantastic job so far?"

Ignoring her, Arthur opened the door to the feasting hall, where he found Pyra bent over her cauldron. The grouchy chef was stuck in a loop, her face bouncing back and forth between scowl and glee—"*Grmph.* Ah! *Grmph.* Ah! *Grmph*"—as she stirred mashed-up beetle carcasses into a potion that sizzled and exploded in the same loop.

"*Right*," Arthur said. "She's making an antidote. Lady Weirdwood is still in her coma from the Scarabs."

He hurried toward the Healing Room.

Tweee. Tweee. Tweee.

On the way, they heard a sound that nearly broke Arthur's heart. He peered into the training room and found Weston, grayed out and motionless, command whistle resting between his lips. *Tweee. Tweee. Tweee.* Each time he blew, his imp-lock doorknobs rolled themselves in different drill patterns on the floor. The patterns were sloppy and inexact.

Arthur wished he could seize the gardener general by the epaulets and take him back with them, saving him from disintegrating in the hands of the Eraser. But Weston was immovable, just like everything else.

They reached the Healing Room and found Lady Weirdwood fast asleep, wrinkles lying flat across her face. Amelia sat beside her, a helpless automaton nurse, dipping a cloth into a copper basin again and again but never bringing it to the old woman's forehead. Arthur studied Lady Weirdwood's sleeping form, hoping to find the yellow tinge of her wedding dress or blue varicose veins, showing that the old architect was still part of the story. No such luck.

Arthur sighed and touched the old woman's liver-spotted hand. "Even if she was in color, she wouldn't be able to help us in this state."

He searched her closed eyes, hoping some sort of answer would come to him and save them from this hopeless place.

"I hate to be a bother . . . ," Audrey said, "but where's the kid?"

Arthur whipped around, searching the Healing Room for KW. "What do you mean, 'where's the kid'?"

"She was holding my apron strings until we got to this room!" Audrey said.

"How could you let her out of your sight?"

"Don't you put your guilt on me!" Audrey said, pointing a claw in his face. "I was very clear when I told you I was no kind of babysitter for a human ch—"

TWEEEEEEEEEEEE!

A sound screeched through the room, scaring them off their paws and feet. In the doorway stood KW, Weston's whistle in her lips.

Arthur strode straight toward her and yanked the whistle from her mouth. "Where were you? You can't just go sneaking off like that! Audrey and I were worried sick!"

KW gave him an exaggerated frown.

Audrey snorted. "Your father's very upset. We might have to ground you."

Arthur scowled back at Audrey. "This isn't funny." He held up the whistle. "We need to go put this back where we found it before we change the story perm . . . an . . . ently."

Arthur stared at the whistle. He shouldn't be able to hold it at all. It was part of the story fabric. And yet, its silver metal reflected colors that were absent from the rest of the room.

"How did you get this?" he asked KW.

KW shrugged.

Arthur studied her constellation eyes. Was KW able to remove objects from the story because she had once been the

Manor's architect? Or was it because they were off the page? Did the whistle's colors mean it was part of their story now?

"Arthur," Audrey whispered, pointing toward Lady Weirdwood's hospital bed. "*Look*."

Arthur turned and found the blanket was *squirming*. The old woman's snake uncoiled itself from beneath the sheets, flicking its tongue toward KW . . .

"Mac!" KW squeaked in delight and ran to the bedside. "Hiya, Mac," she whispered, holding out her hand.

The snake stretched, winding up her arm, its scales rippling greenish-yellow. It was reentering the story.

"Wait!" Arthur said, heart hammering.

KW yanked back her hand, and the snake plopped onto the bed, the color in its scales dimming.

"Don't . . . hold it yet." Arthur shut his eyes. "I need to think."

"What's going on, Arthur?" Audrey said. "Let her hold her pet."

His mind was a mess of thoughts. "If KW picks up that snake, it will revert her back to her old self."

Audrey gave him a look. "Isn't that what we came here for? Getting the fancy old architect back on our team?"

"Well, yeah, but . . . there's no Manor for her to control anymore."

"It sounds like there wouldn't be no harm in it, either." Audrey patted KW's shoulder. "Go ahead, darlin'."

KW reached out for the snake again.

"*Wait*," Arthur said, catching her little arm. "That isn't the only problem. If we take the snake, we could change a key part of the story we're currently in. *Thieves of Weirdwood* could end differently than it did. And who knows what kind of problems that could create? Maybe worse than the Eraser."

"So," Audrey said, folding her paws, "this *is* like time travel."

Arthur shook his head. "It's like editing a story whose earlier events can ripple through pages and—"

There was a sound in the distance, loud and vibrant. Voices echoed down the hall. Wally had made his marshmallow landing and returned to the Manor. The story was blazing back in.

"We better hustle outta here," Audrey said. "I've had enough of being hurled out of buildings today, thank you very much."

Arthur, panicked, looked to the snake, whose scales had dulled back to gray. He had to figure this out fast. Any moment, Pyra would come into the Healing Room to administer the Scarab antidote to Lady Weirdwood. The revived old woman would summon Arthur's and Wally's past selves to the Throne Room. There, she would make Wally a Novitiate before presenting Arthur with a copy of the very book they were currently inside . . .

"Lady Weirdwood didn't have her snake!" Arthur said.

"Huh?" Audrey said.

"When I saw her at this point in the story," Arthur said, "she was sitting on her throne and her snake was nowhere in sight . . . I'm pretty sure." He gritted his teeth, wishing he had the copy of *Thieves of Weirdwood* to double-check. "I remember because it was the first time I'd seen the old woman without her pet. I think. That means the current versions of ourselves must have already traveled back in—" Audrey grinned, and he quickly changed direction. "I mean, entered this part of the story and taken the snake to make Lady Weirdwood old again! We can take the snake!"

KW reached for her pet, but this time it was Audrey who caught her hand.

"Snakes don't make people older," the ferret said. "In fact, they *claim* to do the opposite. This slippery oil salessnake used to roll through the Dapplewood every few seasons, promising his tinctures would restore any bird, rodent, or reptile to their former glory. The tinctures were expensive, and as you can see"—she held out her arm, sprouting with white hairs—"they did not work. One of the many reasons I don't trust snakes."

"Of course . . . ," Arthur said. "Snakes are symbols of *regeneration*. They shed their skins, becoming like new." He gasped. "Audrey, let me see your claws!"

She offered her paw, confused. Sure enough, her claws had shrunk to the quaint sewing size they had been before he had altered them in the Whirling City to save them both from dragon prison. *After* Audrey had held the snake back in the crumbling Manor.

"This snake doesn't make people older," Arthur said, gazing into the narrow slits of the serpent's blind eyes. "It restores them to their rightful forms."

"Can I hold Mac now?" KW asked.

"Not yet," Arthur and Audrey said at the same time.

Audrey looked to the snake, and her muzzle wrinkled with disgust. "First time I saw this thing was on the rooftop when

Lady Weirdwood was fighting that dragon. It certainly wasn't shedding its skin then. In fact, it looked"—she placed her paws over KW's ears—"*dead*. I remember because it's always a relief to have one less serpent in the world."

"It was *dead*?" Arthur whispered.

"As a fallen branch."

"If the snake was missing in the Throne Room and then dead on the rooftop, it must die sometime after we take it."

Audrey tilted her head in thought. "I am . . . not following."

Arthur barely had a grasp on it himself. "This snake seems to become the opposite of whatever changes it makes to the person who holds it. If Lady Weirdwood grows older, the snake gets younger . . ."

Audrey's eyebrows rose in understanding. KW squirmed between her paws.

"What if that means we're supposed to bring someone back to life with it?" Arthur asked.

"Who?"

"*Garnett Lacroix*," Arthur said with all the hope he could muster. "Maybe this snake can restore the Eraser to its original form."

The sounds in the hall were growing louder, the colors brighter.

Audrey removed her paws from KW's ears. "What if you're wrong?"

"Then we'll be just as bad off as we are right now," Arthur said. "But if I'm right, then we'll undo the most destructive thing ever to be unleashed on the Fae and the Real." He ruffled the child's hair. "And then we'll make her grow up again."

KW combed her fingers through her hair, fixing it.

"You hear that, darlin'?" Audrey said, giving the child's shoulders a squeeze. "Your pet Mac is gonna save the world. Then we'll give it back to you."

KW gave the slightest of nods as Arthur and Audrey gave each other a wary look. The Eraser could just as easily erase her beloved snake.

They stared at the gray serpent like it was a live wire. The first time Arthur had touched it, he had felt an ache in his bones, a collapsing in his heart, the opposite of the tingling he felt whenever writing spells. Now he understood that the snake had been *changing* him—rolling him back to the person he was before the start of this magical adventure. Arthur didn't know how far back it had brought him, but he didn't want it to go any further.

"Can you carry it?" he asked Audrey.

The ferret's paws leapt to her chest. "Uh-uh! No, *sir*. I may have neglected to mention this, but I despise snakes. When they aren't selling me useless oils, they have a habit of eating my kind."

"But you've already been turned back to your original self!" Arthur said. "You're the only one who can carry it without changing."

"It has *fangs*!" Audrey hissed.

"Audrey," Arthur said, taking the ferret by the shoulders. "I learned to stop calling you a rat. You can learn to trust snakes."

"Oh, you say that like it's the same thing!" Audrey said, crossing her arms. She sighed. "If that thing so much as looks at me wrong, I'll chew it to pieces."

"No!" KW said.

Audrey gave her a half-hearted smile. "Only kidding, darlin'." She shuddered as she draped the snake around her shoulders.

As the story swooped into the Manor like a colorful storm, Arthur, Audrey, and KW snuck into the Abyssment, where they found the mirror, in color and fully operational. Arthur used the blank book on the stand to write the DappleWood—*in all its storybook glory*—hoping to find the Wardens safe and sound, having escaped from the erased Manor.

"I cannot wait to be tucked away in my own little house," Audrey said. "Er, whatever your version of my little house is, I guess."

But for all of Arthur's descriptions of the quaint little cottages and the rustling forest and all its creature comforts . . . on the other side of the mirror was nothing but a blank void.

The DappleWood had been erased again.

19
THE TRACKDRAGON

Wally watched pocket-worlds pass the Trackdragon window.

And Breeth watched him watching.

"*Wallyyyyyy*," she said, dangling from the compartment above his seat. "This is *booooooring*. We don't have time for this! You're supposed to be saving the world, and I need to be out there ghosting all good like I do!"

"We have plenty of time, Breeth," Wally said, not taking his eyes from the window. "It will take another few weeks for us to catch up to where Arthur and the others are in the story. You just have to be patient."

"*Ugggggggg.*" Breeth oozed over the edge of the compartment into the seat across from him. "Let's see you be patient after being locked in a Manor for several years and then in fake heaven for *months*!"

"This is important, Breeth."

"But *whyyyy*?"

Wally's eyes remained fixed on the window. "I don't know yet." He drew a contented breath. "Isn't it nice not to do something for a while? No fighting. No arguing. Just . . . watching."

"Nope!" Breeth said. "You just described my worst nightmare. Blech. Yuck. Sick."

They had boarded the Trackdragon shortly after Lady Weirdwood grew a Shadowrail platform in the Manor. Wally had entered an open cabin near the back, had plopped himself down by the window, and had been watching cities and pocket-worlds flicker past ever since. To Breeth, it might as well have been paint drying.

Thump! Thump! Thump! Thump! She tried kicking Wally's armrest, but her feet kept bouncing off. "*Rrg!*"

Wally didn't even blink. The Trackdragon had stopped in another pocket-world, as gray as every other that had come before it. They were in a vast desert lit by stars. Torn into the steep slope of a dune was a Rift that looked onto a snowy village. Camel-like creatures with thorn-skinned riders approached the Rift to greet humans dressed in thick furs as they stepped out of a blizzard onto dry sand.

The people in furs gave water to the desert travelers while the camel riders showed the children of the snowy village a wicker cage that seemed to hold pet fireworks. The kids warmed their hands by the fireworks' light, which sparkled gray in their eyes, as the camel riders gulped the water as if it was the first drink they'd had in weeks.

"So, what are we doing about this?" Breeth said. "You want me to beat up those camels?"

"No one needs to get beaten up, Breeth," Wally said with a smile. "*Look.* The Rift is letting both sides share things the other didn't have before. The people and the Fae-born are figuring it out all by themselves."

Breeth smooshed her nose against the glass. "Well, can we at least go out there and *pretend* to ride the camels? They won't even know we're there."

"Sorry," Wally said. "We have to do as much research as we can before we catch up with the story."

Breeth dragged her fingers down her face. "Do you *hear* yourself? If I'd wanted to do research, I would've stayed in Lady Weirdwood's huge, boring library!"

With a screech and a whistle, the Trackdragon started rolling again. It chugged out of the desert, passing through the seam that separated the Real from the Fae, and into the boring infinite depths of stupid, starry space.

"*Fine*. You wanna stare?" Breeth stuck her entire face between Wally's nose and the window. "Let's *stare*. I can stare *much* longer than you can. I named *spores*, Wally. That's how bored I got. You ever name *spores* before?"

Wally sighed. "I can see through your face, y'know. It's like glass."

"Oh yeah? Can you see through *this*?" She made every face she could think of: happy, miserable, scared, pig, tongue wiggle, and zombie.

Wally's eyes went wide. "*Breeth*."

Grudgingly, she spun in the air and faced the window. The Trackdragon had arrived at another Rift. This one was smaller. *Newer*. And much more horrifying than the last.

They were in the Real this time. A bank. Hippo-like humanoids in suits were storming the vaults, devouring the bills like salads and washing them down with barrels of coins. If a human banker got in the way, the hippos ate them too. Outside the bank, men with weapons were lining up, ready to hunt the hippos.

"Yeeshk," Breeth said.

Finally, Wally looked away from the carnage. "That's the problem, isn't it? The Fae and the Real can help each other *if* they can get along. But some Fae-born are too wild, and some humans are too selfish. Tearing the Veil might bring about a better world, but so many will get hurt . . . It wouldn't be worth it."

Breeth wasn't really listening. She was daydreaming. "If I could possess those hippos and humans, I'd make them all sit down to a tea party and talk about their feelings. But *nooooo*. Everything has to be *gray* and *boring*, and I have to obey the laws of *time*, or whatever."

"Interesting," Wally whispered to himself as the Track-dragon started to move again.

"Uh, *yeah*," Breeth said. "It *would* be interesting. The only interesting thing that's happened in—"

The compartment began to tremble violently as the window flashed an impossible white. Outside was neither Real nor Fae nor starry between. There was nothing at all. Breeth and Wally had been on the Trackdragon long enough now for the Eraser to begin its mass destruction. The only thing that passed the window now were leftover scraps of the erased Fae. And at the very edges, a rainbow shimmer.

Wally mumbled to himself, "Lady Weirdwood's bubble

sheen didn't keep the Eraser from reentering the Manor. She kept it from entering the *Real*."

Breeth didn't know what he was talking about, but she had to admit that she had a morbid fascination with these erased landscapes. The Eraser was the only force she had come across in her ghosthood that could snuff out her spirit. Staring into this blankness was like staring into true death. She wondered sometimes if the Eraser was just a ghost like she was, searching for a way home. It just didn't know how not to be a jerk about it.

She also wondered about all those ghosts she now knew were locked away in the organic materials of the Real and Fae. And she wondered how many the Eraser had already erased.

Later that day, the Trackdragon huffed to its final stop on the line. Out the window, a bright sunset illuminated an endless ocean and many floating islands. The islands were surrounded by dozens of Rifts.

"*Whirling City!*" the conductor called. "Exit here for the Whirling City!"

Wally got up. "We're getting off."

Breeth blinked. "Wait, whoa, really?"

"Really," he said. "We've got a bird to find."

"Then we get to rejoin the adventure, right?"

"No," Wally said, stepping out of the compartment. "Then we're going to look for more Rifts."

"*Waaaallyyyyyyyyyyyyyyyyyy!*"

20

AUDREY

The DappleWood was gone. The cottages and the lanes. The shops and their wares. Pleasant Pond and the Dozen-Acre Meadow. All that remained was a vast three-dimensional canvas spattered with bare remnants, like spills of paint: some cobblestones, a wall or two, and clumps of trees in the adjoining wood. It seemed even the wind had been erased.

Audrey blinked at the nothingness. She had finally made it home, only to find it gone again. "I . . . I just smelled it yesterday."

"I don't like it here," KW whispered, squeezing Audrey's paw.

Audrey's throat was too tight to answer.

"It was her home," Arthur said, picking up the child. "Audrey . . . I'm so sorry this happened. When Wally's brother led the Eraser away from the Manor, he must have brought it straight . . ."

Audrey took off across the blank landscape, bounding from cobblestone to patch of grass, passing half a streetlamp here, a crooked chunk of house there, as she sniffed for survivors. "Mrs. Chicken? Mr. Frog? *Anybody!*"

She heard a creak ahead. A piece of the blankness, a perfect square, lifted from the ground before flopping back down, leaving a dark hole behind.

A feathery head poked out. "Audrey? Is that you?"

Audrey scampered across the last few cobblestones and threw her arms around Mrs. Chicken's neck. The chicken embraced her in her large, fluffy wings.

"Audrey, it is *lovely* to see you alive and safe, but what on *earth* is between us?"

"Oh," Audrey said, stepping back and collecting herself. "It's a snake. Don't worry. It doesn't bite. Or it hasn't yet, anyway."

Mrs. Chicken eyed the snake warily as Audrey peered down into the pub owner's underground egg storage and found dozens of eyes peering back at her.

"Hello, Audrey!"

"Why, if it isn't Ms. Abbott!"

"Our seamstress has returned!"

"Can you fix my zipper?"

"Forget your zipper! My entire wardrobe was erased!"

Audrey's paw leapt to her mouth. "Are they all down there?"

"Every last one," Mrs. Chicken said. She laid a wing on Audrey's shoulder. "All we were missing was you."

Tears of relief spilled down Audrey's whiskers. The town may have been erased, but the heart of the DappleWood lived on in its citizens.

"I do have some regrettable news," Mrs. Chicken said, folding together her wingtips like fingers.

Audrey's throat clenched up again.

"That little girl . . . ," Mrs. Chicken said. "The Badgers with Badges did as Amelia asked and locked her in the greenhouse. Shortly after, the child fell into a deep sleep, from which she would not wake. When that walking nothingness showed up, we couldn't lift her in time. We barely made it underground ourselves."

Audrey's heart took a tumble. She knew only one young girl who could not be woken. "Breeth was erased?"

"Her body was," a beautiful woman with dark skin and ink-stained fingers said from the underground storage. "We believe Breeth's spirit was elsewhere."

Audrey breathed a little easier, but she still felt a sharp pang of guilt. She'd been the one to help Breeth let go of her anger and leave that body behind. Now that poor, sweet child would be a little ghost girl forever.

"Fear not, everyone!" Arthur's loud voice cut through the blank landscape as he stepped forward with KW, who made mighty hops along the leftover cobblestones. "I'll remake this town before sunset!" He glanced at the blank, white sky. "Er, sunrise. Whatever comes next." He got KW situated on a cobblestone, then rubbed his hands together. "All I need's a pen and paper and a dash of DappleWood inspiration."

"Arthur . . . ," Mrs. Chicken said, not looking him in the eye. "We think it's best if you don't help us anymore."

Arthur went pale. "Wh-what? Why?"

Audrey was also shocked. She had never heard Mrs. Chicken speak an ill word against anyone.

A man Audrey didn't recognize crawled through the trapdoor. He wore drumsticks on his belt, and he held Audrey's diary.

"After I transformed back into myself," the man said, "I found this in the forest." He flipped to the end of the diary. "It seems someone tried to resurrect a certain Gentleman Thief—a fictional character who was retired by a dragon-bone Quill and therefore, according to magical law, could not be resurrected. This action tore a Rift into the Fae's world of the dead and released nightmares into this town. Arthur"—the man opened the diary face out—"is this your handwriting?"

Arthur opened his mouth as if to argue, then simply said, "Yes."

Several townscritters gasped below. A squirrel scout whimpered.

Arthur's head hung heavy. "I thought I could banish the Eraser by resurrecting Garnett Lacroix with my writing. I was trying to prevent this very thing from happening."

"You could have killed everyone here," Cadence said.

"You promised us we'd be safe!" a mouse cried from below.

"You turned our town into a nightmare!" Mr. Mole shouted.

"You said you'd beat the Nothing Man," a squirrel scout said sadly. "We thought you were our hero."

Arthur stared into the underground, eyes traveling around the many disappointed fuzzy, feathered, and scaled faces of the

DappleWood. "I . . ." His expression broke, and he turned to leave.

"Arthur?"

Arthur stopped as the beautiful woman and an injured man who seemed to be her husband crawled through the trapdoor. He did not look back at them, as if he was ashamed.

"Sekhmet . . . ," the man said, leaning to compensate for his bandaged back. He hesitated, as if he couldn't bring himself to ask the question. "Did she make it out?"

Still, Arthur kept his eyes ahead. "I couldn't save her. I couldn't save anyone." He continued toward the blankness.

Audrey was tempted to go after him. To tell the others not to be too rough on the boy. (And that was all he was. A boy.) But it seemed Arthur had hidden his misdeeds from her neighbors so they would see him as some sort of savior. At the same time, he had neglected to give them information about the Eraser they could have used to keep themselves safe. Arthur still needed to learn to let others be the hero sometimes.

Audrey took KW's little hand, and they watched as he vanished into the patchwork forest. Soon after, the other humans, the chef and the drummer, the injured man and his wife, also left the decimated village, following a strange sort of moving map, hoping to find their daughter alive somewhere in all that blankness.

***

Audrey joined the effort to cobble together the DappleWood's leftover pieces. Even KW hopped along the patches of crabgrass, gathering sticks.

Throughout the search, Audrey kept the snake draped over her shoulders so the child could reach out and be tickled by its unnervingly forked tongue. Every time the thing slid its scales along Audrey's fur, she shivered straight to the tip of her tail. But she felt strangely grateful for the horrific serpent. Her discomfort kept her distracted from the devastation her town had experienced, spread it out so she didn't feel it as sharply.

By the time the white of day fell to black of night, the town had set up a pleasant little encampment of odds and ends—half beds, leftover straw, a chair or two—with a bonfire crackling in the center. It was quiet around the camp. A sadness hung in the starless sky. The only thing that could be heard was the crackle of the flames against the aching absence of a windless night.

Something large came rolling toward the encampment. Every head jerked toward the darkness, eyes wide, whiskers perked, worried that whatever it was had come to finish them off. A large object, brown as a boulder, rolled into the fire-light, pushed by Arthur. The townscritters' worried expressions did not soften.

Audrey stood from the fire and met Arthur in the half darkness. "What's this?" she asked of the boulder-like object.

"I think it's Ludwig," Arthur said softly. "The Manor's woodworker." He rotated the object to show a giant hand sticking out of the side like a sprout breaking through the shell of a seed. "I found this—er, *him*, in what's left of the forest. It was buried beneath the soil, so it wasn't erased." Arthur nodded toward the DappleWood citizens. "I figured if they don't want me to help them rebuild their town, maybe they would welcome the aid of the friendly giant who fixed my sloppy first drafts." He knocked on the seed. "They just have to figure out how to crack it open."

"That's kind of you, Arthur," Audrey said, resting a paw on the seed. "They'll appreciate it."

Arthur gazed back into the darkness. "I also found the Rift the Eraser left behind. I'm going to take the snake and follow it through the pocket-worlds. And I'm going to bring the Eraser down. Tonight."

Audrey felt a flutter of worry. "Now don't go getting yourself killed just because my neighbors ruffled you some."

"It's the only idea we have left, Audrey," Arthur said, desperation in his eyes. "I have to try."

Audrey couldn't keep her whiskers from worrying. "Well, at least take some food and supplies with you."

She returned to the bonfire and told her neighbors what Arthur had found for them.

"We don't want no part of it!" Mr. Mole grumbled.

Mrs. Chicken clucked in agreement. "We discussed it as a town, and we've all agreed that it's best if we never allow anyone from outside the DappleWood in again."

"But . . . ," Audrey said. "It will take *months* to chop the lumber from the forest and rebuild. Years maybe! And that's if there's even enough wood left. Arthur and this woodworker could do it in a day with *zero* building materials."

Mrs. Chicken folded her wings across her breast. "Whatever we build on top of this blankness will be ours and ours alone. No more outsiders. They cause too much trouble." She glanced at KW, then looked away with sadness. "That includes the small ones. We're clearly unable to protect a human child."

Audrey stepped behind KW and pulled her close. "You can't send Arthur and a kid out there alone! Where's that Dapplewood hospitality?"

Mrs. Chicken lowered her beak. "Our hospitality expired the day that thing erased our home for the second time. We must keep our critters safe."

Audrey looked to her other neighbors for support, but none would meet her eye. With a huff, she took KW's hand and turned on her paw.

"*Audrey*," Mrs. Chicken said, stopping her. "If you go with them . . ."

Audrey squeezed her eyes shut, hesitating just a moment. Then, without looking back, she led KW to Arthur.

"What did they say?" he asked, looking concerned. "Why is KW with you?"

Audrey looked down at the child, who had reached up to secretly pet her snake.

"I'm a simple ferret," she finally said. "All I want is a quiet life with a happy ending. Not some huge battle between the worlds and an Erasery whozeewhatzit." She stared into the nothingness of night, which frightened her more deeply than her darkest dreams. "Like my ma used to tell me and my siblings when we were just little slinks of fur: *When you see trouble comin', it's best to keep out of the way and let the Great Seamstress sort it out.*"

"Audrey, I would never ask you to risk—"

"I'm not finished," Audrey said. "On the other paw, no

one will have a happy ending while that thing's at large. And I still believe the Veil should stay *right* where it is"—she looked back toward her neighbors, huddled cozy and close around the firelight—"even if it does make those who live behind it scared and mistrustful." She lowered her muzzle before Arthur could see the tears. "So I'm coming with you." She sniffed and adjusted the snake around her shoulders. "Who else is going to carry this disgusting serpent?"

Arthur stared at her, clearly too shocked to speak.

There. She'd managed to convince him without having to get into all that mushy emotional stuff or admit that her neighbors were the type to cast a child into the night to keep themselves safe.

"Come on, sugar," Audrey said to KW. "It's past your bedtime, and we have a ways to go before we rest."

She took one last look at the DappleWood citizens, then clasped the child's hand and strode into the darkness as if it were a park on a sunny day.

***

After a long journey through the nonexistent night, they heard a faint slurping sound and arrived at a dark, purple opening—a tunnel burrowed through black canvas. The Eraser had walked straight through the DappleWood's border and continued to burn through adjoining pocket-worlds.

KW whimpered, and Arthur took the hand Audrey wasn't holding, rolling Ludwig's seed with his free one.

They walked through the tunnel of ragged Rifts, passing partially erased pocket-worlds that looked like paintings left to rot in the rain. With every pawstep, Audrey wondered if she'd made a terrible mistake. She should be back home sewing or mending or—

And just like that, they saw it. The Eraser. It blurred through a star field of heavenly moths, their wings disintegrating like tissue in its wake. Every hair on Audrey's body stood on end. She had never actually seen the thing that had erased her village. It looked like the darkness after a candle had been extinguished. Only it was man-shaped. She had the terrible feeling that if she stared at it too long, it would draw her in whisker-by-whisker, claw-by-claw, until there was nothing left.

Arthur reached for the snake around Audrey's neck.

She caught his hands. "Are you sure you want to do this?"

Arthur didn't answer, only took the snake.

Audrey pulled KW close, and they watched as he marched toward the man-shaped black hole, the snake draped over his arms like a limp sword. Audrey had to admit he looked almost heroic.

"*Garnett Lacroix!*" Arthur cried.

The Eraser whirled, eyes sparking golden in the nothingness as its head deformed into a hat shape.

"To quote my favorite hero," Arthur said, "'That'll be enough of your *gruelty!*'"

He hurled the snake, which caught around the Eraser's neck and coiled tight. The Eraser's hands leapt to grasp the serpent, whose scales started to burn like match heads. KW cried out in alarm, and Audrey quickly scooped her into her arms, pressing her face to her shoulder.

When the snake refused to come loose, the Eraser lashed

at Arthur with its fingers of nothingness. Arthur retreated to Audrey and KW as the horrific thing's jittering form inflated with depth and texture, bones and nerves, followed by muscles and skin.

"It's working!" Arthur called over the chaos.

Audrey hadn't blinked in a full minute.

Details of a dashing Gentleman Thief came through in pulses. But then . . . those handsome features started to bloat and distort. His swooping hat disintegrated like ash, and his long, golden hair started to thin. His eyes drooped as red veins cracked through them.

"It's not stopping at Garnett," Arthur said with a mixture of confusion and awe. "The snake is restoring him back to his author, Alfred Moore."

And it wasn't stopping. The man started to slim, his thin hair grew thick and chestnut brown as his body became curvy in a different way. He was transforming into a woman.

"*Valerie Lucas*," Arthur whispered. "Garnett's true creator. But she's . . ."

"*AAAAUUUUUUUUGGGGGGGHHHHHHHHHH!*"

The woman let out a shattering scream, like the howl of the dead, as her eyes blazed with white fire and her hair and clothes smoldered. The air around her began to ripple . . . then tear. A Rift opened behind her, showing a bustling port city.

"*Kingsport*," Arthur said, a touch of fear in his voice. "It's bringing her home."

Screeching, Valerie Lucas tore the snake from her throat and hurled it lifeless to the ground. The restoration began to reverse as nothingness spread from the woman's head down to her feet, unraveling her skin, muscles, nerves, and bones.

Arthur covered his mouth in horror. "The snake wasn't strong enough. The dragon-bone Quill overpowered it."

Within moments, every inch of the woman named Valerie Lucas was gone. Replaced by the Eraser.

It jerked like it was going to come at them, disintegrate them one layer at a time. But it saw the snake lying dead at its feet and hesitated. It turned its staticky eyes on the Rift and blurred into the streets of the port city, melting buildings in its wake.

"No," Arthur whispered. "No, no, *no*."

The Eraser had erased Audrey's home. And now it was going to erase Arthur's.

21
CONSTELLATIONS

ingsport was in chaos. The Eraser blurred down the busy streets, waves of nothingness rising on either side, cresting over the buildings and disintegrating them like burnt paper. The waves of whiteness never crashed; they only rose higher into the sky. The screaming citizens shut themselves inside. But it was no use. They couldn't hide from this.

The bookstore had fallen. There was no trace of the theater. The orphanage had a chunk taken out of it. The sight was too much for Arthur's heart. He'd seen pocket-worlds erased. But this was his *home*.

He squeezed his eyes shut, relishing the darkness after all that white.

Sharp claws grabbed his shoulders. "We need to do something."

Arthur flinched away.

A fuzzy paw slapped his cheek, forcing his eyes open. He saw the ferret's face.

"I can't do this anymore, Audrey. I created the Eraser.

Now I've brought it to Kingsport. All my ideas are the wrong ones."

"From what I've seen, Arthur," Audrey said, "your ideas are wrong until they're right. Remember when you made me jump off a floating island? I'm going to make you do the same." She turned him toward the Eraser. "That's the fall. Now, what are we going to do about it?"

Arthur blinked at the expanding whiteness. He couldn't cast magic in the Real. He didn't have a dragon-bone Quill. And the snake was dead. KW had collected it from the ground and was cradling it in her little arms.

"No need to fear!" a voice bellowed. "Help is here, folks!"

"Clear the streets!"

A group of Oakers trooped in to see what all the panic was about. They froze when they saw the Eraser.

"What in hell's name is *that*?"

"Never seen the like! But I'd like to see it try that melting business with me!"

The Oaker ran toward the Eraser, club raised. Before he could swing it, the Eraser vaporized him with a swipe of its hand.

"Dustin!" an Oaker cried.

The others kept an eye on the Eraser. "It's headed toward the Gilded Quarter!"

"We gotta derail it! Them folks pay our wages."

"Come on, ya creepy bastard! This way!"

The Oakers hollered and clacked their nightsticks against the shop fronts, quickly retreating toward the steep path that led to the port's cliffs. The Eraser blurred after them.

Arthur's breath caught. "They're leading it to Greyridge Mental Hospital."

"Away from the rich and toward the helpless," Audrey said, covering her mouth in shock.

Arthur had known patients in Greyridge: Wally's brother and Valerie Lucas, his favorite author of all time. Even Harry had spent some time there. The patients were trapped in their cells and couldn't escape.

"I have to save them," Arthur whispered.

"*You*," Audrey said, "need to figure out how to stop *that thing* from erasing folks. I'll go warn the poor people in that hospital." She pulled the scraps of KW's wedding dress from her apron and wrapped them around her fuzzy ears, making a cowl. She turned to KW, who was sitting on Ludwig's giant seed, and ran her paw down the child's cheek. "Stay close to Arthur, okay?"

KW's frown only steepened.

Audrey looked at the Eraser, then down at her paws, which looked so small and helpless. "Arthur, would you . . . change me somehow? No big muscles or anything like that. Just . . . make me braver?"

"I wish I could," Arthur said, "but I can't use my magic in the Real."

Audrey cocked an eye at the Rifts surrounding the city street. "I'd say the lines between real and imaginary have been blurred *mightily*."

Arthur's eyebrows rose in realization. He searched the half-erased street until he spotted a notary with half a door missing. He slipped inside, found a quill and a pad of paper, and stepped back out. He wrote something quick and dotted it with a period. "*There.* How do you feel?"

Audrey drew a deep breath and gave her shoulders a wriggle. "Better actually."

She scampered on four paws, around the Eraser and Oakers and up the craggy cliffs of Greyridge. Arthur looked down at what he'd written: *Audrey remained exactly as she is.*

He flipped to the next page and froze. With Rifts opening around the city, he had his magic back. He could write anything he wanted, so long as it played by the rules of Kingsport's imagination. But was anything in the Mirror City powerful enough to stop the Eraser? How could he possibly defeat nothing?

"*Snff!*" A nearby sniffle startled him.

"*Right,*" Arthur said, blinking at KW. "You're still here. Um . . . any ideas?"

KW wiped her nose, spreading a streak of snot across her cheek.

"*Great,*" Arthur said. "I can totally babysit while defeating the scariest bad guy of all time. No problem."

A horrific crumbling drew his attention back to the cliffs. The Eraser was passing through Greyridge, cleaving it in two, the remaining stones tumbling into the sea. Arthur prayed Audrey had gotten the patients out in time.

He was about to focus back on his writing when he noticed a large Rift had opened just above the cliffs. Through it, he could see the inky black sea of the Mirror City. But the Rift continued to peel back like an onion skin, showing the starry expanse between the pocket-worlds, which also peeled away, revealing . . . nothing at all.

Arthur blinked at the spot, seeing it in a way he never had before. The nothingness was a *clean slate*. An empty page. A blank canvas. The Eraser may have been destroying everything in sight, but it was also creating *infinite* potential.

Arthur looked from the blank spot to his notebook to the giant seed . . . and he quirked an eyebrow. "Dry those tears, KW! The only person who will be crying today will be Garnett Lacroix when we free him from that prison of nothingness! And those will be tears of *relief*."

KW tried to put on a brave face and failed.

Arthur crouched to her level. "Hey, it's going to be okay. I promise." He looked to the lifeless snake in her arms and felt a sting in his throat. He'd been so neglectful. "I'm sorry about what happened to Mac. He was very brave, and I promise he won't have died in vain."

KW petted her pet's scales. "He's not dead," she said in a quiet voice. "He's just sleeping."

Arthur couldn't tell if this was a normal kid thing to say or if the young lady somehow sensed the power her pet snake held.

"Hey." Arthur smiled and patted Ludwig's seed. "Think you can help me get this up those cliffs?"

KW gave a hesitant nod, and together they rolled the seed down the street, through the port, and up the cliffs, carefully balancing along the slim section of craggy path that still existed. On the way, they passed Greyridge's rescued patients, and Audrey, still cowled, scampered along with them. "Where y'all going with your tails on fire?"

"No time to explain!" Arthur said.

The trio reached the top of the crags where Greyridge once stood. The Eraser had continued over the edge of the cliffs and was erasing the water itself, sending massive geysers into the sky. It could come back at any moment.

"Ludwig?" Arthur said, frantically knocking on the seed's shell. "*Ludwig!* I don't know if you're ripe yet, but I need you to *wake up.*"

The seed didn't stir.

"Ludwig, *please*. We need to build a new Manor. I'll write while you fix, just like we did in the DappleWood."

Nothing.

Tweeeeeeeee!

Arthur flinched, expecting to see the Eraser crawling over the cliffs' edge to vaporize him. When he remained in one piece, he looked up to find KW had Weston's whistle in her mouth.

"*KW?*" Arthur said, touching his chest to ease his hammering heart. "I know you love that whistle, but you can't just blow it *straight into my ear* when there are horrific things around trying to *kill us.*"

Crrkkt! The seed cracked, and Ludwig's wide, sticky face peeked out. "Veston?"

"Ludwig!" Arthur cried. "Boy, am I happy to see you. I need you to help me build a new Manor. And by that I mean clean up all my mistakes."

The carpenter blinked his sappy eyes. Then he flexed his giant muscles, cracking open the rest of the seed and unfurling himself. Arthur was about to cover KW's eyes, but Ludwig was already wearing overalls.

Arthur slapped his forehead. "We didn't bring any tools!"

"No need," Ludwig said, reaching back into the seed shell. "I grow vis zem. You see, vhen Veston removed me from his subconscious, he—"

"Let's stick a bookmark in the personal histories for now," Arthur said. "We're building a new Manor. I write, you fix, okay?"

Ludwig saluted with a hammer. "Ja."

"Now for the hard part," Arthur said, and opened his notebook. Never had a blank page been so intimidating.

"Don't think," he whispered to himself. "Just write."

And he did just that.

> *In a land that was neither Real nor Fae,*
> *Neither Kingsport nor Mirror Kingsport*
> *Not Veil nor starry between . . .*
> *A Manor began to grow. Tendrils and roots twined out of the earth,*
> *spinning into supports and fanning out into walls.*

In Arthur's periphery, roots coiled along the empty cliffs.

"Little mouse?" Ludwig asked Audrey. "Vould you be so kind as to tveet zat vhistle?"

Audrey didn't correct him for calling her a mouse. She just took the whistle from KW and whistled when Ludwig said *whistle* as the carpenter expertly guided the roots into a foresty foundation.

"Now for the layout," Arthur said.

He placed his pen back on the paper but drew a blank. He tried to remember the Manor's layout, but the many interconnected hallways were a mess in his mind—like a maze of crumpled spiderwebs. And he hadn't even started thinking about the colors or the smells or the style of the wood carvings or rugs or paintings or decorations or every last exquisite detail. How could he possibly capture it all?

"What are you doing?" a small voice whispered beside him.

"I'm trying to write a story about a Manor," Arthur said, pinching the bridge of his nose.

"Why?"

"*Because*," he said, and left it at that.

He focused on the page. Why hadn't he paid better attention while he was in the Manor instead of spending all his time worrying about what the Wardens thought of him?

"*Because* isn't really a reason."

"KW?" Arthur said, clenching his fist. "I'm trying to be patient, but I really don't have time to explain right n—"

He looked up and his mouth snapped shut. Sitting beside him was one of the most beautiful girls he had ever seen. Brown curls tumbled around a heart-shaped face and smirk-shaped lips. And her *eyes*. They were as dark and blue as the twilit heavens and seemed to sparkle with a wisdom not of this earth.

Arthur felt a falling sensation and quickly looked away. That's when he noticed the hem of the girl's wedding dress . . . It was KW. An invisible energy wafted from the Rifts around them, aging the lady in waves. Months passed like minutes across the girl's face and hair. Her limbs were growing longer. Her dress more worn.

She was Teen Weirdwood now. TW. *And*, Arthur thought with a pinch in his heart, *she wasn't stopping there.*

"Sorry," TW said. "I'll be quiet and let you work."

"No!" Arthur said, his voice cracking. "You can interrupt. I'm, um, trying to rebuild *your* Manor, actually."

"I have a Manor?"

"The most beautiful Manor you'll ever see," Arthur said, not daring to look back into her eyes. "It grows like a tree. Each room is like a fruit dedicated to a different idea within our collective imagination. The passages are its branches that represent the trials a person must traverse to reach them. And the basement is its roots that stretch into the darkness of our subconscious."

Arthur took notes as he spoke. It was much easier to describe something to a cute girl than it was to write it.

"It sounds perfect," TW said.

"It is," Arthur said. He looked at the blank page and started to feel overwhelmed again. "But there are so many *details*. The art, the furniture, the themes of the rooms. I couldn't possibly remember it all."

"Do you need to?"

"What do you mean?" He still couldn't bring himself to look TW directly in the eye.

"I mean, do you need to rebuild the Manor exactly how it was?"

"Well, *yeah*," Arthur said. He gazed out to sea, where the Eraser was still sending plumes of water into the clouds. "Otherwise, it might not work right."

"Well, if it's *my* Manor," TW said, "I think you should make it however you want. You're the most creative person I've ever met."

Arthur finally looked at her. "I am?"

"Of course," TW said with a cute shrug. "When I was little, you got us out of that terrifying place with all those broken stairs and floating halls by escaping through a *book*. You led us through that bat building, somehow saved us from falling out of the sky, and navigated that creepy gray city." She smiled in a way that sent Arthur's heart fluttering. "You're also one of the bravest people I know."

Arthur swallowed. "Thank you. I haven't felt that way recently."

He fell into her eyes again. He saw the constellations shimmering there and realized . . . they weren't constellations at all. He leaned in to get a better look, and TW flinched back.

"Sorry!" Arthur said. "I'm so sorry. I wasn't trying to kiss you. I just . . . I need to look in your eyes for a second. If—if that's okay."

TW gave him a questioning look, then put her face closer. The nebula she'd had in her eyes as a baby and the microscopic galaxy of her childhood had developed not into a universe . . . but *blueprints*.

"TW," Arthur whispered. "You have the whole Manor laid out in your eyes!"

She smirked. "Sounds like you'd better get writing then."

The flutter in Arthur's heart died away. "Guess I'd better," he said with a sad smile.

He would never see TW's beautiful face again. He gave her

one last look before tearing his eyes away and returning to his notebook.

Maybe TW was right. Maybe the only way forward was to fill the Manor with things he loved, like he'd done with the DappleWood and the Great Elsewhere. He started by writing one room for each exciting moment in his adventure: a Dapplewood garden in the courtyard, a re-creation of the StormCrow in the feasting hall, and a Gentleman Thief–themed study, complete with pun-filled skeletons. Next, he worked on some darker moments, dedicating a small library to Alfred Moore and Valerie Lucas, a rookery for Liza and her father, and finally an indoor salt pool for Huamei, the dragon boy. Every so often, Arthur briefly glanced into TW's aging eyes to make sure he had the layout right.

As the Eraser cut a trench of nothingness through the ocean, the author, the woodworker, the ferret, and the architect slowly rebuilt Weirdwood Manor, filling the whiteness above the cliffs. The bones of the first floor were nearly complete when a claw tapped him on the shoulder.

"Yeah?" Arthur said, not looking up from his notebook.

"*Arthur*," Audrey said, pointing.

Arthur looked to the horizon and saw a wide, black shape sailing through the fountains of ocean water and the staticky blankness.

"What . . . is that?" Arthur asked.

"Looks like a . . . bird," Audrey said, squinting.

Sure enough, as the shape grew closer, it developed wings.

Arthur slowly stood, dropping his pen. "*Liza*." And she wasn't alone. Someone was riding on her back. "*Cooper!*"

A grin burst across his face. There was no problem in the Real or the Fae that he and his old friend couldn't figure out together.

"Vhy have ve stopped ze vorking?" Ludwig asked, peeking out from the foundation.

"We're about to get a lot more help," Arthur said, still beaming.

But as Liza flapped closer, his heart began to sink. Something golden was spilling from her black wings. Arthur swallowed in fear. *Spores.* And in the spores, Breeth, cackling with delight. Even more horrifying, in the great bird's wake, the entirety of Kingsport's bright blue sky was *unzipping*, revealing the gray sky of the Mirror City behind it. Almost like Wally was *intentionally* tearing the biggest Rift Arthur had ever seen.

"Arthur?" Audrey said. "That Eraser thing is headed back toward the city. Shouldn't we keep building?"

Arthur couldn't take his eyes from Wally and Liza. He didn't understand. The last time he'd seen his friend, Wally had betrayed him. Where had he been since? And what in the infinite pocket-worlds was he doing now?

"Arthur?" TW said, lightly touching his arm.

Arthur finally looked, and his heart broke when he saw the crow's-feet spreading from the corners of TW's eyes. *LW's* eyes. The lady was almost back to her old self.

He looked to Ludwig and Audrey, who had their hammer and whistle at the ready. What was more important? Completing the Manor or stopping his friend from making a terrible mistake?

"Hold this," he said, handing Lady Weirdwood his notebook. "I'll be back as soon as I can."

He took off down the craggy path, unsure he was making the right choice.

"Arthur!" Audrey called to him. "What about the rest of the Manor?"

"Ve need you here to vrite ze details!"

Arthur skidded to a stop. He looked back at the partially built Manor jutting up into the sky.

22
THE ROOFTOP

Wally soared over Kingsport on Liza's back, her feathers soft and fluttering beneath him. Above, massive Rifts tore across the sky, unveiling the Mirror City's strange horizon. On either side, spores spilled from Liza's long black wings. And below, Kingsport wavered like a mirage, bringing forth the dreams and the nightmares that had been hiding beneath.

Magic clashed with reality as the shops and streets merged with their mirror counterparts, steepening the alleys and contorting the buildings into their exaggerated counterparts. Some of the citizens gasped in delight to find miracles sprouting through the cobblestones. Others screamed in terror when they suddenly found themselves walking beside beastly figures in human clothing.

Wally remained focused on the task at hand. "How's it going down there, Breeth?"

"Weird! Scary! Funny! All the things!" Breeth said, her sporey form soaring beside him. Her face contorted as she made straining sounds. "*Rrrrr!* It's sorta like patting your head and rubbing your stomach at the same time—*Rrg!*—only I've got a hundred paws and claws and scaled and furry tummies and horned and slimy heads!"

Directly below, in Market Square, a gang of centaurs had appeared. They drew their bows, aiming arrows at the terrified shoppers. Breeth grunted and wriggled, and soon, a golden cloud of spores swept into the market, enveloping the centaurs, who immediately dropped their bows and arrows and waved pleasantly to the confused shoppers.

Once they'd caught up with the story and returned to the present, Breeth had used the single spore in her heart to connect to millions more throughout the disintegrating pocket-worlds. And now she was using them to corral as many Fae-born as her ghostly brain could handle. Under normal circumstances, Wally was against Breeth controlling anyone, but the ghost girl had promised to only make the most dangerous creatures behave themselves and not, in her words, *make them do weird things to each another and stuff.*

Breeth's misuse of magic was also tearing Rifts by the dozens. Just as Wally intended.

"Good work, Breeth," he said. "That's all I need for now."

Breeth's face lit up like New Year's Eve. "You mean I'm free to . . ."

"Knock yourself out. Just don't forget to swing by Kingsport's General Hospital and pick up you-know-who."

"I won't! *Ee hee hee hee hee!*"

Breeth's spores started to fall, her shape melting with them. Far below, the shop fronts of Market Square rattled as the ghost girl shot through the city.

Wally pulled back on Liza's feathers, and the great black bird flapped higher into the rending sky. He scanned the city and spotted a streak of staticky white on Kingsport's Port. He angled Liza toward the sea, heart pounding in his throat.

The moment they had caught up with the story, he, Liza, and Breeth had followed the Eraser's path of nothingness through the pocket-worlds, rescuing Fae-born wherever they could. At the path's end, Wally discovered the Eraser had entered his own city. He was terrified to discover what it had destroyed.

But as Liza sailed closer to port, he saw that the only building that had been erased was Greyridge. The mental hospital was gone. Obliterated. Erased. As if it had never existed. And there were Greyridge's patients, standing safe on the coast.

Wally's heart soared. How appropriate that this adventure would end with the destruction of the place that had started it all by treating Graham poorly and driving Wally to drastic action. As Liza circled back, Wally saw that some Mirror City structure was already growing in Greyridge's place. It bloomed through the blankness, a branchy foundation stretching a nascent framework over the white. Wally was excited to see what sort of building would replace that cursed hospital.

He traced the staticky path along the cliffs and over their edge. The Eraser was cutting a vast arc through the ocean, erasing fish and seaweed and carving a deep trench through the waves. The water seemed to slow the Eraser's movement. That was good. It gave Wally time to take care of some things.

He pointed to a rooftop and called over the rushing wind, "There, Liza!"

Liza angled her great wings downward, and with a powerful flapping came to perch on the roof with a waft of ash.

Wally slid off her wing and walked to her beak, smoothing the feathers between her eyes. "Will you keep an eye on the Eraser and let me know if it gets close to the shore?"

Liza puffed her feathers in agreement, then flapped her wings toward the boiling ocean.

Wally drew a long breath and took in the roof—the tiles and chimney pots, the ash and fire escape—so quaint and simple now. The last time he'd climbed up here, he'd nearly thrown up he was so afraid of heights. But in the last few months, Liza had carried him across the clouds of a hundred pocket-worlds. A rooftop was nothing.

Someone came huffing up the fire escape.

Right on time, Wally thought as Arthur Benton climbed up and over the roof's edge.

"Hello, Arthur," Wally said. "I figured you'd know to come here."

"Wally!" Arthur said, dusting the ash from his shirt. "Where have you been? What's happening to the sky? What's happening to our *city*? Was that *Liza* I saw?"

Wally gave him a trembling smile. "It's nice to see you too."

He tried to hold himself with more confidence than he felt. He had Breeth and Liza on his side. A million spores as well. But Arthur had a pen sticking out of his jacket pocket. With a single scribble, he could bend the very fabric of reality to his whim, undoing everything Wally, Breeth, and Liza had fought for.

"Breeth isn't here," Wally said. "And I sent Liza away." He nodded to the pen in Arthur's pocket. "You mind?"

Arthur drew out the pen and a single piece of paper. "I need these, Wally," he said, still out of breath from the climb. "I have to stop . . ." He nodded at the sky, growing more mirror-like with each passing minute.

"I think I know how to beat the Eraser," Wally said. "But I need you to listen to me. And I need to be able to trust you."

Arthur gave Wally a wary look, then gazed over their city with furrowed eyebrows.

"We have time, Arthur," Wally said. "The Eraser is stuck in the ocean for the time being. And Breeth's making sure the Fae-born behave themselves."

Arthur considered his pen and paper for a moment, then tossed them both over the edge. Once again, Wally and Arthur were just two kids standing on a rooftop.

Wally's muscles relaxed a bit. He sat between the chimney pots, exactly where he'd found Arthur on that fateful day that had changed their lives.

"The moment you stepped through that mirror," Wally began, "I realized I couldn't go with you. My thoughts were all tangled up. I didn't know what was right. So, I went to see my brother in Greyridge. At the beginning of the story."

"Let me guess," Arthur said. "You couldn't talk to him."

Wally nodded. "I realized at that moment—well, a moment *later* in the story—you were discovering the same thing." He looked Arthur in the eye. "I sent you into a dangerous place all alone. I'm so sorry."

Arthur seemed to grow uncomfortable in his skin and broke Wally's gaze. He looked into the sky and saw Liza, a black smudge, circling the horizon. "You saved us, didn't you? When Audrey, KW, and I fell out of the monster hospital. You and Liza swept in and caught us at the last second."

Wally smiled. "Even Arthur Benton wouldn't survive a fall like that."

Arthur didn't smile back. "*How*, though? How did you change the past—er, *story*? I tried, but it . . . it's impossible!"

"I thought so too," Wally said, then looked toward the blank spot where Greyridge once stood. "My brother was painting his cell wall, as always. When I couldn't get him to respond, I studied his art instead. For the first time, I *really* looked at it. And I realized he was painting Mirror Kingsport. It wasn't the work of a madman at all. It was the *truth*. I told him I was sorry I hadn't seen how beautiful his painting was before. And then . . . something changed. Graham flashed with color and then drew something that wasn't there before— three shapes falling through the sky toward something like a thundercloud."

Arthur looked more flustered and confused than Wally had ever seen him.

"I knew you and the others were going to fall out of that hospital," Wally said. "But I had no idea how to save you in a grayed-out story when I couldn't even bend a single flower petal. So I asked myself, what if Graham was sending me a message? What if those three smudges were you, Audrey, and Lady Weirdwood falling through the sky? And what if what

Graham had drawn below you wasn't a storm cloud at all? What if they were black wings?"

"Liza," Arthur whispered. Then he shook his head. "But she hadn't turned into a bird in that part of the story." He sounded angry. "How did she get there?"

"Breeth and I got off the Trackdragon around the time you were leaving the Great Elsewhere. We found Liza, and I used the same trick I did with my brother, talking to her until the blue shimmer returned to her feathers."

Wally didn't mention that he'd done this by telling Liza he knew what it was like to love a family member who endangered others' lives—that Graham and the Rook were not so different. He didn't think Arthur would like that.

"I hopped on her back," Wally continued, "and we followed the dragon duchess's guards back to the Whirling City, where we had access to Rifts that led to every pocket-world in the Fae. From there we just had to find the one that contained our first adventure, *Thieves of Weirdwood*, where you three were currently falling to your deaths."

Arthur started to pace the roof, rubbing the back of his head. Wally couldn't tell if his friend refused to believe what had happened or if he was just upset that Wally had figured out a major magical solution that Arthur could not.

"I can't spin stories like you do, Arthur," Wally said. "I can't create pocket-worlds or change people's minds with my words. What I *can* do is notice the little things you and I didn't see when we were living the adventure. And I can sort of read them in a new way. You, Audrey, and KW weren't in the actual story, so it was like your fate was open to interpretation. And that meant it was open to *change*. Who's to say what does and doesn't happen off the page of a story? Who's to say Liza and I didn't swoop in and save your lives?"

Arthur stopped pacing and stepped to the roof's edge. "And you think this new power of yours is going to help defeat the Eraser?"

Wally stepped beside him and drew a deep breath, trying to banish the nervousness. How much should he tell his friend? "Figuring out how to change what happens off the page got me here. But this . . ." He gestured to the white splotch expanding across the colorful horizon. "This is *on* the page. It needs a whole different solution."

Arthur folded his arms. "So, what do you think we should do?"

Wally opened his mouth to explain, then closed it again. He didn't think Arthur was ready to hear what he had to say. So he cleared his throat and tried a different approach.

"Before we found Liza, Breeth and I found a Shadowrail station in the grayed-out Fae and boarded a Trackdragon. And then . . . we just rode it. That's it. For the first time in months, I didn't have to do anything. I didn't have to act. Didn't have to fight. Didn't have to make any life-changing decisions. I could just sit and watch through the window." Wally felt a soothing breeze through his soul. "I saw things, Arthur. Unbelievable things . . ."

The Trackdragon had chugged through the starry expanse, in and out of hundreds of pocket-worlds. And Wally watched them pass from his train compartment. He saw a Fae kingdom of glass that was close to shattering. And on the Real side, a desert with all the sand needed to melt down and build more skyscrapers. He saw a Real city whose river was choked with sewage and dead rats. And on the Fae side, a pocket-world of cats and crystalline rivers.

"Every city, every pocket-world, was *riddled* with problems," Wally said. "Chaos. Starvation. Wilting forests. And in every instance, a solution waited right on the other side of the Veil."

Arthur's expression didn't change an inch.

Wally scratched the back of his neck. "I've never been great at describing stuff. That was always your thing." He looked to the clouds. "Let me show you instead."

He placed his fingers to his lips and whistled. A few moments later, Liza swooped back onto the roof, her great wings stirring up ash and ruffling their clothes. Arthur was so startled, he tripped and fell backward. He quickly hopped up and smoothed his shirt.

"Liza," he said, tears in his eyes. "I was afraid I'd never see you again."

Liza's feathers remained sleek and cold. Now that the Veil was tearing, Wally knew she could turn back into a human any time she wanted. But Liza clearly still didn't want to speak to Arthur after he had killed her father. Even if it was an accident.

Wally stroked the giant bird's beak. "Will you take us above the city? I need to show Arthur something."

Liza quirked her head. The real test was whether she would allow Arthur to step onto her wing or if she would snip him in two. She clicked her bill in thought, then extended her wing like a ramp, allowing both boys to step up onto her feathery back.

Liza flapped her wings, lifting them off the roof and high into the clouds until they could see Kingsport's four quarters laid out in a circle below them.

"I don't see the point of this, Cooper!" Arthur called. "We should be on the ground, helping—"

"Just watch, Arthur!" Wally shouted back. "For once. Just watch."

The two sailed over Kingsport, gazing down at the breathtaking chaos of the melding cities. In the Wretch, a gang of Corvidians flew circles over a gang of armed Black Feathers. In the Gilded Quarter, the rich panicked while peacocks in tuxedos and ball gowns appeared in the gardens of their stately houses. On the Port, fishermen dumped nets full of mermaids onto the docks. And in the Bliss, church leaders shouted sermons to the masses as demon-red fingers reached up through the drains.

Every situation was ready to break out into chaos. But the Fae-born glowed golden with spores as Breeth kept them reined in.

"The Wardens always talked about keeping the Balance between the Fae and the Real," Wally said. "But I see suffering on both sides. Starving orphans. Dying forests. Crumbling cities. The *Pox*. Are you really happy with the Balance as it is, Arthur?"

"Of course I'm not happy about the *bad* things. I just don't want any more porcelain dolls or Corvidians or tentacle monsters destroying our city."

"That was a *planned* attack by Alfred Moore," Wally said. "And *we* stopped him. Not the Wardens. You, me, and Breeth."

"Mirror Kingsport is *dangerous*, Wally. We almost died every twenty minutes!"

"You think our city is a walk in the park? How many times were we beaten by Oakers? How many nights did we starve? Our friends died. Our *parents* died." Wally drew a deep breath, preparing his heart for what came next. "People will always get hurt, Arthur. Veil or no Veil."

Arthur didn't respond, and Wally looked back to find his friend staring across the ripping horizon, now a patchwork of Kingsport's bright blue and the Mirror City's slate gray.

"The Eraser isn't tearing these Rifts," Arthur whispered with a horrified expression. "It's *you*."

Wally looked at the same horizon and smiled. His brother's dream—*his* dream—was finally coming true. "Lady Weirdwood gave me the solution a long time ago when she told me about Voids. They're created when a beloved character in the Fae is forcefully ripped from the imaginations of the people in the Real. Like when Garnett Lacroix was written out of existence by a dragon-bone Quill. But with enough Rifts, that missing feeling will leave, and the Eraser will vanish like it never existed."

"But that missing feeling *won't* leave, Cooper," Arthur said. "In case, you forgot, there isn't a Garnett Lacroix on the other side!"

"That's where you come in, Arthur," Wally said. "Without a Veil, you'll be able to write a new Gentleman Thief wherever you want. Your fictions will be *realities*."

The horrified expression didn't leave Arthur's face. "What do you mean '*without a Veil*'?"

Wally sighed with a smile. This was it. It was time to tell his friend the truth.

After watching the interactions created by hundreds of Rifts, Wally had decided that bringing down the Veil was the right thing to do. But he still had had no idea *how* to do it, let alone how to make sure no one would be hurt in the initial chaos that would follow. Meanwhile, Breeth hadn't stopped bouncing off the walls of the Trackdragon compartment, complaining about how frustrating it was that she had finally learned how to possess multiple Fae-born but was unable to show off in the grayed-out past. Once they found Liza, it had all clicked, and Wally realized he had everything he needed to safely bring down the Veil.

Liza, happy to complete her father's work, would spread the Mycopath's spores with her wings while Breeth, ready to play and eager to find as many lonely ghosts as she could, would possess every Fae-born in sight, misusing magic and tearing enough Rifts in the Veil to bring the entire thing crashing down.

"Combining the Real and the Fae might be the only way to save everyone in our city from being erased," Wally said. "But if a better city emerges once Kingsport and the Mirror City combine, I'm going to keep tearing the Veil until it spreads across the whole world."

"Wally," Arthur said in shock. "That's not funny. Usually when people say things like that, they break out in evil laughter."

Wally bit his lip. He was doing his best not to sound like

Graham—so full of frustrating certainty about a vision that couldn't be confirmed by anyone but himself.

"I'm not some villain in one of your adventure stories, Arthur."

"You sure about that?" Arthur said, gesturing to the Rifts tearing throughout the city. "Looks to me like you're still blindly following your brother."

Wally drew a breath, trying to get on top of his frustration. He didn't want to fight his friend. He just wanted Arthur to listen.

"Graham was convinced the Veil did more good than harm," Wally said, "but I didn't take his word for it. I went and found out for myself. By boarding that Trackdragon at the beginning of the story, I've been able to study this stuff as long as you and I have been on these adventures. I wasn't looking at the Real and the Fae in bits and pieces the way Graham saw them whenever he gazed into the future. I was seeing them as they are right now. I'm not tearing the Veil because it's my fate. I'm tearing it because it's the right thing to do."

Liza glided through a golden spore cloud, and Wally noticed that Arthur didn't hold his breath as usual. He wondered if his friend was so angry with him that he had forgotten his fear of the Mycopath.

"Let me get this straight," Arthur said. "You're ready to gamble away the safety of every person in our city just because you saw some pocket-worlds with cracked glass and dirty water?"

"It's not a gamble when I have Breeth to help keep things calm," Wally said.

Arthur still looked upset, so Wally steered Liza toward their old stomping grounds.

"Remember that knot in your stomach?" Wally asked. "The hunger that turned your morals to mush, making it so you never thought twice about stealing?"

Arthur sighed, his anger relenting a bit. "After we got to the Manor, I still hid food from the feasting hall in my pockets."

Wally nodded. "We're lucky that we got to leave our thieving days behind, Arthur. We accidentally stumbled into magic, and it changed our lives. We can do the same thing for our friends. It's just like a Garnett Lacroix story, stealing from the rich to feed the orphans. Only we're giving them *magic*."

Arthur folded his arms, his anger clearly returning. "What would you know about Garnett Lacroix?"

"I know he wouldn't like Kingsport the way it was when we lived here," Wally said.

Liza swooped low, and Paradise/Parasite Lane rushed beneath them.

Wally pointed out interactions that Breeth's spores were not controlling. On the street where the Battle of the Barrows had raged, a garden grew. Near the officers' watering hole, a dozen Oakers were trying to arrest a single Ogre Oaker, who was comically trying and failing to arrest them back. And outside the StormCrow Pub, which Liza had cleaned up in her human form, a reformed werewolf exchanged recipes with Charlie, the Rook's ex-bodyguard. Finally, Wally pointed out the Ghastly Courtyard where the dreams of doomed Black Feathers spouted into the sky, dazzling those who lost them.

"See?" Wally said. "Good things are happening all by themselves. No heroes needed."

Arthur didn't so much as crack a smile.

Wally searched the horizon for more evidence that his plan was working. "Look what's happening where Greyridge used to be," he said, pointing toward the Port's cliffs where the skeletal frame of the strange new building was continuing to blossom. It was starting to look *familiar*. "I can't tell what's growing in its place, but it's gotta be better than a hospital."

Arthur pointed over Liza's opposite wing. "What about *that*?"

Wally looked down at Meadow/Mildew Street and saw a giant ball of elephant trunks, dripping and sniffling as it rolled like a boulder after a crowd of screaming people.

"Or that?" Arthur said, pointing to a different emergency. "Or *that*?"

Directly below, a gang of goblins smashed the window of a restaurant, sending the customers scattering and urchins scrambling inside. One street over, a bloody fight had broken out between a scarred weasel and one of the Black Feathers' old gang captains. They were going to kill each other.

Wally anxiously searched the scenes for the telltale glow of spores. Where was Breeth and why wasn't she taking care of this?

"You're *forcing* this new life on our city," Arthur said. "And now people are getting hurt."

Wally closed his eyes and steadied himself. "I'm not saying it's perfect, Arthur. Of course it will be chaotic at first. That happens in every revolution. But I still believe that humans and Fae-born can learn to work together and that both sides will be better in the end."

"Make it stop, Cooper," Arthur said behind him.

"I can't do that, Arthur," Wally said sadly. Even with all the evidence sprawled out before them, Arthur couldn't see the bright future that awaited them.

"I said make it *stop*!" Arthur shouted.

"*Oof!*"

The air was knocked from Wally's lungs as Arthur tackled him from behind. Without thinking, Wally threw an elbow into Arthur's stomach, then rolled and tried to get his friend into a headlock, hoping to stop this stupid fight before it began. But Arthur threw back his head, cracking Wally's jaw. The boys wrestled along Liza's feathered back, coming dangerously close to spilling off one wing, then the other.

"What are you gonna do?" Wally shouted, struggling to pry Arthur's fingers from his shirt. "Throw me to my *death*? That won't stop Breeth from tearing the Veil!"

The fury didn't leave Arthur's eyes. "I'm just trying to show you how *evil* you're being!"

His hands whirled back as Liza tipped her wings, trying to make Arthur fall to the street below.

Wally leapt forward and grabbed hold of Arthur's suspenders, saving him from a fatal fall. "We're not trying to kill him, Liza!"

She leveled her wings, and Arthur grabbed Wally's shirt in his fists while Wally held Arthur's wrists. They breathed heavily, staring into each other's eyes.

"It's already done. The Veil is torn. I just . . ." Wally sniffed blood back into his nose. "I just wanted you to be a part of it."

"Never."

The two continued to struggle against each other as Liza swooped down and perched at their destination.

"*Look*, Arthur," Wally said.

Arthur looked.

Liza had landed on a roof directly across from the tenements where the boys had grown up. The building looked halfway through a magical renovation. What had been a patchwork of crumbling bricks and rotting wood was now growing ivory columns, multicolored Fae bulbs, and living gargoyles and grotesques.

One of the windows glowed with pearly light. Inside was Harry. Arthur's dad seemed to be back on his feet, having paid the owed rent. But that wasn't the important part. Harry was dancing with a breathtaking woman of blue glass.

Arthur looked away, a pained expression on his face. "Nice try, Cooper. But you can't pull on my heartstrings with a sappy scene like this. I created that ghost in the Great Elsewhere."

"Look again, Arthur," Wally said.

Arthur furrowed his eyebrows in confusion, then looked back toward the pearly window. He released Wally's shirt as his angry expression melted into that of a young boy who had been lost for a very long time.

"Breeth heard her weeping in the hospital walls before we left gray Kingsport," Wally said. "She's been there since the day she died. I don't think she wanted to leave the city you were in."

Arthur stared at the ghost of his mom. His *real* mom. No tears streamed down his cheeks.

Wally continued. "After the Battle of the Barrows, you made me believe my parents were in a good place. That they were happy. Your words made me feel safe for the first time in . . . I don't know how long. That was what made us friends, Arthur." He smiled at Harry and the ghost in the window. "I wanted to repay the favor. By giving you the real thing."

Arthur looked away as if embarrassed.

Wally placed a hand on his friend's back. "Just think of the good your magic could do in a Veil-less world. You can use your writing to help Breeth maintain the new Balance, keeping people safe while they have experiences like the one your dad is having right now."

Arthur still wouldn't look at him. He was staring toward the cliffs of Greyridge.

"I know it's scary," Wally said. "I'm terrified. But back in the Impossible Wood, you told me yourself that fear is good. Those words guided me when I was riding the Trackdragon, looking for answers. I realized that fear keeps you sharp. It makes you pay attention. If you're afraid, it means you're doing something that's important to you. And you're extra careful about the decisions you make."

Arthur stared at his hands. "I said fear is good, huh?"

"You did."

Arthur sniffed. "Are you saying I can be pretty smart sometimes?"

A laugh burst out of Wally. "If it will get you to stop being so mad at me."

For the first time that day, Arthur smiled at Wally, tears finally spilling down his cheeks. "I guess if it's the difference between having my mom back and total nothingness"—he gazed up into the unzipping sky, the Rifts gaping wider and wider—"you and I had better go tear ourselves a Veil."

Wally smiled back, a little shocked and a lot relieved that he had finally gotten his friend to see what he saw. He didn't want to give Arthur another second to change his mind, so he reached into his back pocket and pulled out a paper and pen.

Arthur's eyebrows raised. "You realize this is like handing me a weapon, right?"

"To fight beside me."

Arthur took the pen and paper and arched a gentlemanly eyebrow. "From Thieves to Novitiates to Maverick Heralds of Magic. Who could ask for a better ending?"

"Not me," Wally said quietly. He crawled across the feathers and straddled the great bird's neck. "Come on, Liza. Let's go kill the Eraser."

They soared away from the tenements and toward the coast.

"Wanna hear something funny?" Arthur called over the screaming wind. "When I went to see Harry after we first visited the Manor, your brother's hand told me *I* would bring the Veil down. Later, I thought maybe Graham was hedging his bets, hoping someone would make his fake prophecy come true for him. But well, here we are. I never told you that because I was terrified he was right."

Wally chuckled. "I know the feeling!"

They descended toward the sea, whose waves surged and

frothed as the Eraser finally exited onto the beach. On the coast, armed and waiting, were the Wardens of Weirdwood.

"Amelia!" Arthur said with relief. "Linus and Ahura! Willa and Cadence! And . . . *Sekhmet*! She's okay!"

"Like I said"—Wally smiled back at him—"I'm not following my brother."

After rescuing Arthur, Wally and Liza had returned to the disintegrating Manor, found Sekhmet, and flown her to safety. They'd found the others wandering through the blank DappleWood. A part of Wally had worried the Wardens might interfere with his efforts to bring down the Veil. But he couldn't let any harm come to the people who had given him this magical life. Even if they were in the wrong.

"Wait," Arthur said. "Who's that?"

As Liza glided closer, he noticed the other figures on the coast: a tall man with ill-fitting clothing, a wisp of a woman, and a hulking stone figure.

"You . . . You saved the Order too?"

"They're humans, Arthur," Wally said. "They were in the wrong place at the wrong time. Just like us. And the Eraser's been erasing the Fae wares they need to survive. They have just as much interest in defeating the Eraser as the Wardens do."

Arthur gritted his teeth.

The Order and the Wardens closed in on the Eraser from opposite sides of the beach, their mutual enemy seemingly causing a temporary alliance. Silver Tongue had replenished her flask and was thirstily gulping her mercury. Cadence drummed a steady war beat while Willa released her tin kites into the air. Rustmouth licked his brown teeth as Linus and Sekhmet ignited their swords. And finally, the Astonishment beat together her stony fists, stomping craters in the sand.

The Eraser reached the shore, and the Wardens swept in, attacking with fire and fireworks, with kites and rhythmic bursts of sand, throwing everything they could at the Void to keep it away from the city. The Astonishment stepped beside the Wardens, hurling giant beach rocks at the man-shaped nothingness.

Every spell and rock vanished into the Eraser as it came toward them, unimpeded. It reached the Astonishment and seized her arm, slowly disintegrating her rocky fingers.

"No!" Wally cried. He knew the Astonishment's story now. She had a wife and children. She hadn't chosen this life. He looked to the Wardens, hoping they could save the poor stone woman from being erased.

But something terrible was happening. Willa had turned her furry wings on the Wardens and was commanding her sharp kites to slice their arms and faces. A high-pitched cackle pierced through the frothing waves as Silver Tongue used her mercurial voice not against the Eraser but the *Wardens*.

"Still happy you saved the Order?" Arthur asked.

Wally watched, terrified. The Astonishment's arm had been erased to the elbow. No one was saving her.

Rustmouth seized Silver Tongue's fist and seemed to be admonishing her. But she spit her silvery words, making the man punch himself in the face and knocking him flat. Silver

Tongue giggled in delight, then turned back to the Wardens to continue her tortures.

Wally was tempted to angle Liza toward the beach so she could snap up the awful woman in her giant bill. But with a single slash of the Eraser's fingers, they would never take flight again.

Rustmouth hefted himself to his feet. He snuck up behind Silver Tongue and snatched her flask from her hand. Wally expected him to dump it on the sand, putting a stop to his girlfriend's wickedness once and for all. But instead, Rustmouth tipped the flask to his lips. He guzzled every last drop, silvery liquid running with the rust-brown saliva that spilled down his chin.

"Ain't nobody obliterases my pal!" he screamed at the Eraser. "*Let her go, you starry excuse for a shillhouette!*"

The words, a mixture of shrieking silver and crumbling rust, tore through the air, knocking back the Eraser and allowing the Astonishment to wrench what remained of her arm away. The mercury spent, the Wardens were finally able to get past Willa's kites and reach the injured stone woman, whom they dragged to safety up the beach.

The Astonishment was alive, but the spell had been too much for its caster. Rustmouth screamed in pain as the mercury rusted inside him, cracking his skin and crumbling his body to ash. Soon, there was nothing left of the man but a burnt silhouette in the sand.

Wally stared at it, heart aching. Rustmouth had sacrificed himself to save the Astonishment's life.

Silver Tongue, flaskless and outmatched, skipped down the beach, giggling at the destruction she had caused. Wally wanted to chase after her, but they had a much bigger problem on their hands. The Eraser had reached the first of Kingsport's coastal buildings.

Wally leaned forward, angling Liza's wings steeply downward, swooping toward the Eraser.

"What's the plan, Cooper?" Arthur shouted over the screaming wind.

"We need to get the Eraser to hold still while the Veil tears above it!" Wally shouted back. "You distract it while I take care of the Veil. Then use that paper and pen to fill in the Eraser with Garnett Lacroix." He turned to look his friend in the eye. "You get to write the Gentleman Thief story that will save Kingsport and every last soul in it."

Arthur smiled. "You stole my line."

Liza landed on the beach with a whirl of sand, and Arthur slid off her feathers.

He reached up and clasped Wally's hand. "See you at the end of the story, Cooper."

"Let's make it a happy one, Benton."

Arthur ran toward the Eraser while Liza carried Wally back into the clouds. Spores spilled from her wings, sprinkling over the city. The more Fae-born breathed them in, the more the sky tore wide, blending the silver Mirror light with Kingsport's blue as a massive Rift opened above the ocean, filling half the sky and splitting toward the beach.

Wally's part, the *easy* part, was done. He peeked over

Liza's wing, heart hammering. Back on the beach, Arthur approached the Eraser, taking out the pen and paper Wally had given him. The Eraser stopped in its tracks, its chaotic eyes drawn toward Arthur like magnets. It blurred toward him, its body pulsing like a dark star. It drew closer and closer to the Real and Fae light overlapping on the sand.

Arthur began to write, and Wally watched the Eraser for signs of change. But there were no golden eyes. No hat. Arthur scribbled frantically, and Wally started to panic. Did the tearing Veil make it so Arthur couldn't do magic anymore?

"*Arthur, run!*" Wally shouted from the sky. "Forget the Veil! Get out of there!"

The Eraser was yards away now. But Arthur didn't budge. He stopped writing and stared at the nothingness rushing toward him, as if lost in its spell.

"Dive, Liza!" Wally screamed. "*Dive!*"

She dove. The cutting wind made tears stream from Wally's eyes, blurring the beach below, making it impossible to see what was happening. The Eraser had reached Arthur, enveloping him in its nothingness as sand and Rifts rose around them in a blinding whirlwind.

Before Liza landed, Wally leapt from her back, hitting the beach hard and sprinting into the sandstorm. At its center he found a mass of jittering energy that shone with blue and silver light, unspooling like a ball of string. The Eraser was dying.

Squinting, Wally continued through the stinging sands toward the spot where his friend had stood. But as the air cleared, Arthur Benton was nowhere in sight. Only a pair of suspenders lay in the sand.

Wally collapsed to his knees in disbelief.

The wind brought a lone piece of paper tumbling across the beach. Wally caught it and read his friend's final words:

Forgive me, Harry.

23

THE GIRL WITHOUT SHAPE

Cleaning up messes had never been so fun.

Breeth whisked her spores throughout the city, taming Fae-born left and right. It was like being a dog walker for the weirdest zoo in the universe, simultaneously keeping the Corvidians from pecking out eyeballs, the alligatormen from chomping off feet that wandered too close to the sewer drains, and the werewolves from peeing on innocents.

Some Fae-born behaved themselves perfectly. Like the nest of otter children, who sat on the coast and stared wide-eyed at the bountiful fish that awaited them in Kingsport's seas. Or the caterpillar trolley that quietly munched the park's greenery while it waited for passengers. Other Fae-born were even *helpful*. Like the sky flora that landed on the factory's smokestacks, absorbing the billowing ash into its wings like pollen.

But the nice Fae-born were boring. Breeth preferred the dangerous ones.

She searched for signs of distress and spotted a swarm of toupees flopping down a shopping lane, searching for unsuspecting heads. She swooped low, possessed the hairpieces, then herded them to a bank, finding men's bald heads for the toupees to clamp on to.

"Suckle *these* brains, my darlings!"

Next, she spotted an army of scarecrows, which hopped their poles toward a preschool full of shrieking children. She possessed the scarecrows' straw-stuffed bodies and diverted them toward a flock of Corvidians who had begun terrorizing the fish-factory workers. The bird children shrieked when they saw the scarecrows coming and flocked to a less populated part of the city, where they would no longer harass or poop on anyone.

Breeth cackled in delight, then blasted off like a firework above the city.

"I am Breeth!" she screamed. "Tamer of the Fae!"

Shhhrrrrrrrk!

The more Fae-born she possessed, the more the sky tore. It was satisfying in a naughty sort of way. She hadn't quite understood what Wally had seen through that Trackdragon's window. And she couldn't forget the many undisturbed pocket-worlds she'd stumbled across where the creatures, fairies, and sloth monsters were all as content as clams.

But she trusted Wally when he said the new Balance would bring better lives to people and Fae-born alike. Besides, Breeth had her own reasons for wanting to bring down the Veil.

"Come out, come out, little ghosteses!" she called to the buildings.

Ever since she had freed Huamei and the mouse thing from Weirdwood's walls, she had realized there had to be *millions* of ghosts trapped in musty planks and starchy sheets throughout the Fae and the Real, each as lonely as she'd once been. After that Rift in the Manor had made her skin sparkle glassy blue, allowing others to see and hear her, she couldn't help but wonder . . . how many more ghosts would be freed with the fall of the Veil?

Arthur's mom had been the first.

Breeth passed a cobbler's shop and sensed a familiar tremor in its walls. She followed the tremor to a blue glow where she found a little old woman, peeking her head out of the ugly wallpaper.

"Hello, and welcome to the afterlife!" Breeth said, curtsying her spores. "My name is Breeth. I shall be your ghost host."

The little old woman vanished back into the wallpaper.

"I won't hurt you!" she told the wallpaper. "I'm just a ghost, same as you. But, um, you're free to go and stuff. Trust me when I say it beats living in a wall all your afterlife."

"Free to go . . . where?" the ugly wallpaper asked.

"Wherever ya want!" Breeth said. "The park. Under the sea. Your enemy's house to haunt them."

"I . . . believe I'll remain here."

"Whuuhhwhy would you want to do *that*?"

The woman's face pressed out of the wallpaper. She nodded back into the cobbler's shop, where a spectral old man was fixing not rubber to the soles of shoes but cloud stuff.

"I have my Joe here now," the old woman said. "All is well."

Breeth blinked at the old woman's husband. His skin wasn't blue like theirs was. It was rainy like the fake ghosts in the Great Elsewhere. But Breeth wasn't about to break the old woman's heart.

"He's *very* rainy," she said. "You should be proud. Welp. Have a nice afterlife."

She floated off, feeling a little worried for the ghost lady.

She was on her way toward some screaming when she spotted Audrey, who was using her scissors to cut away a tuxedo that was trying to squeeze a gentleman—currently a purplish hue—to death.

"Hiya, Audrey!" Breeth said, floating up. "How fun is this?"

"Breeth! At last I found you," Audrey said, snipping the last of a strangling collar free. The freed gentleman ran away, clutching his throat. "I think you and I need to have a talk about the definition of *fun*."

"There are good things happening too!" Breeth said, turning in a circle. "Look how happy the rainbow eels in that fountain are! And those people are getting their wishes granted!" She completed her circle. "And I've been freeing ghosts from walls like the world's sweetest exorcist. Who knows? Maybe some of them have a body waiting in a greenhouse somewhere for them to repossess!"

Audrey's eyes grew wide and shiny.

"Don't worry!" Breeth told her. "I'm not possessing anyone but monsters who don't know how to behave themselves. And even then, I'm being *real* nice. For the most part."

"It isn't that," Audrey said, considering her paws. "I, um, have some news."

"This sounds serious," Breeth said. She settled her spores in a sitting position on a garbage can and cradled her chin, all while reining in dozens of Fae-born in the background.

She tried to keep her face still so the nice ferret lady wouldn't notice.

"Breeth . . . ," Audrey said. "Your body. It was in the DappleWood when the Eraser came through. The townsfolk were able to get to safety, but . . ."

"Oh," Breeth said.

An emptiness opened in the center of her spores. The invisible leashes released from her mind, and the wild Fae-born broke free across the city. She couldn't make herself care right then.

Her body, the only one she had ever had, was gone. The last time she'd put it on, she had immediately taken it off again because it felt too constricting. She hadn't realized that would be the last time she had a body. The last time she'd be able to sneeze or scratch an itch or feel the wind through her hair. Or eat normal food. She really liked normal food.

"I'm so sorry, Breeth," Audrey said.

Breeth noticed that her spores were sagging. She perked them back into her shape and forced them into a smile. "It's okay! I'm real good at not having a body now. Who needs all those annoying aches and itches, anyway?"

"Breeth . . ."

"Besides!" Breeth let the spores spill from her arm, show-ing her blue-glass skin beneath. "Now that the Veil is coming down, people can actually *see* me."

Audrey frowned at the tearing sky, then looked into Breeth's eyes in a way that made her spores squirm. "You sure this whole bringing down the Veil is a good idea? Has Wally led you astray?"

Breeth twirled spores around her fingers in thought. "I know Wally wants to bring down the Veil and make a new Balance, and that all sounds good and stuff. But *I* get to save a bunch of ghosts! They deserve to be seen just as much as me."

"Sure they do," Audrey said. She gazed down the city's chaotic streets. "But how many more ghosts are you gonna make in the process?"

Breeth remembered the rampaging Fae-born and quickly re-leashed them with her spores. "I'll keep everyone safe!" she said. "That means every last critter in the DappleWood."

"You can't be everywhere at once, Breeth," Audrey said. She took Breeth's spore hand in her paws and gave it a squeeze. "All I ask is that you think about it."

An ungodly sound reverberated from the beach. A storm-sized scream that seemed to be made of many screams. High above the waves, Liza was circling, Wally and Arthur on her back.

"We should probably quit this chitchat," Audrey said. "Someone sent me to find you."

She pointed a claw toward the craggy cliffs where the creepy hospital had been replaced by a slash of staticky white.

"Who?" Breeth said. "Not Valerie Lucas? She's dead by now. And her ghost is long gone."

Audrey shrugged. "I was told not to tell."

Breeth floated toward the cliffs, questions swirling through her spores. What would it be like to be a little ghost girl forever? Did she have to be? Was there another empty body somewhere in the vastness of the Fae? Could Arthur write her a new one? Would either be as cozy as her old body had been?

She floated faster, trying to escape the terrifying realization that the moment her body had been erased, she had died for good. But that was the thing about realizations. No matter how fast she flew, they always kept up.

She reached the cliffs and was startled to find what looked like a sketch of Weirdwood Manor, its bare frame stretched across the nothingness like a branchy skeleton. But it wasn't growing and even seemed to be wilting some. As if its gardeners had neglected to water it.

She breezed through the doorless entrance and past the half-blossomed foyer. *Funny*, she thought with a squeeze in her chest. The Manor had been another kind of body to her once.

A vast creaky one that had become as familiar as her own. Now it was gone too.

Breeth explored the new, barely built Manor, looking for whoever was looking for her. She noticed the Thorny Passage—the place where Rose had murdered her—was not part of this new Manor's layout. She was grateful to whoever designed it and hoped they got to finish it someday.

She sensed a warmth coming from the part of the foundation where the Room of Fathers had been. She floated to it and found Lady Weirdwood, gray-haired and wrinkle-eyed, dressed in her disintegrating wedding gown, which had also returned to its former uncut glory thanks to her pet snake.

"Hi," Breeth said quietly, feeling a little nervous for some reason. "You're old again."

"Hello, Breeth," the architect said with a smile. "Astute of you to notice. You and I need to talk."

Breeth's spores started to sag again. "It isn't serious, is it? I don't think I can take any more serious today."

"I'm afraid it is," Lady Weirdwood said. "It's the most serious thing in the world."

24
ARTHUR BENTON

25
WALLY COOPER

As the sun set, the last remnants of the Veil disintegrated across the sky. Strange stars shimmered to life, one by one, illuminating a city that was not Kingsport, not Mirror Kingsport, but something in between. The screaming in the streets faded as the citizens began to adjust to their new magical reality.

Wally Cooper did not feel triumphant. He sat on the beach and watched the crab constellations scuttle across the green horizon, catching meteorites with their claws to eat them.

"We did it, Graham," he whispered. His head sank between his knees. "It wasn't worth it."

He held his friend's suspenders in one hand, his final words in the other: *Forgive me, Harry.* He didn't understand why Arthur hadn't even tried to write a Garnett Lacroix story. Did he know something Wally didn't? Had Arthur's sacrifice been the thing to finally bring the Eraser down?

"You were the true hero," Wally said. "I'll make sure everyone knows your story."

His eyes filled with tears as he had a quiet moment for Arthur Benton.

When Wally raised his head again, he spotted the strange structure growing in the white space above the cliffs where Greyridge had been. With nowhere else in the world to go, Wally went to investigate.

It was only when he stepped into the structure's unfinished foyer that he realized it was a nascent version of Weirdwood Manor. A rough draft of the first magical room he and Arthur had ever entered. It seemed to have only just started growing and was in frail condition. A strong breeze would blow the bare branch structure into the sea.

Wally wandered the roofless halls, trying to trace his usual path through the rooms. But the layout had changed. Like someone with much different taste than Lady Weirdwood had redesigned it. He found his way to the Throne Room, a hollow shell of its former glory. The walls drooped like dead wet leaves. The floor was strewn with snakeskins. And sitting on the waxen throne . . . was Arthur Benton.

Wally's mouth fell open. Had Arthur escaped the Eraser? Had the fall of the Veil somehow brought his friend back to life? Wally wanted to run and throw his arms around his friend's neck, pulling him into the tightest hug he'd ever given. But something made him hesitate.

"I'm sorry, Wally," Arthur said.

Wally swallowed. "About what?"

Arthur stared at the notebook in his lap. "It was a decoy. That's why it couldn't cast magic. I wrote a version of myself to go talk to you so I could stay here and work on . . . this." He gazed around the sprouting walls of the Throne Room.

Wally blinked in shock. The person he'd talked to on the rooftop, the person he'd fought with, fought *alongside* . . . wasn't a person at all. It was a Fae-born version of Arthur. And Wally had bought it, just like he had his fake ghostly parents.

"I didn't want you to have to see me die," Arthur said sadly. "But I didn't have any choice."

Wally squeezed his fists. "What are you saying?"

"Again, Wally," Arthur said. "I'm sorry."

He lifted his notebook, crossed out the writing there, and the nascent Manor began to grow. The frame swelled and crackled like tree trunks while the branches interlaced into solid walls, their tops popping into leaves, which fanned into a canopy roof.

Wally backed away in horror. He'd been tricked by *two* of Arthur's lies. "*Breeth!*"

He sprinted from the room, searching for the ghost girl. She could tear down this Manor before Arthur could fix the Veil. The border between worlds hadn't been rebuilt yet. The fight for a better future wasn't lost.

As Wally ran down the corridors, the Manor continued to bloom around him, coming into its full grandeur. It was bigger than before. More stylized and garish and overstuffed. Clearly a work of Arthur Benton's.

Wally found Breeth in the Room of Fathers, whose walls shone bright with a cloudless sky. She had left her spores behind somewhere and was sitting on the grassy carpet, ruffling the blades with her blue-glass fingers.

"Breeth!" Wally said. "Arthur is going to fix the Veil! We have to stop him!"

"Hi, Wally," Breeth said quietly.

His hands dropped to his sides. "What's happening?" he asked, heart pounding. "What's wrong?"

Was she going to tell him she agreed with Arthur? Were all his efforts for nothing?

"So, um . . ." Breeth swallowed, struggling to begin. "Um . . ." She squeezed her eyes shut, drew a ghostly breath, and spoke as quickly as she could. "Lady Weirdwood's spirit is gonna possess this new Manor to give it its power, and that means there's gonna be an open spot in the afterlife, and she asked if I wanted it, and I . . . I said yes." She opened her eyes to look into his. "I get to see my parents again."

Wally's legs gave out beneath him and he sat on the grassy carpet.

Breeth frowned so deep, it broke his heart. "I'm sorry I can't help you bring down the Veil, Wally."

"That's . . . not it," Wally said. It was true the fight was lost. That Arthur had won, and the Veil would remain up. But . . . Wally's face crumpled.

"Don't be sad!" Breeth said, spiriting up to him. "Maybe you can go to the spots where the Real needs the Fae and the Fae needs the Real and tear Rifts there. Professional Rift-tearer. That'll be you."

"You don't understand . . ." He stared into Breeth's eyes. "I'm losing my best friend."

"Oh." Tears of plasma spilled down Breeth's cheeks. They both wept a moment, their sniffs echoing through the Room of Fathers's bright blue day.

"Think about it," Breeth said, wiping her cheeks. "This'll be a happy ending because I'm *dead*. Funny, right?"

Wally cried even harder, so she did too. Wally's tears made her look more ethereal than ever. Like she was already gone. After a moment, Breeth lifted Wally's chin with a blue finger and beamed through her tears. "The boring parts were worth it. Especially if it stopped you from becoming a ghost."

Wally sniffed. "If this whole adventure was about getting you back to her parents"—he tried to smile—"it was also worth it."

Breeth let out a sob and covered her face. "Just promise me that you won't be best friends with any other ghost girls. Otherwise, I'm gonna be real sad in the afterlife."

Wally laughed despite himself. "I promise."

The blue-sky ceiling started to tear like paper, shining with a light he'd never seen before. It was almost too comforting to look at. Breeth got that same shine, and she started to rise, like a piece of silk on an updraft. She kept her eyes on Wally until the moment her head reached the ceiling.

Breeth finally looked up. "Hi, Mom. Hi, Dad."

And she vanished like melted glass.

***

When Wally finally left the Room of Fathers, he found Arthur waiting for him in the hall. The boys stared at each other, nothing to say. Wally remembered the moment back in the disintegrating Manor when he could have asked Breeth to take the baby from Arthur but didn't. He could have changed everything in that moment. He could have made Graham's last and only dream come true. He could have made the world a better place.

"This was the way it had to go, Cooper," Arthur said. "I hope you'll see that someday."

Wally had to keep himself from punching him. "You didn't even hear my argument. You were *hiding*."

Arthur sighed heavily and took out his notebook. "I alternated pages, writing one line for the decoy before writing one for the Manor." He showed him. "I read every word you said."

"But you weren't actually planning on helping me," Wally said. "You were just keeping me distracted."

Arthur thought about this a moment. "It was the right thing to do."

"You only think that because you're coming out on top," Wally said, anger seething inside him. "You get to take off in this Manor and live a magical life as a Novitiate. But what about our friends, who will have to keep stealing to survive? What about the Fae-born who live in dying pocket-worlds? What about our p—"

He was about to mention their parents when it finally hit him what "*Forgive me, Harry*" meant. By reestablishing the Veil, Arthur would be sending the ghost of his own mom to wherever ghosts belonged. And he would be robbing his dad of his wife. Arthur Benton believed in the Wardens of Weirdwood enough to lose his own family. Wally didn't know how to argue with that.

Arthur gave Wally a hopeful look. "We can go back to the Great Elsewhere and find your parents. I can edit them so they're more realistic than ever and—"

"My family's gone, Arthur," Wally interrupted. He gazed past Arthur toward the Manor's exit. "It's time I find a new one."

Arthur's jaw started to tremble. "I . . . I need you around, Wally. You make me a better person."

Wally gazed around at the new, richly decorated hall. "Seems like you're doing just fine without me."

With a flick of his pen, Arthur had undone everything Wally had fought for all these months. Everything his brother had fought for all these years. He didn't know how they could possibly be friends after this.

Arthur's head drooped. "I guess this is one rift I can't fix."

Wally huffed, annoyed. "You gotta work on your lines, Arthur."

Arthur nodded and wiped his tears. "You should get going," he said, stepping out of the way.

Wally crossed his arms. "Are you not gonna tell the Wardens that I'm here? Have them lock me up? I tried to tear down the *Veil*. I'm Weirdwood's number-one threat."

Arthur gave him a surprised look. "You beat the Eraser, Wally. All by yourself. You're a hero. No, you're *the* hero. I won't let anyone forget that."

That made Wally soften. Just a little.

Somewhere in the Manor, Ludwig was singing opera. His voice echoed down the corridor, adding ornate carvings and details to the baseboards and crown molding. Wally had to admit the place was looking nicer by the second. But to what end?

"Come on," Arthur said. "I'll make sure you get out safe."

They walked together and came to the spiral hallway where Arthur had once abandoned Wally. Sekhmet was blocking their way.

"Quick, Cooper!" Arthur yelled. "Dodge around her!"

He grabbed the spiraled rug and gave it a flick, sending a wave toward Sekhmet, who drew her sword. Arthur charged around the spiral, but she was too quick for him, diving up and over his head and using the flat part of her sword to wrap the waving rug around him, binding his arms to his sides before kicking him to the floor.

Sekhmet came toward Wally, sword drawn, and he raised his hands to protect himself. Something metallic clamped around his wrists, and he looked, expecting to find himself bound with magma manacles.

Instead, he was wearing his golden gauntlets.

"Didn't want you to forget those," Sekhmet said. She leaned in and smooched Wally's cheek, which flooded with heat. "Thanks for saving us," she whispered, and limped past him through the door, holding her injured side. "Oh, and I'd get out of here before Amelia sees you."

She turned the corner, and Wally admired his gauntlets in the candlelight, remembering what it was like to put them on for the first time. They had made him feel like a hero.

With a grunt, Arthur managed to untangle himself from the rug. "Won't she be embarrassed when she realizes how openly she flirts with me?"

Wally stifled a laugh.

They arrived in the foyer, and Arthur opened the Manor's front door. On the other side was the demon-headed knocker with the onyx ring, which the boys had once used to break into Weirdwood. Some things hadn't changed in Arthur's new design.

"Look how far we've come, Cooper," Arthur said. "From a couple of thieves who could barely feed ourselves, to Novitiates, to . . . whatever we are now."

Wally's pain and anger were still there, burning deep. But he was too exhausted to hold on to them right then. And something about Arthur's words made him feel nostalgic.

Wally peeked outside at the burnt façade of Hazelrigg House and sighed. "I guess it's true what they say. Arthur Benton sure knows a score when he sees one."

They stood in the doorway in awkward silence, neither sure what to say.

Arthur took off his pants.

Wally laughed. "*Why?*"

Arthur shrugged. "I thought it would be funny," he said, tears welling in his eyes. "Y'know, one last time."

Wally felt a welling up of emotion and turned away before Arthur could see. "See you around, man."

"Yeah," Arthur whispered. "S-see you around."

Wally stepped out of Weirdwood Manor and into the city that was not quite Kingsport and not quite Mirror Kingsport. The Wardens hadn't begun mending the Rifts yet, so he walked the enchanted streets beneath a quilted sky, taking in the interactions between humans and Fae-born before everyone woke up from the dream and this beautiful vision melted away forever.

He came to the spot where Kingsport's train station stood and found a Rift that looked onto the starry expanse. Gauntlets in hand, Wally Cooper ambled toward it . . . and he vanished into the Fae.

26
THE ARCHITECT

Arthur watched Wally walk into the otherworldly hues of the Mirror-melded city, an emptiness opening in his chest. People had left Arthur before. His mom had passed away from the Pox. Harry had gotten lost at the bottom of a mead barrel. But no one had ever left Arthur because of what he believed in. Finding a way to defeat his best friend was the first puzzle on this adventure that he had hated to solve.

"It's time, Arthur," Amelia said behind him.

Arthur turned and saw the acrobat's face. He tried to match its braveness. "Time to sew up the Rifts?"

"No," Amelia said, looking down. "It's too late for Kingsport, I'm afraid."

Arthur's stomach flipped. "What?"

Her blue eye assessed the ragged sky. "The Rift has spread too far. It's encompassed the border of the city. The citizens have seen too much, and they have fallen into Daymare. We have no choice but to sever Kingsport from the Real."

"What about the trade ships?" Arthur asked. "Or—or the sewer system? What about the people's relatives outside the city?"

"It's not going to be easy," Amelia said. "But for the time being, Kingsport will have the Mirror City to trade with. They'll need to get used to stranger wares."

Arthur, in shock, stepped through the Manor's entrance and gazed over his city, now trapped in the Fae forever. He'd thought he could save it by rebuilding Weirdwood. But Kingsport had been doomed the moment Wally Cooper flew in on black wings.

In a way, his friend had won. Did Wally know it?

A movement caught Arthur's eye, just beyond the Port. A forest had grown around the library, the building's old stones jutting up through enchanted treetops. By the light of a thousand fireflies, fairies and elves and cats on two paws were dancing with Kingsport's less fortunate. The sight reminded him of all the lovely things Wally had tried to point out from Liza's feathery back. The things Arthur had been too stubborn to see.

Maybe *doomed* wasn't the right word for what was happening to Kingsport.

Arthur's heart began to thump. "Does that mean everything will stay the same?"

"It does," Amelia answered, as if it were a tragedy and nothing more.

Arthur swallowed deep. His mom's ghost would stay. Harry wouldn't lose her. But the thought of visiting the tenements right now, after everything Arthur had just been through, was enough to make his legs shake. He would visit his mom when he was good and ready.

"Perhaps, Arthur," Amelia said, "next time you'll think twice about messing with magic you do not understand."

Arthur turned slowly and met her eye. He had taken

responsibility for his mistakes. He had apologized profusely and done everything he could to fix it. Even creating a new Manor. It seemed there was no pleasing the acrobat.

"Y-you were the one who told me to try resurrecting Garnett," he said, voice trembling. "And then you had me *lie* for you."

Amelia shrugged. "The Veil is intact, and we have a new Manor," she said. "What would you change?"

Arthur's lips sealed shut, leaving a bad taste in his mouth.

"Come," Amelia said. "The others are waiting."

Confused, Arthur followed her to the Room of Fathers where Sekhmet, Linus, Ludwig, and Pyra stood in a sort of circle against the bright sky walls. In the center was Lady Weirdwood, seated on a simple wooden chair, her dead snake draped over her lap. She smiled at him.

Arthur froze. "You're . . ."

Lady Weirdwood nodded. "Old again."

"I was going to say beautiful."

The architect blushed. "A *wrinkly* sort of beautiful."

Arthur smiled. He could see the youth in the old architect's face now. The baby, the kid, and the teenager he'd known were still looking out through those starry, blueprint eyes, now growing cloudy with cataracts.

Amelia stepped before the lady, and Arthur took a place by Ludwig near the wall.

"Ahura, Willa, and Cadence are securing the border," Amelia said, "hemming the citizens in."

"And Wally?"

"Escaped, ma'am," Amelia said.

LW nodded. "Here's hoping he doesn't inherit his brother's more meddling traits."

Arthur shifted his stance.

"Now," LW said, mindlessly stroking her pet snake's lifeless scales. "It's time for me to shed this old skin of mine and be absorbed into this new, lovely Manor."

"*What?*" Arthur said, stepping forward.

Lady Weirdwood smiled at him. "Being absorbed into the Manor is the destiny of every Weirdwood architect once their work is finished. And after this most recent adventure"—she sighed a tired sigh—"boy, is my work ever finished."

"But—but . . . the snake!" Arthur pointed to the pet lying limp in her lap. "You can use it to become young again!"

"That's not how it works, Arthur," LW said. "You know that. Besides, the snake must go back earlier in the story to the moment you took it."

Arthur tried to think of a way they could come up with another solution, keep the snake and LW, but Amelia flashed him a searing look, so he stepped back beside Ludwig, who gently rubbed his shoulder. Arthur was too devastated for words. He couldn't stop thinking about TW's eyes.

LW moved to stand, and Amelia collected the snake from her lap. "All that's left," the old woman said, getting up with a grunt, "is for me to choose my inheritor." She looked at the faces in the room. "Arthur? Please come stand before me."

Arthur's eyes went wide. "Hmm?"

"You're inheriting Weirdwood Manor."

A jolt swept through Arthur's body. "You're kidding."

"I am not," Lady Weirdwood said.

He looked around at the others, who all looked as shocked as he felt. Ludwig was beaming. Amelia looked furious.

"Why don't you give it to Linus?" Arthur asked. "Or Sekhmet? Or literally anyone else?"

Linus put up his hands as if not wanting to touch the position.

Sekhmet shook her head. "I'd rather be out in the field."

"But . . . ," Arthur said, stepping before Lady Weirdwood. "This is a *terrible* idea, right? Everyone can see that, right? How terrible this would be? I mean, I made a *lot* of mistakes. And— and I'm just a *kid*. I always hated it when fantasy books give kids too much power. And finally, to be perfectly honest, now that I think about it, I'm not even sure I see eye to eye with—"

"Relax," LW said. "Amelia will act as regent and Ludwig as the Manor's caretaker while you learn the position's ins and outs and inside-outs. You will continue to receive commands from both until the day you turn eighteen or they deem you responsible enough to take over. Whichever comes last. Until that day, you will study magic as if it were your air and water."

Arthur was numb from head to toe. When he had first stepped into this Manor, he would have taken the position of architect in a heartbeat. He remembered even bragging to Wally that he would do that very thing someday. But now that he understood just how complex magic and the Balance and the Manor really were, he was beyond intimidated by the responsibility that came with the waxen throne.

"You can turn it down, you know," Lady Weirdwood said.

"Great," Arthur said. "I turn it down."

The old architect glanced at the others, whose shocked expressions softened. Only Amelia's expression remained wound tight.

"You have made terrible mistakes, Arthur," Lady Weirdwood said. "But you've also fought tooth and nail to repair those mistakes." She nodded toward the door. "I told you on the cliffs outside that you were one of the bravest and most creative people I've ever met. Those weren't the empty words of a teenager. I meant them. When I was briefly a child, I watched you save this Manor and its legacy. Weirdwood would no longer exist were it not for you."

Arthur's insides were still surging with doubt.

The old woman took his hand. "Finally, and most important, you just fought a war against your best friend to save the Veil. If that doesn't make you the most qualified to protect it, I don't know what does."

Arthur pulled his hand away. He still wasn't sure he had done the right thing, ignoring Wally's evidence and advice to save something he barely understood.

He glanced at Amelia, whose furious expression had turned into something more dangerous: *jealousy.* He wondered what Weirdwood would be like if the acrobat were in charge. Cold. Militaristic. Possibly full of lies. And he wondered if anyone who had spent their life in the Manor would do any better. With their current rules, the Wardens could never make Wally Cooper proud.

But Arthur Benton could.

"I'll take it," he said before he could stop himself.

"Good," LW said solemnly. She nodded to Amelia. "Please hand Arthur the sacrificial knife."

Arthur stepped back. "What? No! I'm not stabbing you!"

LW winked at him.

Arthur frowned. "That wasn't funny."

His anger quickly broke when he realized that he was going to lose this person who had been like a grandma and a child and a crush all at once. "I . . . I don't want you to die."

"Just think of me as an old lady," LW said softly. "Then it's not so sad."

She handed Arthur the lifeless snake. Then she closed her eyes, and vines began to grow through the floor. They coiled around LW's ankles, then up her legs and around her torso. Her sleeves. Her throat. They were about to encase her completely when—

"*Wait,*" Arthur said.

The vines stopped growing, and LW opened her eyes. "You're interrupting a solemn moment, you know."

"I know," Arthur said, breathless. "I gotta say something. And I realize this might make you take the position away from me, but . . . if I really am the heir to Weirdwood Manor, then . . . I'm going to change some things."

"Oh?" The vines around LW unspooled a little.

Arthur tried to gather his thoughts, but his nerves were a mess. So he channeled Wally's voice instead. "The Manor can't go back to the way it was. We can't lock up artists anymore." He didn't look up, in case LW's eyes threw him off track. "And . . . maybe we need to change our thinking about the Veil. No matter what it does to protect us and the Fae-born, it still separates us. Maybe we can relax on that a bit. Become more like ambassadors instead of border guards. Maybe the Balance is . . . whatever we say it is."

There was a long moment of silence as the clouds drifted across the walls.

"I think I made the right decision," Lady Weirdwood said with a smile in her voice. "Now. Let me go in peace."

Arthur glanced up just in time to catch the architect's beautiful constellation eyes as the vines continued their coiling up and around her head until not one bit of the old architect was visible. The vines crackled. Their leaves turned brown and fell to the floor. Beneath was nothing but dead plant matter.

Arthur held the snake close while he tried to control the waves of emotion crashing in his chest. He turned and found the others grieving in their own ways. Linus's and Sekhmet's heads were bowed. Ludwig and Pyra had tears in their eyes. Amelia was glaring at Arthur.

"You're fired," he told her.

Her blue eye went wide. "Excuse me?"

The others looked equally shocked.

Arthur's skin crawled with discomfort, but he pushed forward. "You manipulated me. You tricked me into doing your dirty work, and then you lied to the Wardens about tearing Rifts. Worst of all, you didn't tell anyone that you knew Rose was in Breeth's body. We could have stopped her from stabbing Linus."

Now it was the others' turn to glare at the acrobat.

Amelia licked her teeth as she uncoiled her whip from her

holster. Arthur winced, expecting her to crack it around his neck, to take her revenge. But instead, she tossed it to the grassy carpet and marched out of the room. A few moments later, the distant entrance was slammed shut.

"Vell?" Ludwig said. "Vhat now, your lordship?"

Arthur grimaced at that word. "Well, first off, you can just call me Arthur . . . please. And second, I guess someone needs to reconnect the Abyssment to the Manor?"

Ludwig nodded. "Ja. I vill do zis sing." The woodworker departed the room, the new floorboards squeaking pleasantly beneath his giant feet.

Arthur looked at the dead serpent in his arms. "And I guess we've got to get this snake back to earlier in the story. I'd do it myself, but . . ." He wasn't sure his heart could handle seeing LW again.

Pyra stepped forward and took the snake with a grunt. The chef also departed.

Arthur gave Linus and Sekhmet a sheepish look. "As for the rest of us . . . I guess we teach the citizens of Kingsport how to survive in the Fae. They're scared right now. We need to show them that becoming part of the Mirror City isn't the end of the world. Just the start of a new one."

Sekhmet looked to her father, who looked back to her and nodded. The two sword fighters left.

Now that he was alone, Arthur got an anxious feeling in his bones. Unsure what to do, he walked the halls of the Manor. *His* Manor, he supposed, though he didn't think he'd ever get used to that thought. His legs brought him to the zigzag staircase, which he scaled to the rooftop, just in time for sunset. The turrets glowed golden and the weather vane burned copper. It pointed to the inky sea, which sparkled with silver waves.

Arthur nestled himself between two flowering towers and opened his notebook. *I can't do this*, he wrote. *I don't know enough. I'm too selfish. My best friend hates me right now. I—*

The bones of the Manor released an aching groan, and the weather vane began to spin. There was no wind.

"Is that . . . *you*?" Arthur whispered.

The weather vane stopped spinning. Now it pointed east, toward the city, whose streets had flooded with wild mist. Arthur heard shuffling and giggles in the night as urchins, human and Fae-born alike, snuck through the cobbled streets.

He imagined younger versions of himself and Wally stepping out of the mist, attempting to break into this Manor. The young Arthur was full of himself, overstuffed with adventure stories and confident he could solve the world's problems with the arch of an eyebrow and a few clever remarks.

He looked down and crossed out what he had written. Beside it, he wrote, *Listen.*

He considered the city below—the mirror architecture filling in the erased spaces. Kingsport was almost unrecognizable. And yet, it felt as familiar as a dream. In a strange way, this new city stood as a testament to what he and Wally both believed in. It needed a name that captured that.

Arthur wrote, *New Kingsport.*

"Blech," he said, and scribbled that out too.

He closed his notebook. He could figure the name out later. For the time being, Arthur Benton's writing was complete.

27
THE TRAVELER

In the DappleWood—the *third* DappleWood—the critter citizens were planting trees in the nothingness, regrowing their home from the roots up. The blank little village was filling in almost like a coloring book, brown and gray stones stacked one by one to remake the cottages. Green seeped up from the fields, adding blue to the sky and yellow to the sun, which shone through the sprouting trees, making the land more dappled by the day.

***

A few pocket-worlds over, in the Fiery Plains, Sekhmet was defending a herd of endangered fire bulls. When Arthur, the surprisingly quiet new architect, had asked what she wanted to do, she had told him she wanted to be out in the pocket-worlds, defending the most vulnerable Fae-born.

Done, he had said.

Sekhmet raised her flaming sword and screamed, "Lend me your horns!"

And she led the flaming, galloping charge against the iceberg-sized ice bear.

Never had she loved being a Warden so much.

✳✳✳

Several more pocket-worlds over, in the newly founded *Huameia*, a blue-glass dragon and his pet ghost mouse coiled through the sky and over the floating islands inspired by the Whirling City. Each island was filled with a different type of Fae-born whose pocket-world had been erased. Someday, they would find proper homes for them. But until then, Huamei and the little mouse would keep them safe.

✳✳✳

Atop the crumbled rooftops of the Untitled City, the Black Feathers conspired with the Corvidians.

"Here's the plan," Alec said, a smile on his face and some meat on his bones. "The Black Feathers will keep the driver distracted while the others swoop in and—"

"Wait, are we talking black feathers or *Black Feathers*?" Sam asked. His wounds had healed, and he hadn't been beaten by an Oaker in weeks. "Things've gotten confusing since these birdbrains showed up."

One of the birds squawked, eyeing the boy menacingly.

"Try it and see what it gets ya!" the boy said, making fists.

"*Boys*," Alec said, quickly getting between them. "And birds. Just please try and cooperate. There's plenty of food to go around, and we don't even eat the same things."

Alec had become the gang's de facto leader, with or

without feathers, after he'd convinced the Corvidians to stop stealing babies and canes and shown them where the fishing tackle was stored on the Port. Turned out a swarm of bird children was the perfect distraction for the human thieves, who raided the fishing nets.

The boys and birds would eat well that night. Just as they had for a dozen nights before.

***

Down the street, a little old woman was helping a rainy child named Maddie tie the laces on her new cloud shoes. She didn't want them getting caught up in the spokes of her starlight bike. Joe, the woman's husband, was back in his shop, working on the next pair. He still accepted payment in butterscotch. And his wife encouraged him to eat every last one.

***

One district over, in the StormCrow Pub, Silver Tongue was flirting.

"See, I say the Order had it all wrong," she said, licking her spilled drink from her fingertips. "We was always chasin' after money. But money don't mean nothin' these days. Whatcha *need* is influence."

The gentleman she was talking to was handsome in an exhausted sort of way. But she had dated Rusty for years, and heaven knew he was no looker. Besides, he had drunk her precious mercury and that had gotten him killed like a real nincompoop.

"Ma'am," the exhausted man said. "I've told you a hundred

times, I'm not interested. I just woke up from . . . I don't know what. A coma maybe. I've been in bad straits."

Silver Tongue ignored him. "What we *shoulda* been doing the whole time was tearing down the Veil, y'know? Create a little *chaos*."

"I have had enough chaos," the man said, moving to stand and rubbing his bloodshot eyes. "Now, if you'll excuse me, I must try to find my writing desk."

Silver Tongue took another sip from her drink. "*Sit down, cutie,*" she said with a silvery shriek.

The man abruptly sat as if his legs had been broken.

Silver Tongue draped a blue-veined arm around his slumped shoulders. "See," she explained sweetly, "you and me is gonna start a new Order. One that knows what it's about. But if we's gonna take on them pesky Wardens, we're gonna need all the help we can get. And correct me if I'm wrong, but you got a talent, dontcha? A talent for the art. A talent for the *strange*."

The man stared at his immobile legs, afraid. "I can't move. What have you *done* to me?"

"Just bein' persuasive." She poked her teeth with her tongue and pinched his nose. "Ah, don't look so frightened, sweetie. Tell the kiddies at home your name."

"I-I-I'm Alfred Moore."

"Yes, you are," Silver Tongue said. "And no one makes a monster like you, amirite?"

***

Once the man and woman left the pub, Liza locked up for the night. The customers had been rowdy that day. She'd had to remove a splinter from a werewolf's paw, rescue a woman from one of the flytraps, and stop one of the ceiling vultures from eating Pancake Jack's remaining leg. But that was the job.

As Liza stepped away from the pub, she raised her arms and threw them down, sprouting feathers with each additional wave. She sailed up into the moony sky and found the other giant rook that soared there. The two flew through the misty night.

***

Elsewhere, in a small forest encampment, Garnett Lacroix roused his Merry Rogues.

"Gus! Tuck! Mim! Up and at 'em!"

Mim sat up like a jackknife and rubbed her eye. Tuck unwrapped his arm from Gus, who pretended to stay asleep.

The Gentleman Thief breathed deep the night air, the golden buttons on his shirt shining like suns. "Come, my dears. Now that I have returned from cruel oblivion, and you are back from bony abandon, it's time for **adventure**."

Mim patted her stomach. "Least there was no hunger when we was skeletons."

"Or scrapes," *said Tuck, looking at the scars that crisscrossed his arms.*

"Or smells," *said Gus, sniffing his own armpit.*

"A quest awaits us, haunted and strange!" *Garnett said, rolling up his sleeping bag.* "Her royal highness, Princess Pumpkinface, has requested that we track down her squiggly little squashes. I call it . . . The Case of the Purloined Pumpkin Princess."

"How's about the Stately Stolen Squashes?" *Mim offered.*

"Or the Gallant Grabbed Gourds!" *said Tuck.*

Gus finally sat up with a yawn and a scratch. "Ah, come on. You took all the good ones."

The others gave him a deflated look.

Gus guffawed. "Only kidding. The Jacked Jack-o'-lanterns of Judiciousness!"

"Ha!" Garnett said. "Come! Let us seize this city by its suspenders and make it spill its secrets."

The Gentleman Thief strode gallantly away from the camp, and the Merry Rogues followed him, singing all the way.

***

On the cliffs where Greyridge once sat, in a beautiful, new Manor, Arthur Weirdwood closed his notebook. It was tentatively titled *The New Adventures of Garnett Lacroix*. They were just for him, really—a way to think about what it meant to be a gentleman and a thief while he navigated his new duties as architect. He hoped the new stories would make Valerie Lucas proud.

Arthur went to the DappleWood Hall to check on Audrey, who was currently sewing his new suit. He had tried to get her to make him the outfit that the Gentleman Thief wore in his adventures, but she had kindly pointed out that purple tails and garish buttons, while certainly eye-catching, weren't very practical.

"How's it coming, Audrey?" he asked.

Audrey set down her sewing and shook out her paws. "Sometimes, *just sometimes*, I wish I'd kept those longer claws you gave me. Purely for sewing purposes, of course."

Arthur smiled and twirled his pen around his fingers. "Just say the word."

Audrey waved him away and picked up her needle. "Less blabbin', more jabbin'. Otherwise, you'll be runnin' this Manor naked as the day you were born."

Arthur chuckled and left the Hall, passing Huamei's room, which now had a permanent Rift that led to Huameia. Whenever the Wardens found Fae-born in need of a home, they sent them there.

He came to the kitchen and peeked inside. "How's she doing, Pyra?"

The chef grunted. She wore gloves and held a beaker filled with a lovely pink goo, which she delicately applied to the Astonishment's skin. The gray was fading into a light brown, becoming more supple.

"Does it hurt?" Arthur asked.

The Astonishment rocked her head side to side.

"Well, that's good," Arthur said.

He couldn't wait until the Astonishment's vocal cords were freed from their rocky prison so he could hear what she sounded like. He would ask her if she wanted to join the Wardens. The Manor could use her strength, rocky or no.

"Pyra will take good care of you," Arthur told the Astonishment, and the chef grunted.

He continued on, passing through the new Bookcropolis. High on the wall, under the main dome, was a portrait of Graham Cooper. Arthur had placed it there to remind himself that there were other ways of thinking about the Veil. He'd been keeping an eye on Kingsport ever since it slipped into the Fae. And he had to admit Wally had been right. Things hadn't turned out too bad. The nightmare, if that's what it had been, was over.

Arthur reached the western exit of the Bookcropolis and found Ludwig putting the final touches on the new Judgment Passage, which no longer swallowed liars into the Abyssment but bound them in place.

"Looking good, Ludwig."

"Ah, sank you, Arsur!" Ludwig said, wiping sappy sweat from his forehead. "Ve do ze lady proud, ja?"

He blew Weston's whistle and grew more vines, which he shaped with his tools. The giant woodworker was slowly but surely learning his twin's trade.

"Keep up the good work," Arthur said.

Finally, he went to the Throne Room, where he found Linus, whom he had asked to replace Amelia as regent.

"We all set?" Arthur asked.

"She's finally ready to fly," Linus said. "Just say the word."

Arthur sat on the waxen throne and breathed deep. "The word."

Linus smirked.

And Weirdwood Manor sailed off between the worlds.

❈❈❈

Wally Cooper stepped onto the Trackdragon and gave a ticket to the conductor for the first time, no longer an invisible stowaway.

"Where ya headed?" the conductor asked, inspecting the ticket.

Wally smiled. "Wherever you'll take me."

The conductor punched his ticket and handed it over. "You're in the right place then."

Wally went to find his seat. Being on rails felt soothing. A one-way track, guiding him toward a singular future, much like his brother's vision for a new world. After leaving Kingsport, or whatever it was now, Wally had realized that if the Veil was going to stay up, there would be a lot of people and Fae-born who could use some help. He wanted to be there for them.

He reached his compartment and set his bag beside the skinny closet. He brought down the foldaway bed, ready to

collapse and sleep for a dozen hours at least. But something stole his breath. There, on the pillow, was a puppet. A baby. The last character from Punch and Judy.

Wally blinked at it. Had Graham known all along that this was where he would end up? Failing to bring down the Veil? *Possibly* changing the mind of Weirdwood Manor's new architect? It seemed so insignificant. And yet . . . maybe he hadn't failed his brother's expectations after all.

Wally picked up the puppet, half expecting to find Graham's hand beneath it, waiting to surprise him. Of course, there was nothing there.

Wally flopped onto the bed and set the baby puppet on his stomach. He watched it move up and down as he breathed, and he considered the countless pocket-worlds ahead, each with a unique problem to solve. He was intimidated. He was terrified. But he was here because he'd chosen it. This was his.

As the Trackdragon roared to life, his eyes fluttered shut. Wally Cooper drifted off to the sounds of the rumbling engine as he was carried through the stars.

The End

AFTERWEIRD

Deep in the bowels of the Abyssment, in the brain of a demon lamb, Rose's ghost was scheming.

The last few weeks had been pure agony. Being trapped inside the skull of a demon was an infinite torture, and the creature still hadn't grown used to her presence. It was constantly bucking, *shrieking*, trying to kick her out. Rose screamed in agony along with the lamb, adding her voice to its cacophony of hellish voices.

The pain was nothing compared to how much Rose missed her son. But she knew the damned struggled for eternity, and that meant she had an eternity to break free. And when she did, she would find those Wardens. She would make them pay. After that, she would find that little girl, Breeth, wherever she was, and she would—

"Stop sporin' on me, Fun Gus! I'm your *queen*, remember?"

A voice came from outside the demon lamb. A *young* voice, echoing through the Abyssment.

"*Knock knock!* Anybody home?"

Rose startled. The demon lamb startled. The voice was in its skull now. As bright and bubbly as it was familiar.

"Woof!" the voice said. "You should clean up in here. These thoughts are *filthy*. And it's *so hot*. Do demon brains not have any fans? Ha ha. Just kidding."

"Breeth?" Rose said.

"In the flesh! Er, *spirit*. You know what I mean."

"Wha . . . ?"

"What am I doing here?" Breeth asked. "Great. Question. See, Lady Weirdwood was nice enough to let me take her spot in heaven so I could go be with my parents. They're great. You'd like them. But they got real sad when they saw me because it meant I was dead, and I guess they were hoping I was gonna live a long life and stuff. You get it. And honestly? If I'm being honest? The afterlife is kinda *boring*. Like, not as boring as the Great Elsewhere, but still. I mean, how could it not be after you have the whole Real and Fae as your playground? So I thought to myself, who would really appreciate being here? And then I was like, Oh! *Duh.* Rose."

"You've come to . . . free me?"

"And send you to the afterlife," Breeth said. "To see your son. I saw him up there. Cute kid."

The fuming in Rose steamed away. She had been plotting *revenge* against this child.

"Breeth . . ."

"Don't say thank you," Breeth said. "It's awkward for both of us, right? What with you murdering me and all. But I figure if your kid didn't get to live a very long life, he at least deserves to have his momma around."

Rose was speechless.

"Welp!" Breeth said. "You're free! All you gotta do is leave."

She exited the skull of the demon lamb, leaving the back door open for Rose to let herself out.

Breeth took off, up into the Manor, where she spun Arthur's tie, made Ludwig's tools skitter away, and splashed Pyra with her own cauldron concoction before soaring out the exit and into the Fae.

She was off to find Wally.